# THE
# MAKER

Book **Ten** in the
**Munro Family** Series

# CHRIS TAYLOR

Copyright © 2015 by Chris Taylor

All Rights Reserved



LCT Productions Pty Ltd
18364 Kamilaroi Highway, Narrabri NSW 2390


ISBN. 978-1-925119-22-0 (Paperback)
ISBN. 978-1-925119-21-3 (Ebook)

**The Maker** is a work of fiction. Names, characters, places, brands, media and incidents either are the product of the author's imagination or are used fictitiously. Any resemblance to actual persons, living or dead, events, or locales, is entirely coincidental.

Published in the United States of America

Be careful what you wish for…

Chanel Munro has landed her dream job as a junior resident doctor at the prestigious Sydney Harbour Hospital. Only two years out from medical school, she can't believe she's been chosen by the highly respected Doctor Leo Baker to be part of his elite team.

But an esteemed position on Doctor Baker's team doesn't come without sacrifice. It soon becomes clear her boss expects her to provide him with certain favors and he's not talking about volunteering for the coffee run.

Scared, angry and confused, Chanel is at a loss what to do. She refuses to give in to blackmail, but if she takes her complaint to the medical board and they don't believe her, her career will be in ruins. The years of study and sacrifice will be for nothing. Vowing to steer clear of him, she keeps a low profile and puts all of her energies into the job that she loves.

But patients are dying strange and unpredictable deaths under Doctor Baker's care and she can't help but wonder why. It's ludicrous to suggest he's at fault. Notwithstanding his personal failings, he's an exceptional doctor. As the death toll continues to climb, Chanel takes her concerns to the police.

Detective Sergeant Bryce Sutcliffe of the City of Sydney Police Station is sceptical of Chanel's claims. Despite the fact he's drawn to her earthly beauty, he can't help but wonder if there isn't more behind her complaint. When the wife of a New South Wales senator dies under Doctor Baker's care, Bryce is forced to pay attention.

Could the girl with the compelling eyes have been telling the truth? Could the Sydney Harbour Hospital's most highly respected doctor be a murderer?

# The Munro Family Series

THE PROFILER
(Book One—Clayton and Ellie)

THE INVESTIGATOR
(Book Two—Riley and Kate)

THE PREDATOR
(Book Three—Brandon and Alex)

THE BETRAYAL
(Book Four—Declan and Chloe)

THE DECEPTION
(Book Five—Will and Savannah)

THE NEGOTIATOR
(Book Six—Andy and Cally)

THE CHRISTMAS VIGIL
(A Munro Family Series Novella)

THE RANSOM
(Book Seven—Lane and Zara)

THE DEFENDANT
(Book Eight—Chase and Josie)

THE SHOOTING
(Book Nine—Tom and Lily)

THE MAKER
(Book Ten—Bryce and Chanel)

# DEDICATION

*This book is dedicated to all of the doctors and nurses who daily give their all to help ease the suffering of the sick and dying in our busy hospitals and as always, to my sexy, real life hero, my husband, Linden.*

# Acknowledgments

As usual, no book comes into being without a lot of help and support by my friends and family. A world of thanks must go to my friend critique partner extraordinaire, Grace Anselmo. Thank you for all that you do.

To Pat Thomas, the best editor in the world. I love working with you. You turn my humble offerings into something truly amazing. I couldn't do it without you. To Detective Superintendent Michael Kilfoyle, thank you for lending my story credibility. Any mistakes are wholly my own.

To Grady, Alisha and all of the staff at damonza.com, thank you for yet another fantastic cover. To my sister, Nicole Guihot, thank you for your excellent editorial comments and suggestions. Nic, I hope you like the final result.

To Amy Atwell and her dedicated staff at Author EMS who are so much more than book formatters. Amy, once again, thank you for your magic.

To the fantastic writer organizations such as Romance Writers of Australia, Romance Writers of America and Romance Writers of New Zealand for all the help, support and encouragement they offer new and aspiring writers, including me.

To my readers, thank you for your support and love for my stories. Your encouragement and enjoyment make this journey all worthwhile.

And lastly, to my friends and family, especially my husband and children. Thank you for putting up with late dinners and even later conversations as I've emerged day after day from the sometimes scary but always enthralling world I've created on my computer.

# PROLOGUE

His measured footsteps made no sound on the shiny, linoleum-covered floor of the hushed hospital ward. He walked, unhurried, toward the room where she lay. Night had fallen a few hours earlier and the only sounds came from the occasional cough or groan from a patient and the muted murmur of voices from the skeleton nursing staff rostered on the evening shift. He'd passed right by them on his way to the ward. They stood in a huddle at the nurses' station, engrossed in catching up on the latest gossip, the latest scandal on TV—anything but the patients in their care.

It wasn't a reflection of their nursing ability. They were among some of the hospital's best. But by that time of the evening, most patients had been made comfortable for the night and were asleep, or close to it. It was no accident that he'd chosen this time to be there.

He rounded the corner. Ever careful, he snuck a look over his shoulder, just to be certain. The way was clear. He drew in a deep breath and did his best to steady the persistent thump of his heart. The anticipation of what was to come sent a fresh wave of excitement thudding through his veins and despite his attempt to calm his thoughts, his pulse leaped forward again.

He'd been given a sign from God and the sign was crystal clear. There was no doubt in his mind what needed to be done and he was pleased to have been trusted with the task. He'd been handpicked by God to carry out His wishes and the thought of ending the dying woman's suffering filled him with immeasurable joy.

The woman in question shuddered and moaned in the bed, even in her sleep. He'd done all he could to ease her pain, but short of increasing her dosage of morphine until she was unconscious, there was nothing more he could do. That was, until God had given him the sign. That had changed everything. Soon, very soon, Frances Daniels would find everlasting peace.

At sixty-eight, Frances was dying from terminal cancer. It had started in her lungs and had quickly spread to several parts of her body. In the beginning, they'd tried a combination of chemo and radiotherapy, but nothing seemed to work. No one wanted to admit defeat, but the medical team were fast losing hope.

Now he stared down at the woman, thin and pale against the twisted cotton sheets. She stirred restlessly, almost as if she could sense him and his purpose for being there. Renewed anger surged through him at the pain God had inflicted upon her. It wasn't right that He gave her this awful cross to bear. It wasn't right that He made her suffer.

All of a sudden, it wasn't Frances, but his mother lying there. Muttering and moaning in her sleep with a pain that even the strongest of sedatives couldn't touch. And he, no more than a child, helpless and weighed down by sadness, stood by and watched her die. Slowly, painfully, each breath a ragged whisper, she died with an anguish no child should have witnessed. The familiar feelings of helplessness and loss washed over him and he closed his eyes against the pain.

"No!" he whispered, his voice harsh in the silence of the room. "I'm no longer that helpless child. I won't stand by again. God has given me His orders. It's up to me to end this woman's pain."

He stepped closer to the bed and reached into his pocket, retrieving the vial he'd brought with him. His movements were tender when he gently shook Frances awake. She opened her eyes with a start and blinked, unsure for a moment where she was and then she smiled.

"Oh, it's you. I thought you would have left long ago. You work too hard." She smiled through the pain that had been with her for far too long and his lips turned up in response. He let the joy of what was to come flood through him once again. Soon, she'd feel so much better. Soon, there'd be no pain.

"Frances, God has sent me to do his bidding. I'm here to set you free." He brought the vial closer and held it beneath her nose.

She frowned in confusion and turned her head away. He followed the movement, keeping his hand firmly in place. She breathed and coughed and breathed again and he made sure she inhaled what he held. When he was certain it was enough, he carefully sealed the vial and slipped it back into his pocket.

"Doctor—"

"*Shh*, Frances. It's okay. Everything's going to be perfect. You'll see." He smiled down at her again and whispered, "It's time to meet your Maker."

# CHAPTER 1

Chanel Munro took a moment to surreptitiously swipe her sweat-dampened palms down the sides of her white lab coat. The impressive sixteen-storey, sandstone building that housed the patients of the Sydney Harbour Hospital towered before her. Butterflies churned in her stomach and she breathed deeply, hoping to calm her nerves. It was her first day as a junior medical resident under the esteemed Doctor Leo Baker. She'd die if he were to guess how anxious she was.

It was ridiculous, really. It wasn't like she was a fresh-faced intern straight out of medical school, who'd barely seen the inside of a hospital. She'd worked in the largest hospital in Brisbane for more than two years. The place had become her second home and she'd loved every minute of it.

But while she loved Brisbane and its laid-back lifestyle, she was more than three hours' drive away from her parents and only sister and at least a day's drive away from her brothers. After supporting her oldest brother through a recent health crisis, she'd realized how important it was to be close to her family and surrounded by their love.

Her numerous nieces and nephews were getting older and she'd missed many of their milestones. Her birthday had come and gone a month earlier and the reality she was only three years shy of thirty had come as a bit of a surprise.

*Where had the time gone?* It seemed like only yesterday that she'd graduated high school and stood outside the hallowed walls of the medical school at Brisbane University, her stomach taut with nerves. And here she was in Sydney, outside the city's most prestigious hospital, with stomach-churning fear, excitement and anticipation—just as strong and familiar as all those years ago.

She'd applied for the residency position on Doctor Baker's medical team without any real hope of success and was stunned when an email came through congratulating her on her appointment. While she'd graduated top of her class in Brisbane, it was rumored more than a thousand young doctors had competed for the ten, much-coveted places on Doctor Baker's team.

The fact that she now lived within a ten-mile radius of three of her older brothers was almost as important as the realization she was finally living her dream. Having scoured the classified advertisements online and in the Sydney newspapers for weeks prior to her move, she'd been fortunate to find a cosy two-bedroom apartment in North Sydney, only minutes from the train station. While the rent was pretty steep, the proximity to her work in the city and the fantastic harbor views more than compensated. Besides, she was optimistic she'd be able to find a roommate to help offset the costs.

She'd already prepared an advertisement to pin on the staff noticeboard at the hospital as soon as she could. But first, she had to find the courage to walk inside.

With another deep breath, she adjusted her backpack on her shoulder and made her way down the cobblestoned path that led to the wide front doors. A little ways past the entryway, stood an information desk manned by a white-haired volunteer. Chanel smiled at the woman behind the counter.

"Hello, I was wondering if you could tell me where I could find Doctor Leo Baker?"

"Good morning, and welcome to the Sydney Harbour Hospital. I take it you're one of our lovely Doctor Baker's fresh recruits?" The woman's twinkling eyes almost disappeared into the folds of soft skin around her eyes.

Chanel nodded. "Yes. I'm Chanel Munro. This is my first day."

"Pleased to meet you, Chanel. I'm Marjorie Campbell. You can find me most mornings right here at the information desk. I share it with Dottie Featherdale. Between the two of us, there's nothing we don't know about this place." She winked and Chanel couldn't help but chuckle.

"That's good to know, Marjorie. I'm from the country. I've only visited Sydney on the odd occasion. It's a little overwhelming to a newcomer."

"I could tell you were a country girl the moment I spotted you standing outside the door. There's something so fresh and wholesome about you."

Chanel blushed. "Actually, I was born and bred in the country, but I've been living in Brisbane the last few years. I attended university there, and afterwards, I worked in the Brisbane Hospital."

"Oh, I meant no offense. I was born in the country, too. My family came from the north coast, up near Byron Bay. I moved to Sydney when I married my Ron." She sighed softly. "That was nearly fifty years ago."

Chanel smiled. "You must have been a child bride."

Marjorie blushed with pleasure, but waved her compliment away. "Get away with you now."

Chanel glanced at her watch and noted the time. She bit her lip. It wouldn't do to be late on her first day. Marjorie noticed her frown.

"I'm sorry, honey. I've been rambling on about nothing and you need to find Doctor Baker. Please excuse an old lady her memories. Now, if you go to the end of this corridor, you'll find a bank of elevators. Take one to Level Three. You'll find his rooms on the left, right around the corner. He's one of our finest doctors," she added, puffing up with pride. "You'll learn much from him."

"Yes, so I've heard. I can't wait to begin."

"He's also easy on the eye," she added and gave Chanel a wink. "It always makes for a more interesting day when there's a little eye candy around."

Heat rushed into Chanel's cheeks, but she giggled at the old lady's insights. From what Chanel knew of Doctor Baker, he was young enough to be Marjorie's son. The fact that he was old enough to be Chanel's father also didn't seem to matter to the woman. Pushing aside that thought, Chanel smiled again.

"It was lovely to meet you, Marjorie, and thank you for making me feel so welcome. I'm going to love working here. I just know it."

The tight white curls bobbed around the older woman's head and her face filled with good cheer.

"My pleasure, Chanel Munro. You have a great day."

---

Chanel hefted her backpack over her shoulder and stepped out of the elevator. Rounding the corner, she found Doctor Baker's rooms as Marjorie had described. His name was engraved on a brass nameplate affixed to the outside of the closed door. She swallowed a fresh wave of nerves and knocked.

"Come in."

Chanel's breath caught at the sharp command. It had come from a woman. She scrambled to adjust her thinking and her approach. She'd been worried about offending the doctor, but offending his secretary was probably just as bad. She opened the door and offered a hesitant smile to the woman who gave her a narrow-eyed stare from behind the counter.

The woman's skin was flawless, though she had to be in her fifties. She wore a designer suit and her hair was thick and luxurious. It hung over her shoulder in a stylish ponytail and was made up of so many shades of blond, it was obvious she employed an expert colorist. Despite the woman's unfriendly demeanor, Chanel felt a burst of admiration.

"Hi, I'm—"

"Chanel Munro. You're late."

Chanel nodded and slid her backpack off her shoulder. "I'm sorry. I was—"

"Doctor Baker has a reputation for excellence. He is held in the highest esteem in medical circles right around Australia. He's also a very busy man. He doesn't tolerate excuses, Doctor Munro, no matter what the circumstance. Let this be your one and only warning. Don't be late again."

"No, of course not. I promise I—"

"Take a seat. Everyone else is here. Doctor Baker will be out shortly."

Chanel gathered her backpack and turned away. She glanced at the other people who almost filled the modest waiting room. Apart from a man reading a newspaper who looked like he was in his forties and a woman graying at the temples, engrossed in texting on her phone, they were young, like she was.

Chanel nodded polite acknowledgements to the other members of Doctor Baker's team and took the only remaining chair. She smiled at the girl seated on her right.

"Hi, I'm Chanel Munro," she said and offered the girl her hand.

"Tanya Singh," the girl responded in a voice without a trace of an accent, despite the fact her glossy black hair and midnight eyes appeared to indicate she was of East Indian heritage.

"Nice to meet you, Tanya. Are you part of Doctor Baker's new team of residents?"

"Yes, we all are." Tanya lowered her voice to a whisper. "Don't worry. I only got here a minute or so before you. I think she only growled at you because you're so young and beautiful. You probably remind the old hag of what she used to look like."

Chanel swallowed a gasp of surprise, but Tanya only giggled behind her hand.

Chanel's lips twitched upward in response. "*Shh*," she admonished, stifling a grin. "She'll hear you."

Tanya shrugged, unconcerned. "She thinks because she's

Doctor Baker's wife she can lord it over his students. Ha! I'll show her. She's nothing but a bully. Wait until—"

"She's Doctor Baker's *wife?* Are you kidding? And she *works* for him?"

"Yeah, weird, huh? You'd think with all the money he must make she'd be whiling away her time at soirees and society lunches. Perhaps she doesn't trust him around his young and beautiful medical students?" Tanya winked and Chanel was reminded of Marjorie's comments about the doctor.

Tanya lowered her head conspiratorially. "I've heard rumors that he—"

Her words halted abruptly when an inner door opened and Doctor Baker strode into the room. Chanel had seen images of him on Google, but none of them had done justice to the way he appeared in the flesh. Apart from being above average height and in peak physical condition, he had an air of charm and charisma that no photo could properly capture. His blue eyes twinkled with warmth and humor and his teeth showed white and straight and perfect amidst the fullness of his smile.

*The man was gorgeous.* If she were the kind of girl who was attracted to older men, she'd be a goner, for sure. Aware that she'd been staring, Chanel dragged her gaze away from him and studied the carpet.

"Good morning to all of you. I hope I haven't kept you waiting?"

A murmur of 'No, Doctor' ran through the group.

"For those of you who are new to Sydney Harbour Hospital, I'd like to welcome you, and in particular, I'd like to congratulate you on making it onto my team. There were many of you who competed for a place. You have a right to feel proud that you made it through."

Chanel nodded in agreement. She looked up and her gaze tangled with his. He stared at her, his expression intense. Her heart skipped a beat and heat rushed into her cheeks. After what seemed like forever, he looked away and she drew in a shaky breath. She snuck a peek at Tanya, but it seemed the girl hadn't noticed.

"Anyway, enough of that," Doctor Baker continued, his tone dismissive. "Why don't you come through to the boardroom? We can get to know each other a little better and I can fill you in on what I expect." He swung around and spoke to his wife. "Susan, bring in some coffee. Or perhaps some of you would prefer tea?"

"Coffee's fine," Chanel murmured, along with the nine others.

"Coffee it is, then." With that, he turned on his heel and headed toward a room adjacent to the one he'd come from. He opened the door and then stood back to allow them to enter. Chanel stared straight ahead and followed behind Tanya.

"Hey, what's your name?"

The doctor's voice was a low murmur in Chanel's ear. His warm hand on her bare arm startled her. Her mouth went dry and her tongue refused to work.

"Ch-Chanel Munro," she stammered and silently cursed the fresh wave of heat that flooded her cheeks.

"Chanel Munro. A beautiful name. Welcome; it's good to have you on my team. I'm looking forward to getting to know you."

"Th-thank you, Doctor Baker. I-I'm very grateful to be here."

His voice dropped to a husky drawl. "We all have much to be grateful for, Chanel Munro."

Someone behind her cleared their throat and Chanel lowered her head in embarrassment. No doubt he told all of his recruits how pleased he was they'd joined his team. He'd handpicked them, after all. She hurried after the others and took a place beside Tanya in the boardroom.

A large oval table made from some kind of dark, polished wood filled most of the room. High-backed black leather chairs provided seating for at least twenty. Floor-to-ceiling bookshelves filled with numerous leather-bound medical journals stood against two walls. A third wall held a large flat-screen television, projector screen and sophisticated-looking audio equipment. Pale morning sunlight filtered in through the windows that were set against the fourth wall. The room was darkly masculine and perfectly suited the charismatic doctor who took the place at the head of the table.

Chanel was a little alarmed to discover she sat directly across from him. She felt off balance, uncertain of how to proceed. She was grateful for the vastness of the table that separated them—even though that distance didn't seem near enough.

She frowned and did her best to quell her nerves. She'd been around good-looking men before. She'd worked with a lot of doctors who were easy on the eye and she'd even dated one or two. What was it about Doctor Baker that had her so nervous inside? He was nothing more than her boss— albeit an attractive one.

The door to the boardroom swung open and Susan Baker walked in carrying a large tray laden with a silver coffee service and cups to match. Chanel eased out her breath in relief and vowed silently to keep her wayward emotions under control. She was there to learn under the best. A year under the tutelage of Doctor Baker would set her up for life. She'd be guaranteed entry into whatever post-graduate medical career she chose. She refused to allow her nerves to jeopardize everything she'd worked for. With that resolution in mind, she kept her gaze focused on the table before her.

"Thank you, Susan." He turned his attention to his new team. "People, we have fresh coffee, cream and sugar. Come and help yourselves."

The others pushed back their chairs and headed toward the tray that had been left on one corner of the table, not far from where the doctor sat. Chanel remained where she was. The aroma of freshly brewed beans wafted toward her, tantalizing her and warring with her need to keep her distance from Doctor Baker.

"Do you want one?" Tanya asked and Chanel swallowed a sigh of relief.

"Yes, thank you. Cream and one sugar would be great."

A few moments later, Tanya returned with a cup in either

hand and set one down before Chanel who offered the girl a grateful smile.

"Thank you. You're a lifesaver! It's my first hit of caffeine for the day."

Tanya smiled. "Really? I can't get out of bed without at least one cup in my belly. I'm lucky. My dad brings it in to me every morning."

"You still live with your dad?" Chanel asked in surprise. She'd gauged Tanya's age to be close to her own.

"Yes. I still live with my dad. I think I'm the only thirty-year-old in Sydney who does so, but there you have it."

Chanel shrugged. "I guess if there isn't a reason for you to move out, it's a sensible thing to do. The rents in Sydney aren't cheap, particularly close to the city. I bet you save a ton of money."

"Yes, I've managed to save up and buy my first investment property." Tanya winked. "There are some perks to living with your family at my advanced age, although it plays havoc with your love life."

"I think I could handle living with one of my brothers, if they had the room," Chanel replied. "Three of them are scattered around Sydney. Each is married with a handful of kids. Their houses are full to bursting. Too bad, because my love life's non-existent. I'm twenty-seven years old and can count the number of boyfriends I've had on one hand."

"You look a lot younger. Fresh and beautiful. Your skin's so clear and your hair—there's no way you'd get a color like that out of a bottle."

Chanel touched the single long braid a little self-consciously. People were always commenting on the color of her hair. Her father still referred to her having a 'head of pure sunshine.' She preferred to describe it as blond.

"Thanks," she muttered. "You're right. The color's natural. My mother's fair. Even in her mid-sixties, she still has gorgeous hair."

"Like the doctor's wife," Tanya whispered on a giggle. "But you can bet hers came from a bottle. She's plastic from head to toe."

Chanel snuck a peek in Susan's direction and hid a smile behind her hand. The woman had an enviable figure and looked like she was devoted to her gym. A firm-looking pair of breasts large enough to put Pamela Anderson to shame were shown to full advantage in a tailored blouse with three of the top buttons undone. She leaned across her husband, giving him the opportunity to look his fill, but his gaze remained fixed on Chanel. She blushed and looked away and busied herself by taking a quick gulp of her coffee.

A moment later, the doctor clapped his hands together to capture everyone's attention. "All right, now that we have a shot of caffeine on board, let's get started. Thank you, Susan. You can take that away now." He barely spared his wife a glance.

Her mouth tightened, but she made no reply. Instead, she removed the tray of coffee things, as directed. Chanel watched with interest as she closed the door behind her.

Doctor Baker cleared his throat. "I've allocated everyone a pager. Make sure it's switched on at all times, unless you're on rostered days off. Speaking of rosters, I've prepared one for each of you. You'll find you're scheduled for twelve-hour shifts and then you'll be on call for another twelve. If you're lucky, you might snatch an hour or two of sleep between emergencies."

A chorus of groans rippled around the room, but were quickly silenced with a stern look.

"Let me remind you, you were the ones who applied to be considered for my team. I took only the best, but now you're here, I expect you to earn it. Anyone who can't keep up will fall by the wayside. Be warned, I won't be here to pick up the pieces. If you want to work under the best, you have to be the best. Anything less is unacceptable." He drilled them with hard eyes, his gaze slowly scanning the room. "Are we clear?"

"Yes, Doctor," Chanel murmured, along with her colleagues.

The doctor stared at her and a little smile curled up his lips. "Good. Now, let's go have some fun."

# CHAPTER 2

The doctor's idea of fun was doing rounds on a medical ward. The beds were filled with his patients and all of them were grateful to see him. They clung to his words with almost as much vigor as they clung to his hand and it was obvious they thought very highly of him. Even their relatives looked upon him with admiration, gratitude and respect.

Chanel pulled a notepad out of her backpack and scrawled down details of each bed and the patient contained therein, taking time to note their particular maladies and the treatment that had either been administered or would be in the near future.

The majority of patients were well into their seventies and many of them suffered common complaints that came from aging: diabetes, ulcers, heart disease. A couple of them had come in with pneumonia. Doctor Baker took the time to listen to each one of them, often perching himself on the side of their bed. Chanel watched him squeeze old hands and pat wrinkled cheeks and couldn't help but be impressed. He even helped one woman spoon yoghurt into her mouth.

No wonder he was loved and adored by everyone he came into contact with. Chanel had never seen such devotion from a doctor. He was kindly, caring and more than generous with his time, speaking with his elderly patients in tones gentle, respectful and considerate. It was only when he turned his attention to his students that his demeanor changed.

That's when his eyes narrowed and his gaze turned hard. He fired one question after another at them, demanding answers that most of them struggled to give. Chanel fought to keep up with her notes and inched her way toward the back of the group.

"Doctor Munro, please step forward."

Her heart skipped a beat. She quaked inwardly at the thought of being subjected to his harsh glare, but was left with no choice but to comply. She felt like an intern on her first ward rounds all over again.

"Yes, Doctor Baker?"

"This is Mrs Amelia Arncliffe. She was admitted last night. With Mrs Arncliffe's permission, I want you to carry out an examination and then tell the rest of us what ails her."

Chanel bit her lip against a sudden rush of nerves, but quickly answered him. "Yes, Doctor."

Stepping forward, she fielded a sympathetic look from Tanya and moved closer to the bed. A cloud of snowy white hair framed the old lady's petite face. She smiled up at Chanel and nodded her consent.

"Hi, Mrs Arncliffe. I'm Doctor Munro. Now, what seems to be the matter?"

"That's what you're here to find out, Doctor Munro," Doctor Baker said dryly.

Chanel blushed, but refused to be intimidated. She'd been treating patients under the guidance of her superiors for the last two years. She was hardly a novice. Drawing in a surreptitious breath, she tried again.

"Are you in pain, Mrs Arncliffe?"

"Yes, Doctor. It's my tailbone. I can hardly bear to lie on it."

"Did you suffer a fall?"

"No. It's been sore for a while and it's gradually gotten worse. Now the pain's so bad I can't stand it. It feels like I'm on fire."

"Do you mind if I take a look?"

"No, not at all." The woman rolled further onto her side and Chanel moved away to close the curtains. There wasn't enough room for all ten of Doctor Baker's students to fit around the bed.

"Half of you will have to wait outside. You can sit in on the next one. The rest of you, gather close," he said and moved until he stood right next to Chanel.

Her heart rate skittered, but this time it wasn't from the stress of getting the answer wrong. The smell of his expensive cologne tickled her nostrils. She could feel the heat of him through her white lab coat. With her gaze fixed on the patient, she pulled away the bedspread and sheet.

"I'm going to have to lift up your nightdress, Mrs Arncliffe. Is that okay?"

"Do what you need to do, honey. I have nothing you haven't seen before although I bet it's a bit more wrinkly than what you're used to."

Chanel smiled at the woman's sense of humor and proceeded to lift up her nightie. The elderly woman's legs were slim and pale and hairless. Her skin was mottled with age. Raising the nightdress above the woman's buttocks, Chanel spied a dark and angry wound, raw and festering with pus. She stifled a gasp. Her gaze flew up to meet Doctor Baker's. He stared at her, his eyes dark with the same anger that stirred inside her.

"Mrs Arncliffe," she said, striving to keep her voice normal. "Do you live at home? Who cares for you?"

"For over fifty years my dear old Edward looked after me. Every morning that we were married, he brought me tea and the papers in bed. He treated me like a queen. When he died last year, I couldn't cope without him. My children thought it best for me to move into a home."

"You mean, a nursing home?"

"Yes. I have my own room and a bookshelf and small closet to store my things, but I hate it. I've hated every minute of it since I moved there. Too much death and sickness. It feels like we're all in a holding pattern and they're just waiting for us to die."

She sniffed. "I can't leave, even if I wanted to. My son sold my house within a month of me moving out. He says he's invested the money in the share market, but I haven't seen any proof of it. I know he has my best interests at heart and I'm not accusing him of any wrongdoing, but I wish I'd been given a chance to decide if I liked living in the home before my choices were taken away."

"*Mm*," Chanel murmured, unable to say anything else. If she voiced her real feelings on the subject, she'd be reprimanded for speaking her mind. It wasn't her place to have an opinion on Mrs Arncliffe's living arrangements. Her family had done what they thought was best. At least, she hoped they'd acted with noble intent.

"How often do the nurses take you for a walk, Mrs Arncliffe? It seems to me that you've been sitting or lying down for extended periods of time."

"Yes, you're right about that, honey. I spend a lot of time in my room. Our meals are served out in the common room, but often I don't bother getting up. Most of the time, the food is flavorless slop. It tastes nothing like what my Edward used to serve. The nurses don't care if I don't make it out for meals."

"What about showering? Do you need assistance for that?"

"Yes, I'm afraid I do. My legs don't work like they should. A nurse usually takes me to the showers in a commode chair and gives me a wash."

Chanel gently lowered the woman's nightgown and pulled the sheet and bedspread over her legs. She glanced at Doctor Baker.

"So, Doctor Munro. What's your diagnosis?"

"She has an abscess on her sacrum, Doctor. It's been there for some time. I'm not sure how it was overlooked by the staff in the nursing home. The hole's almost as big as my fist."

Fresh anger lit the depths of Doctor Baker's eyes and Chanel knew exactly how he felt. She'd never seen such neglect. And to think the poor lady was in the care of health professionals... There hadn't been any caring going on for a long, long time.

"How's your pain, Mrs Arncliffe?" Chanel asked gently, keeping her anger in check.

"Not too bad, honey. Whatever Doctor Baker prescribed for me last night seems to have done the trick. My pain hasn't been this controlled for weeks."

Chanel looked up at the doctor and in silence, tried to convey her gratitude. She was beginning to understand the reaction he elicited from everyone around him. He was nothing short of a hero.

"How would you treat Mrs Arncliffe, Doctor Munro?" he asked.

"The wound needs debriding, preferably under a general anaesthetic. Once the dead skin has been removed and the wound properly cleaned, it needs to be packed with antibiotic-infused gauze and the dressing needs to be changed twice a day. I would also prescribe IV antibiotics to deal with infection. It has already set in around the wound. We need to take care it doesn't get a further hold. With proper care and attention, she should make a full recovery."

"Very good, Doctor Munro. And when Mrs Arncliffe returns to the nursing home, what then?"

Anger and frustration welled up inside her and her chest went tight. Chanel stared up at him and blinked hard at a sudden surge of tears. The thought of the poor little lady returning to the place of neglect was almost too much to bear. She opened her mouth, but no words came out.

"It's okay, Doctor Munro," Doctor Baker said, his voice low. "We'll leave it there for now. You did well. Exactly the treatment I've prescribed. Congratulations. We might make a decent doctor out of you yet."

His fingers brushed up against her arm and despite the fact she'd never been attracted to men who were old enough to be her father, she shivered from the contact. Her body's instinctive response annoyed her. Even if he were twenty years younger, the fact remained that he was her boss. Her married boss. She had strict rules against dating both types of men. It wouldn't do to offer him any encouragement. She moved away and turned to open the curtains. The other members of the team stared at her curiously.

"How did you know what it was?" the woman with the graying hair asked.

"What did it look like? It sounded gross," one of the young men asked.

Tanya was madly scribbling notes.

"You'll all get your turn to examine a patient and provide me with your diagnoses," Doctor Baker interjected. "Doctor Munro performed very well, but I'm nothing, if not fair. You'll all have your chance to wow me with your brilliance."

He smiled and Chanel found herself smiling back. He was an excellent physician who truly cared about his patients. He might have been her married boss, but that didn't mean she couldn't respect and admire him from afar.

---

Detective Sergeant Bryce Sutcliffe pressed the security button that locked the squad car and made his way across the expanse of asphalt parking lot to where it joined the cobblestoned path that ended at the front doors of the Sydney Harbour Hospital. His partner of three months, Detective Jett Craigdon, strode along beside him. A light summer breeze blew up from Circular Quay, ruffling their hair. It provided cool relief from the heat of the day and helped to divert his thoughts from the inevitable feelings of dread that weighed him down whenever he stepped inside the cold and sterile corridors of a hospital.

"Where have they put Wales?" Jett asked, referring to the prisoner who'd been brought in by ambulance after a foiled bank robbery an hour earlier. Bryce was glad for the distraction and answered quickly.

"Ward Five. He's waiting to be operated on. The guard's

bullet sheared off a piece of the asshole's liver on its way through his gut."

"Too bad it didn't hit anything vital. No doubt they'll repair the damage, stitch him up and he'll be as good as new, ready to terrorize another group of innocent citizens."

Bryce grimaced, hating the fact that much of what Jett said was true. "Let's hope the judge slots him for the maximum this time."

At their approach, the automatic doors to the entry of the hospital slid open on a whisper of sound. Bryce spied Marjorie behind the information desk and threw her a wave. Her face broke into a wide smile.

"Good afternoon, Detectives. I hope the day's been treating you well?"

"You, too, Marjorie. How's Dottie? I haven't seen her for a while."

"Oh, she's just dandy, Detective Bryce. She's having a few days off to visit her grandbabies up on the central coast. Her daughter lives up near Gosford. She should be back on board next week."

"Good to hear it," Bryce responded with a grin and a wave and then headed in the direction of the elevators alongside Jett.

Stationed at the City of Sydney Police Station, both of them were more than familiar with the layout of the hospital. Bryce had been alarmed to discover upon his transfer to the busy station that at least three or four times a week, the officers attended the emergency room and other areas of the hospital to take statements from victims of crime. Every now and then, an alleged offender also required hospitalization. Today was one such instance. Over the years, he'd done his best to tolerate being in a hospital but it was not his favorite place.

*Ding.* The elevator doors were barely halfway open when a woman wearing a white lab coat stepped out and ploughed straight into him. The stack of papers in her hands went flying.

"Damn," she muttered and shot him a frown before bending low to collect the scattered paperwork.

Bryce reeled back from the brilliance of her almond-shaped eyes. They were as blue as the Pacific Ocean.

"I'm sorry," he said and automatically bent down to help her.

She flashed him a grimace that was now tinged with laughter, her displeasure of a moment ago no longer visible.

"Don't be. I should have been watching where I was going. It isn't your fault."

Something moved deep in Bryce's gut and warmth spread through him. At the same time, he noticed the identification badge pinned to her lapel: *Doctor Chanel Munro*. A doctor... A surge of irrational anger went through him and he dropped his gaze and turned away, using the excuse he was helping her collect her papers to avoid looking at her. A moment later, holding out a stack in his hand, he had no choice but to make eye contact with her again.

"Here."

She took the proffered paperwork and murmured a thank you and then gave him a smile so genuine he felt it all the way down to his boots. Her blond hair swung in a thick, jaunty plait. Despite himself, his eyes were drawn to its movement. The color of her hair was reflected in the golden tones of her skin. It looked like she spent many lazy weekends at the beach. His gaze skimmed down her body and images of her in a skimpy bikini came to mind. He frowned, annoyed at the direction of his thoughts.

"Bryce, are you coming?"

Jett's voice intruded on his musings and Bryce swung away from the woman and nodded in response.

"Sure." Steadfastly keeping his gaze off her, he followed Jett into the elevator and pressed the number for the fifth floor.

---

Chanel adjusted the paperwork in her arms and strode away from the bank of elevators, her mind on the man she'd collided with. She'd barely stepped out of the elevator and there he was. If she hadn't been so engrossed in the notes she'd made during her first rounds with Doctor Baker, she might have seen him in time.

Thinking of the stranger's sexy good looks, her heart skipped a beat. He'd been much more to her liking and closer to her age. His coloring was as dark as one of her brother's and she wondered fleetingly if he had aboriginal heritage, like she did. His dark hair and even darker eyes certainly pointed toward some interesting ancestry.

She made a noise of impatience at the back of her throat, unable to believe she was wasting even a second thinking about his background. The odds of seeing him again were next to none. Sydney had a population of over four million and a hospital had a huge turnover of patients, visitors and staff.

Besides, why would she *want* to see him? She'd largely shunned dating and boyfriends for all these years. She refused to lose sight of the prize so close to the finish line. She didn't want anything to distract her from her goal of achieving lofty heights in the medical world. Men had a way of complicating things and right now the last thing she needed was another handsome-man-type complication.

"Chanel! Wait up!"

Chanel turned to see Tanya striding as quickly as her short legs would carry her over the polished linoleum floor that stretched across the vast ground level of the hospital. Like Chanel, Tanya also hefted a file under her arm and was headed in the direction of the exit. By the time Tanya caught up with her, the woman was puffing slightly from the exertion.

"Hey, I'm glad I caught you. I was hoping we'd be able to go and get a coffee and dissect the day's events."

Chanel considered Tanya's suggestion and nodded. "Sounds good. My head's still in a spin after Doctor Baker's whirlwind introduction to Sydney Harbour Hospital. Do you have anywhere in mind? I'm new to the city."

"Sure, follow me. There's a great little coffee shop right around the corner. Their tarts are to die for. You wait and see."

Chanel fell in step with her new friend and a comfortable silence ensued. A short time later, Tanya led the way across a quaint stone courtyard and through the door of a small, but cosy café. Its wooden walls were decorated with original paintings of vibrant garden scenes. The colors were reflected in the bright checked tablecloths that graced the dozen or so tables that filled the room. Tanya chose a table beneath a window that looked out upon the busy city street.

"So, what do you think of the scrumptious Doctor Baker? Is he something, or what?" Tanya pulled out a chair and winked at Chanel.

Struggling to keep her blush in check, Chanel busied herself by taking a seat opposite and arranging her handbag and file full of paperwork on the vacant chair beside her. Knowing that Tanya expected some kind of response, she fished around for something to say.

"Yes, I guess so. There's certainly something about him that commands attention."

"I bet he was hot in his younger days. He's still as sexy as hell and he must be in his fifties. I can see why every female within a five-mile radius of the hospital twitters at the mention of his name."

"Too bad he's married."

Tanya shrugged and opened the menu. "Single, married. Does it really make that much difference?"

"It does to me. I guess I'm a little old fashioned in that regard."

"Is that the reason for the lamentable love life you described earlier? Are your standards too high?"

Chanel might have taken offense if it weren't for the teasing sparkle in Tanya's dark brown eyes.

"I'm not sure it has anything to do with my standards. More like my determination to be the very best doctor I can. For years I've done almost nothing but study like crazy and work hard to further my career. I can't complain. It's gotten me this far. Being accepted onto Doctor Baker's team was a dream come true. I never imagined I'd make the cut."

"You and me both, despite the fact my dad assured me I'd get in. He had more confidence in my ability than I did. Lucky for me, he was right."

"He sounds lovely. Very supportive. What about your mom? What does she think about you being a doctor?"

Some of the light faded from Tanya's face. "Mom died when I was young. Breast cancer. It was very sudden. She was thirty-three. I was five. I remember her a little. Odd flashes of memories here and there. I think I mostly remember her presence and how loved I felt. Dad's been on his own for the last twenty-five years."

"They must have loved each other very much."

"Yes, I guess they did. I was too young to understand their relationship, but the fact he hasn't found love with anyone else tells me what they had together must have been very special." She grimaced. "Sometimes I feel guilty for not moving out of the house. Every now and then I wonder if he would have found company with another woman if I weren't still there. Now that I'm more than an adult, I wonder if it isn't time he had his life back again. He's spent the past two decades watching over me."

"He loves you," Chanel guessed.

"Yes, he does. And I love him. But I'm thirty years old. Maybe it's time I stood on my own two feet and gave him some space..."

"But what about all that money you've managed to save? You wouldn't be able to do that if you were renting or paying a mortgage elsewhere."

"You're right, but how much money do I need? I already own an investment property and I'm an only child. Everything Dad owns will come to me eventually and he's done very well for himself." Her eyes began to sparkle with good humor. "And that's before I find an even richer husband to support me in my dotage."

"Ah, so you're not progressive enough to thumb your nose at a traditional institution such as marriage?"

"Of course not, but it doesn't mean I don't intend to enjoy myself along the way." She grinned and Chanel couldn't help but respond.

The waitress arrived and Tanya ordered for them both. "Trust me," she said. "You're going to love their custard tarts. The pastry melts in your mouth and the filling is beyond divine."

After the waitress had disappeared with their order, Tanya eyed Chanel curiously. "So, tell me more about yourself. You mentioned three brothers who live in Sydney. Where do you fit in the family?"

"I'm the baby. Five older brothers and one sister. My parents are still alive and still together. A big traditional family."

"Ah, so you're the spoiled one," Tanya joked.

Chanel gave a mock gasp of outrage. "No way! Mom and Dad made sure none of us grew up feeling entitled. We were far from poor, but we were made aware of how fortunate we were, don't worry. All of my brothers are in law enforcement and my sister's a child psychologist and married to a police officer. We were raised with a sense of the importance of giving back to our community. I guess it's one of the reasons why I became a doctor. Helping and healing people when they're ill seemed like a noble thing to do."

"And it is. I wish my reasons for applying to med school were as noble as yours."

Chanel smiled. "Okay, so tell me Tanya Singh, what was it that inspired you to become a doctor?"

"I wanted to make my dad proud," she said simply. "He and my mother left India for Australia as a newly married couple, seeking a better life. They wanted to raise their family away from the poverty and desperation that infiltrated so much of the Indian way of life. They wanted more for me." She shrugged and looked away. "The least I could do was study hard and do something with my life that would make them proud. It's sad that my mom didn't live to see the outcome of her sacrifice, but my dad tells everyone he comes into contact with about his daughter who's a doctor."

Chanel swallowed the lump that had formed in her throat. "That's a wonderful story and just as noble a reason as mine to become a doctor. Your dad must be a very special man."

"He is and I'd love him to find someone to love again. Let's face it, I'm going to have to move out some time. I hate the thought of him living there all on his own."

"Have you ever spoken to him about it?"

"Not really, but maybe it's time?"

"Maybe he's even wondering himself whether he should get out again? He must realize he won't have you home forever."

"Yes, maybe you're right. I'm going to talk to him about it. I don't know what I'll do if he agrees it's time I found a place of my own," she laughed.

"I'm sure he's not about to kick you out on the street. Besides, you could always share with me. I'm about to advertise for a roommate. I'm renting an apartment on the north shore. It's a great little two-bedroom place with fantastic views of the harbor and it's only fifteen minutes from the hospital... But all of that doesn't come cheap. I need someone to share the expenses."

Tanya's expression sharpened. "You're kidding, right? You're looking for a roommate?"

"Yes, I have the advertisement in my backpack. I meant to find the staff noticeboard and pin it up today. I was so busy doing rounds with Doctor Baker, it slipped my mind."

Tanya stared at her and then nodded, as if coming to a decision. "I'm going to speak with Dad tonight. It's way past time we had the chat. If he's okay with it, I'd love to move in with you."

Chanel grinned. "Really? I won't be bringing you any cups of coffee in bed. You might want to give the idea some thought before you make a drastic change like that."

Tanya laughed. "No coffee in bed? What kind of roommate are you?" Her smile slowly faded. "I think it's way past time I gave Dad some space. Since I was born, he's spent all of his life taking care of me. It's time he took care of himself."

The waitress arrived with two mugs of steaming coffee and a small tray containing cream and sugar.

"I'll be right back with your tarts," she said and disappeared in the direction of the kitchen.

Tanya picked up one of the mugs. "Here's to new friendships and new roommates."

Chanel touched her mug to Tanya's and echoed the toast. "And here's to surviving a year working under the esteemed Doctor Baker. May his bark be worse than his bite."

Tanya winked. "To Doctor Baker."

# Chapter 3

With his arms loaded, Bryce used his hip to shut the door of his unmarked squad car and headed toward the front gate of the old weatherboard terrace he called home. Juggling the briefcase and paperwork he held in his hands, he unlocked the front door and shoved it open with his shoulder.

"Hi, Grandma, I'm home. How was your day?"

He was met with silence, but forced himself to remain calm. She was eighty-three and rather frail, but that didn't mean she'd suddenly up and left this world. With increasing frequency, he cautioned himself to be prepared for that day, but it didn't mean the moment was upon him now. She was probably in the back of the house, unable to hear him.

The sound of the television, tuned to her favorite sitcom, reassured him somewhat and he made his way further into the house. A moment later, he heard the flush of a toilet and by the time his grandmother appeared in the corridor, his face was wreathed in smiles.

"Bryce, you scared me nearly half to death. I didn't hear you come in." The tender look she gave him softened the harshness of her words and he stepped forward and gave her a hug.

"Sorry, Grandma. I didn't mean to startle you. I'm home a little later than I expected."

"Another busy day at the office?"

"Aren't they all?"

Virginia Tilocca patted her head in an effort to contain the few strands of snowy white hair that had come loose from her usual bun nestled low on the back of her neck. With measured footsteps, she made her way slowly past Bryce and into the vintage *circa* 1950s kitchen. As she opened drawers and looked for utensils, Bryce couldn't help but notice how much she favored her left foot.

"How's your foot feeling today?"

"A little sore. My own silly fault, no doubt. It was such a lovely day. I decided to go for a walk. I only went down the hill and around the corner to that little park. I sat and enjoyed the sunshine for bit and then headed home. I think it was the uphill climb that did the damage."

Bryce frowned in concern. "How's that new antibiotic cream working out? The one your doctor prescribed last week. Is the ulcer getting any better?"

"Well, sometimes I think it looks like it's shrinking and other times I'm not so sure. It was okay last night, but now it feels like my foot's on fire. Like I told you, it's my own silly fault. I shouldn't have overdone it."

Bryce closed the distance between them and turned her gently to face him. "You need to take care of yourself, Grandma. You know what your doctor told you. You're not as young as you used to be and diabetes takes its toll. It's affecting your circulation, which means it will take longer for that ulcer to heal. You need to take it easy and let your body put its energies into getting better."

"Doctor Baker told me exercise was good for me. He told me it would help stimulate my sluggish circulation," she said, her mouth set into a stubborn line.

Bryce stifled the urge to swear and gritted his teeth. "He wasn't talking about tackling a five-hundred-yard hill climb, Grandma."

Her face softened and she patted his arm. "You worry too much, Bryce. I'm a diabetic. I have a few issues with my circulation, an ulcer here and there. That's nothing and it's far from terminal. Don't worry; I've got a few years left in me yet."

Bryce's shoulders slumped on a sigh and he pulled his grandmother in close for another hug. She was so tiny, the top of her head barely came up to his ribcage, but he'd learned she was tougher than most people credited.

"I know you have, Grandma, but I love you and that means I worry about you. I'm sure you worry about me, too, right?" He winked and offered her a smile.

"Of course I worry about you, you dolt. You head out of here every day, ready to do battle with the world and whatever drug-crazed, armed-and-dangerous idiot you come across and I'm expected to wave you off with a smile and a fare thee well. You're my only grandchild." Her voice roughened with emotion and tears glittered in her pale blue eyes. "I love you, Bryce. I'm not sure what I'd do without you."

Bryce swallowed hard against the lump in his throat and tightened his arms about her. He knew exactly how she felt. He'd been eight when his parents were killed in a car crash. His grandmother had taken him in with open arms and had raised him with patience, good humor and love. She was all he had in the world and he dreaded the day he'd lose her.

---

It was late when Bryce switched off the light in the kitchen and walked down the corridor toward his bed. He'd finished the last of the statements taken from witnesses to the armed robbery earlier in the day and was more than ready to call it quits. A light shone beneath the door to his grandmother's bedroom. He tapped gently on the closed panel.

"I'm going to call it a night, Grandma."

"Come and tell me good night," came the soft reply.

Turning the knob, Bryce eased open the door. His grandmother was propped up on a mountain of pillows, her white hair loose and flowing around her shoulders. A book lay open in her lap.

"What are you reading?"

"*Forever in My Heart,*" she responded with enough melodrama to make him smile. Her eyes sparkled. "A romance novel of the highest order," she added.

He snorted his disbelief and leaned over to kiss her on the forehead. "Well, I hope it brings you the sweetest of dreams."

"Oh, it will, grandson. It will. You ought to read one now and then. It might give you some…let's say, inspiration."

Heat rushed up his neck and with it, a trace of anger. "You of all people know my situation. How can I—?"

The smile faded from her face. "Bryce, honey, I'm sorry. I was teasing, but it's been three years. Don't you think it's time—?"

"Time for what, Grandma? She's still alive. Or have you forgotten?"

The old woman shook her head slowly back and forth and her eyes filled with sadness. Unable to bear it another moment, Bryce turned on his heel and left.

With his heart thumping, he dragged in a quick breath and headed to the shower. Leaving his clothes piled in a heap on the bathroom floor, he turned the spray to the hottest temperature he could bear and stood under the torrent of water. He picked up the soap and lathered his skin, scrubbing away the effects of the day.

At least he could be thankful Wales hadn't gotten away with his attempt to rob a city bank and no innocent bystanders had been injured. The bank staff had acted quickly and Bryce and his team had managed to arrest the offender before he'd cleared the building. The whole incident had been over almost as quickly as it began.

With the man in surgery, there hadn't been much to do at the hospital but sit around and wait—and think about his encounter with the beautiful, blond doctor. Even now, the memory of her stirred a barrage of mixed emotions.

He'd had enough to do with hospitals and doctors to last him a lifetime, not the least his recent battle over what to do with his wife. Still, the kindness and warmth in the blond doctor's eyes pricked at his conscience. It wasn't her fault he'd been scarred by members of the medical profession. Then again, he hadn't asked to be the husband of a patient who clung to life only by the grace and expediency of a machine.

It had been three years since the accident and he was under increasing pressure to make a decision. There had been a message on his voicemail only the day before from Angela's doctor. He wanted Bryce to call. It was the second message the doctor had left that week.

Bryce squeezed his eyes shut and tried to block everything out. He was tired of thinking about what needed to be done. He was tired. Period. Sometimes it felt like he hadn't had a restful night since the morning of the accident. In fact, he was sure he hadn't. As much as he resisted the thought, he wondered if perhaps his grandmother was right. *Perhaps it was time to let Angela go...?*

Sadness flooded through him at the thought. It seemed like only yesterday when he'd asked her to be his wife. He'd spied her from across the room of his best mate's kitchen. He didn't even know what she was doing there. It was like something out of a gooey chick-flick movie. The world had stopped.

He was nineteen and until that moment, had never been in love. One look at her dark glossy hair and smiling brown eyes and he was a goner. All these years later, he could still remember the way she'd made him feel.

His body hardened at the memory of his wife in their early years. She'd been everything he'd ever dreamed. They'd been happier than he'd thought possible. And talk about beautiful. She'd been the most beautiful girl in the world.

His cock stirred and he wished for the hundredth time he had a better way to assuage his need. It had been more than three years since he'd made love to a woman and the enforced abstinence was taking its toll. Like tonight, when he had an erection so thick and hard it was painful and all he wanted to do was bury himself into the wet warmth of a woman.

He leaned his head against the coolness of the tiles and

sighed heavily. Pulling off in the shower had long since lost its appeal. Still, if he didn't want to spend half the night with a hard-on and an ache low in his balls, he had no choice but to deal with it. With images of his wife in the forefront of his mind, he stroked his cock and did what needed to be done.

The water began to cool and Bryce realized he'd probably emptied the hot water tank. Rinsing the last of the soap from his body, he turned off the water and stepped out of the shower. He reached for a towel and scrubbed himself dry. Refreshed but still feeling restless, he slung the towel around his hips and headed for bed.

―――――――――

Chanel tucked a loose strand of hair behind her ear and hurried into the hospital. She'd been assigned the day shift and didn't want to be late. Reaching the bank of elevators, she pressed the up button and waited for it to arrive.

"Chanel! Hey, how are you? Are you on this morning, too?"

Chanel turned to see Tanya hurrying toward her, carrying a hefty briefcase.  "Yes, I am." She nodded toward the bulging briefcase. "What could you possibly have in there? It's only our fourth day."

Tanya grinned. "My notes. I wrote out intensive case studies on every one of Doctor Baker's thirty-nine patients we've seen on rounds this week—so if he happens to call on me, I'll be prepared. I don't know how you manage to think so quickly."

Chanel shrugged. "Instinct, I guess. I did a few stints in the emergency room during my first year of residency. It taught me how to think on my feet. There's no time for prolonged examinations and debates about treatment there. Time's often of the essence."

"Well, I'm going to be a blithering idiot when he asks me, I just know it. I can't afford to take any chances. I need to make a good impression. Dad would be devastated if I was taken off Doctor Baker's team. He hasn't stopped talking on Facebook about my acceptance."

Chanel laughed in surprise. "Your dad's on Facebook?"

Tanya grinned. "Oh, yeah. He told me it's the best way ever to keep in touch with everyone. He knows who's going where, who's unwell, who bought a new pair of shoes, even what they ate for dinner. He doesn't need to telephone to stay in touch. Facebook does it for him."

Chanel chuckled again and shook her head. "I need to meet your father. He sounds like he'd be great fun."

"Yes, he is and you can meet him, if you want to. I talked to him about moving out and I mentioned your offer. He was mostly enthusiastic. He said it was time both of us took charge of our lives."

"That's great. When do you want to move in?"

Tanya grimaced. "He wants to meet you first, to make sure you're suitable to share a house with his beloved and only daughter."

"I'd love to meet him. When should we do it?"

"The sooner the better. How about after work today? You could come home with me and stay for dinner."

"Sounds great. With a bit of luck, we'll finish at the same time. How about I meet you out in front of the hospital?"

"Excellent. We can go in my car. I'll drop you off at the train station afterwards. I'll text Dad and let him know you'll be coming. He'll want to put together some kind of feast, for sure."

"Oh, please tell him not to go to any trouble," Chanel protested.

"Of course he'll go to a lot of trouble. He's very traditional in many ways and you're to be our honored guest." Tanya gave her a wink. "I hope you like curry."

———

"Doctor Munro, may I speak with you a minute?"

Chanel slowed to a stop inside Doctor Baker's office and

turned back to face him. A few minutes earlier, he'd handed out a list of his patients and had divided them up among his students. They were now filing out of the room. Chanel had been pleased to see that she and Tanya had several patients in common. They would be able to share their notes and compare diagnoses, as well as discuss treatment options. It would make life easier all round to have a study buddy. One as well prepared as Tanya would be an added bonus.

"Yes, Doctor Baker?"

The man held her gaze, his bright blue eyes commanding attention. "Just so you know, I have high expectations of you, Doctor Munro. You came very well recommended by two staff specialists I happen to know at the Brisbane Hospital and after your performance with Amelia Arncliffe three days ago, I'm quietly confident I might have discovered a star."

Heat crept up Chanel's neck and she was grateful for the high collar on her blouse. She did her best to keep the blush of pleasure from spreading to her cheeks.

"Thank you, Doctor Baker. Your praise means a good deal to me."

His eyes narrowed on her face. "Does it?"

"O-of course it does. You've reached the pinnacle in your field. A year under your tutelage would mean incredible things for me—the very least is what I'll learn from you over that time. I'm pleased and excited to be here."

He moved closer and Chanel's nerves hitched. The cerulean blue of his eyes deepened and his voice lowered to a growl.

"Good. I like that you're excited. It makes it all the more...exciting for me."

His gaze dipped to the rapid rise and fall of her chest and it was all she could do not to raise her arms and cover herself. With an effort, she kept her hands by her sides.

"You can't imagine how boring it is to choose students who look brilliant on paper, but who, in reality, fall far short of my expectations," he continued in a voice pitched for conversation.

"Take Doctor Singh, for example. She graduated with honors, was lauded from one end of Sydney to the other by members of the medical profession, but I can already tell she's not a star. She needs hours, days, weeks to prepare. She can't think on her feet. A doctor needs to be able to assess a situation and come up with a plan of action in a matter of minutes. Most of the time, we don't have the luxury of taking notes and spending time analyzing, comparing, discussing."

He threw out his arms to emphasize his point and his hand brushed up against her lab coat. She ignored the heat left in its wake and concentrated on his monologue.

"More often than not, we're forced to provide an on-the-spot diagnosis and offer treatment in the very same breath." He paused and moved closer, until they were almost touching.

"Don't you agree, Doctor Munro?"

Chanel licked her dry lips and forced her mouth to work. "Yes, Doctor Baker. A lot of the time, you're right, but I think you're being a little harsh on Doctor Singh. There's always a place to confer with colleagues and double check opinions on optimum treatment."

Something akin to admiration glinted in his eyes. "I applaud your loyalty, Doctor Munro, even if it is a little misplaced. Loyalty is a much-admired trait and one that's close to my heart. Unfortunately, sometimes it's in short supply. When it comes down to it, there are those among us who'll opt to save their own skin over that of a colleague."

Chanel forced herself to hold his gaze. "I hope never to have my loyalty tested in that way, Doctor."

His bark of laughter was harsh and bitterness twisted his mouth. "Don't we all, Doctor Munro, don't we all." He reached out and brushed the back of his hand against her cheek.

"You, on the other hand, Doctor Munro, are a star. I could tell from the moment I saw you. There's something about you, something indefinable. It sets you apart from everyone. When I demanded you examine Amelia Arncliffe, you rose to the challenge. No ifs, no buts, no stumbling. You gave me exactly what I wanted." His hand moved to cup her cheek and Chanel swallowed hard against her rising panic.

*What the hell was going on? Was the Sydney Harbour Hospital's most highly respected doctor caressing her cheek? What was she going to do?*

As tactfully as she could manage, Chanel stepped away and out from beneath his touch. Flustered and more than a little unnerved, she fished around for something to say.

"I-I appreciate your vote of confidence, Doctor Baker. I hope I continue to live up to your expectations."

His gaze traveled over her, lingering once again on her heaving chest. "I hope you do, too, Doctor Munro. If you let me down, I'll be gravely disappointed."

"H-how is Mrs Arncliffe?" she asked, latching onto the first thing that came into her mind. "I've seen her for the past couple of days, but she's not on my patient list this morning. When's the debridement?"

Doctor Baker's expression darkened and he took a step back. In silence, he turned away. Chanel frowned, at a loss to figure out his sudden change in demeanor.

"Unfortunately, we lost Amelia Arncliffe last night."

Chanel's hand flew to her mouth in an effort to contain her gasp. "You mean, she *died?*"

"Yes, Doctor Munro. That's exactly what I mean."

Chanel shook her head in confusion, trying desperately to get a hold of her jumbled thoughts. "But... But *how?* She seemed fine when I last saw her. I mean, not *fine*. She was suffering from that terrible abscess and she must have been in excruciating pain, but it was hardly life threatening. What... What happened?"

Doctor Baker swung slowly around to face her. He drew in a deep breath and let it out on a sigh.

"We don't know exactly, yet. Later the same day, after you'd been to see her, she began complaining of stomach cramps and nausea. By midnight, we couldn't stop the vomiting. It was terrible to see her in so much pain, particularly after all she'd been through." His voice lowered to a husky whisper. "I hated watching her suffering. She begged me to help her, but there was nothing I could do."

Chanel shook her head, still in shock. "Will there be an autopsy?"

"Perhaps, although she was far from well. Apart from the appalling abscess on her sacrum, she was malnourished and extremely low in iron and a number of other essential elements." He looked up at her and shook his head sadly. "I'm afraid the neglect had been going on for some time."

Hot anger surged through Chanel and she clenched her fists, feeling the need to hit something. Hard. The thought of how the woman had been treated in the nursing home left her breathless.

"What will happen? Will there be an investigation? Will the family sue?"

"Such righteous indignation! Such passion for justice! We need more people like you in our world, Doctor Munro. Unfortunately, I can't see much justice for Amelia Arncliffe. There might be some members of the medical profession who don't know anything about loyalty, but like I said, the majority of us tend to stick together, no matter what. Misguided or not, you don't rat out a mate. On any given day, it could be you or me in the firing line—there but for the grace of God and all that... None of us are infallible. We're all capable of fucking up. We need to know we have the support of our colleagues if and when we do."

Chanel stared at him, aghast. "But what about Mrs Arncliffe's needs? Who was seeing to them? Surely, she had a right to good and proper health care, especially in a health facility? How are we going to bring an end to the injustices leveled upon some of the most vulnerable members of our community if we don't take a stand against them?"

She was breathing hard and her heart thumped against her ribs. Her hair had begun to escape the confines of the ponytail she'd secured earlier that morning. She was sure she looked a mess—not exactly how she wanted to present herself in the first week of her residency.

With an effort, she slowed down her breathing and got her heart rate back under control. A few quick swipes at her hair and she hoped she'd restored it to a somewhat tidy arrangement. From the look on Doctor Baker's face, he didn't much care either way. He came toward her with a tender expression on his face.

"You're really something, you know? I thought you were a star, but I was wrong. You're so much more than that. Your fire, your passion, your kindness... Do you have any idea what you do to me? How you make me feel?"

Once again, he moved up close beside her and didn't stop until their clothes were touching. He reached out and took her chin firmly between his fingers and tilted her head up to his. Off balance, she stumbled forward and landed full against him. His arm came around her and pressed her closer. She gasped at the feel of his erection against her stomach.

"Oh, Chanel, Chanel, Chanel, from the moment I saw you, I had to have you. Your skin, your hair, your eyes, your body. There's not a single part of you that isn't beyond exquisite and I have to touch you, taste you, fuck you."

His words finally penetrated her fog of fear and panic and gave sudden movement to her frozen limbs. She pushed hard against his chest. Caught by surprise, the doctor released his hold and she stumbled away from him.

"Stop! You have to stop! This isn't right. Please, Doctor Baker, this isn't right."

"Chanel, come on, you're making too big a deal out of this. You and I would be great together. Can't you see that? And think of all I can do for you over the course of this year. You'll graduate top of the class with my wholehearted support and congratulations. The medical world will be yours for the asking. Any job you desire will be within reach. And in the meantime, the two of us can have a little fun. What's the harm in it?"

Chanel stared at him in confusion. *Was he insane? What nonsense was he talking? He couldn't honestly expect her to sleep with him in return for better grades? Surely that kind of awfulness only happened in the movies?*

But as he continued to advance upon her, she realized with growing unease that he meant every word he said. He'd offered her a proposition. Sleep with him and she'd reap the rewards—in every possible way. The very thought turned her stomach.

She glanced at him and saw the determination in his eyes. It was clear she was going to have to work hard to persuade him otherwise. The trick was doing it without offending him. The thought of failing terrified her.

"Doctor Baker, I'm sorry. I hope I haven't given you the wrong impression. You... You're a very attractive man. But the truth is, I'm here to learn, to grow as a doctor, to be the best medical practitioner I can be. I believe in healing and easing pain and being there to ease patients through their darkest hours, but I need to do it on my own terms, using my own talents, my own instincts, my own deductions. It's the only way it can be. Don't you see? I don't want you to smooth my path or remove obstacles out of my way. I want to earn my place in the medical world. Please, tell me you understand?"

Doctor Baker's expression had darkened more with every moment of her speech and she quaked inside at the thundercloud that developed on his face.

"So, you're rejecting me. Is that what you're trying to say? That not only don't you want me, but you don't need me to help you on your way to this illustrious career?"

His tone had deepened to an angrier growl with every sentence he uttered. Chanel held his gaze, but it took every ounce of courage she possessed.

"I wouldn't put it quite so harshly, Doctor Baker, but...the essence of what you say is correct."

If it were possible, his expression turned blacker and Chanel couldn't help the shiver of apprehension that prickled along her spine. *How had she gotten into such a situation?* Things had moved far out of her control. It was time to take her leave.

"Doctor Baker, if you don't mind, I'd like to go and start my rounds. Thank you once again for your kind words. I promise I'll do my best to earn my place on your team."

"Oh, you'll earn your place, all right. You don't know what you've done by turning me down. I have the power to make all of your paths smooth and if I'm so inclined, as rough and rocky as I like."

The threat in his words was as clear as the menace in his eyes and another shiver of foreboding feathered across Chanel's skin. She hadn't set out to antagonize him, but despite her best efforts, one thing was clear: She'd made a dangerous enemy.

# CHAPTER 4

Bryce glanced at his watch and then pushed away from his desk. It was crowded with the usual assortment of case files, statements, pens and pencils and two large, black, leather-bound volumes of legislation that made up the New South Wales Crimes Act. His younger colleagues chided him for being so old fashioned.

With the legislation easily accessible online, most officers searched with their keyboard, but he preferred the smell of the wafer-thin paper and the feel of it beneath his fingers. Besides, he had so many sticky notes stuck on various pages of the Act, with notations scrawled upon them, he couldn't bear the thought of tossing it all away.

With a brief knock on his superior's half-open door, he poked his head through the gap.

"Ah, boss, do you mind if I duck away for a little bit? My grandmother has a doctor's appointment downtown. I told her I'd transport her to and from."

Detective Superintendent Holt Denman glanced up from his computer screen and nodded. "Sure, Bryce. No problem. So far, so good with the emergency callouts. Nothing more than the usual. How long will you be gone?"

"An hour or two at the most. It won't take me long to get home. Provided the doctor's on time, everything should be sweet."

"We both know there's no guarantee the doctor won't

keep you waiting, but take as long as you need. We have everything covered here."

"Thanks, boss. I appreciate it. I'll work through my breaks to make it up."

Holt waved him away and returned his attention to the screen. Bryce turned and headed toward the exit.

———————

"Grandma, I'm not convinced you need to take two novels to pass the time. It's a fifteen-minute appointment." Bryce tried to keep the exasperation from his voice and grinned in an effort to soften his words. His grandmother merely snorted.

"Ha, for your information, smarty pants, I'm on the last chapter of this book and then I won't have anything to read. Doctor Baker likes to take his time with his patients and some of them take advantage. He's not like the doctors in that medical center on the corner."

Bryce helped her into the car and closed the door behind her. A moment later, he slid behind the wheel. His grandmother continued where she'd left off.

"Those doctors are lucky to give you three minutes of their precious time and all the while they make you feel like they're doing you a favor by seeing you. Doctor Baker might run late, but at least he listens to what you have to say. Besides, he's kind of cute, too."

She winked at Bryce and he groaned. Checking his mirrors, he pulled out into the traffic and headed toward the city, where Doctor Baker's private rooms were located. He was fortunate the home he shared with his grandmother wasn't far away.

Situated in one of the older parts of Paddington, his grandmother's house was close to his work as well as to the distractions offered by the city. With the movie theaters, numerous bars, night clubs and live stage performances all within a short distance of each other, it was a perfect place to live.

Not that he had much time to indulge, but every now and then, he'd enjoy a new release at the movies with his grandmother or spend an hour or two relaxing after work with a colleague in one of the city's many bars. The temperate climate and relaxed lifestyle of Sydney suited him to a tee. Then there was Angela, of course. He'd never leave while she was still here.

Twenty minutes later, the pale brick building that housed Doctor Baker's rooms came into sight. Bryce scoured the lot for a parking spot. One of the disadvantages to the rapidly expanding city was the lack of parking. Occasionally he got lucky, but today wasn't one of those times.

"I'm not going to be able to find a parking spot around here, Grandma. How about I drop you off at the front door and come back and collect you when you're finished?"

"That would be fine, Bryce. But what will you do in the meantime?"

He waved off her question. "Don't worry about me. I have my iPad and a heap of files on the back seat. I have plenty to keep me occupied. Are you sure you don't want me to come in with you?"

She rolled her eyes. "I'm a big girl, Grandson. When have I ever wanted you to come in with me?"

Bryce shook his head. "Okay, okay. I just thought I'd ask. I'm happy to, you know."

"Of course I know. You're the sweetest boy an old woman could ever hope for, but I'm fine. It's nothing important. I'm going to get him to take a look at my foot again. I've been applying that cream for more than a week now. I thought the ulcer was getting better, but it doesn't seem to be healing. With my diabetes complicating matters, I just want to stay on top of it, you know?"

"Yes, Grandma. You're doing the right thing. It's much better to get him to check it out and see what he thinks than wait until you have a real problem. Now, how about you text me when you're finished and I'll come and collect you?"

"That sounds like a great plan."

"You have your phone?"

"Yes, Bryce."

"Is it charged?"

"Yes, Bryce."

"Good."

He smiled and waved good-bye. "I'll see you soon."

Pulling away from the curb, he headed in the direction of a nearby park, thinking he'd spend the time going over some of his open cases. There were always phone calls to make, witnesses to contact, lab results to chase. He wouldn't find it hard to fill the time.

A car reversed out of a parking spot right in front of him and a surge of satisfaction rushed through him. Every now and then, his luck turned around—even if it *was* only a parking spot. Pulling the unmarked squad car into the vacant space, he reached over and collected the files that lay on the back seat. Locking the door, he strode across the wide expanse of freshly mowed green grass and breathed deeply.

Summer in Sydney was his favorite time of the year. The trees towering above him were bursting with new life; the carefully tended garden beds could snatch his breath with their heavy perfume and vibrant colors. The air was hot, but not uncomfortably so and when he found an unoccupied park bench beneath the shade of a huge Moreton Bay fig tree, he sighed with contentment.

Apart from the noise of the traffic from the busy streets that bordered the park, it was easy to believe he was far away from the rush and stress of his daily life. Not that he'd change anything about that—well, not on the career front, anyway.

From the time he knew what a policeman was, he wanted to be one. It wasn't just the smart blue uniform and the shiny black boots. Police officers had an unmistakable air of authority about them. They were "take charge" kind of people and got to help others along the way.

Over the years, it hadn't been all smiles and happy days, but he'd learned to take the good with the bad. No career was without its challenges and he saw those difficulties as opportunities for growth and learning, rather than setbacks. At thirty, he had enough experience behind him to be eligible to apply for more senior positions and he couldn't wait for the day he was the commander of his own station. Yes, his professional life fulfilled him on every level. Too bad he couldn't say the same thing about his personal life.

*Angela.*

At the thought of his wife and all they could have had, his heart filled with sadness. They'd had such hopes and dreams. Together, they were going to conquer the world. And then there was the accident and their lives had come crashing to a halt and broken into so many pieces, he'd never be able to put them together again.

Instead of hopes and dreams, he lived in limbo—a half life that was neither living nor dead. If it weren't for his job, he didn't know where he'd be. His job kept him sane. Not many officers lay claim to that, but that was the way it was. His job and his work colleagues were the constants in his life. All the other things were shadows. Even his beloved grandmother, who'd been the center of his life for so long, had become less dependable. She was getting older. Slower. Forgetful. Once so vital, now her health was beginning to fail. He couldn't bear the thought of the woman he loved above all others not being there one day.

Thinking that way was selfish and some would say immature. Everyone died eventually. It was just the way it was. But he didn't want it to happen to his grandmother. Not her. *Why couldn't she be spared? Set apart? Protected from the indignity of aging and certain death?*

Perhaps, if he had more than his grandmother's love in his life, or even some other female companionship, the thought of her inevitable demise wouldn't have him so panicked. But the truth was, there was no one except Angela and as much as it pained him to accept it, she no longer counted.

Swallowing a sigh, he flipped open the file on the attempted armed robbery that had taken place a week ago. Richard Wales had recovered from his surgery and had been refused bail until his next court appearance. With the man caught red-handed on CCTV, Bryce assumed the germ had nothing more to look forward to than receiving a reduced sentence in return for an early guilty plea—but stranger things had happened.

Against his better judgement, Bryce's thoughts wandered to Chanel Munro and he allowed himself a few moments of fancy before grimacing with annoyance. It was stupid to waste time on foolish daydreams. She was a doctor and he was married. He didn't need a reminder of how cruel life could be.

The depressing thought seeped into Bryce's veins and settled heavily in his gut. With a shake of his head, he snorted with irritation. He normally managed to stay positive, despite the setbacks in his life. He wasn't one to wallow in self-pity. He was a "glass half-full" kind of guy. Always had been. He didn't know what had caused this sudden bout of negativity, although he suspected it might have something to do with his worries about the elderly lady who was even now being attended to by her physician.

As if his thoughts had summoned her up, the phone in his pocket chirped to indicate a new text message. Checking the screen, he smiled at the thumbs-up and smiley face emoji his grandmother had sent. She'd embraced technology like it was a new toy and knew as much about cell phones and tablets as he did. She might have been eighty-three, but she refused to allow her age to dictate the way she led her life.

His grandmother was optimism personified. He didn't have to look far to discover the source of his own positive outlook on life. He had much to be grateful for. More than he could fathom.

---

Chanel hurried along the corridor that led to Ward Three and cursed the narrowness of her knee length skirt that hindered her progress. Her high heels clattered across the polished linoleum, but she paid the sound no heed and picked up her pace. Ward rounds had already started and she dreaded giving Doctor Baker any cause to disparage her.

Four members of Doctor Baker's team had been assigned the patients on Ward Three and she was one of them. It had been a fortnight since her confrontation with him and he'd followed through on his threat by making her life as difficult as possible. His favorite time to humiliate her was during ward rounds where, surrounded by his students and an unwitting patient, he seemed to take immense pleasure putting her on the spot.

Spying the team clustered around a bedside, Chanel did her best to slide in beside Tanya without detection. She should have known Doctor Baker would immediately notice her arrival.

"Doctor Munro, so nice of you to join us. Don't tell me, you slept through your alarm? Or perhaps you've been caught in traffic? No, I've got it! A giant cockroach held you hostage through the night and you've only now managed to escape."

Heat seared Chanel's cheeks, but she didn't dare respond. She'd learned the hard way there was no appeasing him. Silence was her best option. After a long moment, he shifted his hard gaze to the patient in the bed. Like a switch being thrown, Doctor Baker's face relaxed and became wreathed in smiles.

"Mrs Evan, how are you this morning? I'm glad to see there's a little more color in your cheeks today. We must be doing something right."

The elderly woman in the bed smiled up at him, her double chin wobbling with the effort. Chanel nearly choked at the warmth and admiration in Mrs Evan's eyes.

"Please, Doctor. Call me Robyn. And yes, thank you, I'm feeling a little better."

"A long way from fit and healthy, though." Doctor Baker turned to encompass the group of doctors behind him.

"I have a few second-year residents with me, Mrs Evan.

They're part of my medical team. I was wondering, do you mind if they look in on you every now and then?"

"No, of course not."

"Good. I'd like to ask one of them to examine you, if you don't mind. It's the best way for them to learn. I hope that's all right with you?"

"Yes, Doctor. I'm happy to help."

Doctor Baker nodded in satisfaction. He turned to face Chanel and immediately his expression hardened once again.

"Doctor Munro, would you care to examine Mrs Evan and share with the group your diagnosis and prescribed treatment?"

"Yes, Doctor Baker." Chanel stepped forward and smiled down at the white-haired lady in the bed.

"Good morning, Mrs Evan. I'm Doctor Munro."

"Hello, Doctor Munro. My, don't you have pretty hair? A halo of gold and sunshine."

Chanel patted her hair self-consciously and avoided looking at the others. "Thank you, Mrs Evan."

"You're welcome, honey. I'm only stating the truth."

"So, how long have you been feeling unwell?"

"It must be at least two weeks. It started with a cough and a sniffle and progressed from there."

"Do you mind if I listen to your chest?"

"Of course not."

Chanel took the stethoscope from around her neck and fitted the ear pieces. Leaning closer to the woman, she gently pressed the end of the stethoscope against the thin cotton of Mrs Evan's nightgown. The rattle in the old lady's chest was unmistakable.

"Do you mind leaning forward, Mrs Evan? I'd like to listen from the back."

The woman heaved herself upright and then leaned forward enough so Chanel could put the stethoscope against her back. Moving the instrument from side to side, the result was the same.

"Thank you, Mrs Evan. You may get comfortable. I'm finished."

Doctor Baker's gaze narrowed on her. "So, Doctor Munro, what do you think?"

Chanel lifted her head and held his gaze. "She has bilateral pneumonia, Doctor Baker. She needs IV antibiotics. Stat. If all goes well, she should be fine in three or four days. At least, well enough to go home."

The hardness didn't leave Doctor Baker's eyes, but he offered a reluctant nod and turned back to the patient.

"There you go, Robyn. A few days and you'll be feeling a whole lot better than you are right now."

The elderly woman looked up at him with gratitude. "Thank you, Doctor. It can't come soon enough." A hacking cough took hold of her and didn't seem to ease. Chanel stepped forward and patted her on the back.

"It's okay, Mrs Evan. Coughing's going to help. It's your body's way of trying to get rid of the buildup of fluid inside your lungs. I know it's uncomfortable, but just try and remember it's helping you to heal. If we give you something to suppress the cough, it will only slow things down."

"We don't want to do that." The old lady gasped and even attempted a smile.

Chanel smiled back at her and squeezed her soft, wrinkled hand.

"You're going to make a fine doctor," Mrs Evan said. "I can see how much you care. You can have all the smarts in the world, but if you don't care about your patients, what good does it do?"

"You're very sweet, Mrs Evan, and thank you for saying so."

"I used to have hair that color," the woman murmured and reflexively touched the wisps of white that covered her head. "A long, long time ago."

"You were beautiful," Chanel said. "You're still beautiful."

A sad smile turned up the corners of the woman's mottled lips. "Now who's being kind?"

"Not kind at all," Chanel smiled. "Just stating the truth."

"Doctor Munro, are you finished here?"

The stern interruption came from her superior. He glowered at Chanel.

"Yes, Doctor Baker. I'm sorry to keep you waiting."

"We have other patients to see."

"Yes, of course." She turned back to Mrs Evan. "It was lovely to meet you and I'm sure you'll be feeling better soon."

"Thank you, honey. I hope to see you again."

"Oh, you will. I'll make sure of it," Chanel promised and followed Doctor Baker and his students out of the room. She'd barely cleared the room when Tanya pulled her to one side.

"I see Doctor Baker's still using you for his punching bag. Where were you this morning, anyway? You were gone before I got up. I assumed you'd left for work early."

"No, I went for a jog. It was such a beautiful morning. I jogged over the Harbour Bridge and back. I was nearly home when I heard the sound of a kitten. It was caught in a drain."

Tanya rolled her eyes. "Don't tell me you were late for work because you were rescuing a kitten?"

"I couldn't just leave it there! It was cold and wet and looked like it had been there all night. What would you expect me to do?"

"I don't know, leave it for someone else to find. Why do you have to be the Good Samaritan?"

Chanel sighed and shook her head. "I don't know. It's just in me. It's the reason I became a doctor. I can't stand back and let things suffer when I can help."

"It was a kitten, Chanel and probably a stray one at that. What did you do with it?"

Chanel dropped her gaze and tried hard to will away the guilty blush that spread across her cheeks.

Tanya's eyes narrowed. "Chanel Munro, what did you do with that kitten?"

"I-I brought it home with me. That's why I was late. I had to run to the corner shop and buy some milk and cat food."

"You brought it home? To live with us? What if I'm allergic?"

Chanel looked up at her. "Are you?"

"No, but that's not the point. You can't bring stray animals home and not tell me. I'm paying half the rent, remember? I get equal say. It's only fair."

Chanel's shoulders slumped and she looked away. "Yes, you're right. I'm sorry. I should have asked you about it first. It was just that, I was there and it was cold and hungry and..." She looked up at Tanya and silently pleaded for her to understand.

Tanya sighed and shook head. "Chanel Munro, what am I going to do with you?"

"You don't have to do anything with—"

"Is it cute?"

A tiny smile lifted the corners of Chanel's lips. "Yes, it's very cute."

"Is it soft and fluffy?"

"Now that she's dry... Yes, she's very soft and fluffy."

"She?"

Chanel's smile widened to a grin. "I checked."

"Does she have a name?"

"Not yet. Why don't you think of one?"

Tanya's eyes sparkled in delight. "Really?"

Chanel nodded. "Really."

Tanya squealed and gave her a quick hug. "Well, now that I know the reason you were late, I'm well and truly satisfied with your excuse for your tardiness."

"Too bad Doctor Baker didn't see it that way."

Tanya's brow creased into a frown. "I still don't get why he's so hard on you. It's like he takes particular delight in seeing you stumble. None of us get any joy out of it, let me tell you. It's embarrassing as hell to watch him tear into you like that."

"You think it's embarrassing for you? How do you think I feel?"

Tanya shook her head in sympathy. "He seemed to like you at the start. I wonder what happened to make him turn on you?"

Chanel compressed her lips, determined not to share her humiliation with her friend. Even if Tanya believed her, what could either of them do about it? When Chanel had shared a few sparse details of the encounter with her sister, Josie had urged Chanel to report him to the medical board, but Chanel wasn't convinced it would be worth the effort.

*Why would the board believe her?* Doctor Baker was lauded by the medical profession from one end of the state to another. He saved countless lives and was humble, to boot. Who would believe her—a nobody second-year resident doctor? Forcing a smile, she hurried to clear the concern from her friend's eyes.

"It's nothing. I'm fine. H-he's like that with everyone. I can't remember the last time he actually praised one of us for our efforts. It's like he enjoys setting us up to fail."

"I think that's probably a little melodramatic," Tanya laughed. "He's a brilliant doctor with a healthy ego. He didn't get to be where he is without a lot of hard work. Okay, he's a harsh taskmaster, but he probably wants to make sure we work at succeeding as hard as he did. Some people are like that. They don't want anyone to take the ecsy road. It just isn't in them to allow it."

"*Mm*, maybe," Chanel replied with an effort, unable to help thinking once again about his unethical proposition. He was more than happy for them to take the easy way if it suited him. In an attempt to steer the conversation in another direction, she said, "So, whose turn is it to cook dinner?"

"Doctor Munro, if you can bear to drag yourself away from Doctor Singh, who is no doubt catching you up on the latest gossip, I'd like a word."

The harshness of Doctor Baker's tone and the steely-eyed glare he threw their way served to bring an abrupt end to their conversation. Nerves surged through Chanel, but she steadfastly forced them aside. She'd had enough of being intimidated, most especially by her boss. With courage she was far from feeling, she moved closer toward him and bravely held his gaze.

"You wanted to speak with me, Doctor?"

He stared down at her, his expression one of uncompromising granite.

"Yes, as it happens, I took a call from staffing a few moments ago. It seems they're down on doctors in the clinic this morning. Three staff members have called in sick and they have a bunch of police officers booked in for their routine physical exams today. Nothing too demanding, but the clinic needs some help. I've offered to let them have the use of your skills for the day."

Chanel started in surprise. It was the last thing she'd expected. While it wasn't an invitation to carry out brain surgery, it was a definite nod to his confidence in her as a doctor. Up until then, she'd only ever dispensed diagnoses and treatment decisions under supervision. The thrill of being allowed to deal with patients independently was beyond exciting. Perhaps he'd reconsidered his threat to make her life difficult?

"Thank you. I'd love to do it," she said and offered him a sincere smile of gratitude.

"You might not thank me after you've had to deal with a dozen or more irritable police officers. None of them like being told they might not be in the best of health. They all think they're invincible. A bit like us, right?" He grinned and it seemed so genuine, she couldn't help but respond.

"Right."

"The clinic opens in twenty minutes. You'll find it on Level Two. Ask for Janet. She's the nurse in charge."

"Level Two. Janet. Right, no problem. I'll leave right away."

"Don't let me down," he warned.

"I won't. I promise."

# CHAPTER 5

Bryce hunched forward over his desk and pressed his cell phone to his ear. He listened for the third time to yet another voice mail message left by his wife's doctor requesting that Bryce return his call. Biting back a sigh, he did his best to school his features into a mask of indifference. No use in alarming his colleagues unnecessarily or worse, opening himself up to a pile of questions he had no desire to answer.

The pointedness of the doctor's message hadn't gotten any easier to hear, despite the number of times he'd listened to it. The unspoken meaning was clear: The doctor wanted to discuss treatment options for his wife.

He scoffed quietly at the medical-speak. *Treatment options?* As if treatment was a priority. The medical staff had stopped treating Angela years ago. Now she was a patient taking up room in a much-needed hospital bed, caught up in a health system that was stressed to its limits. *Treatment options, my ass. They wanted to talk about turning off the machine.*

With another sigh, he ended the call and then immediately called his grandmother. He'd been trying to reach her all afternoon, but her phone continued to ring out. It concerned him when he couldn't reach her. It wasn't that he immediately assumed the worst, but she was an elderly woman in failing health. The facts couldn't be denied.

He left yet another message on his grandmother's

message bank and then dropped the phone back into his shirt pocket. On top of the call from his wife's doctor, it had been a shit of an afternoon.

"Bryce, you haven't forgotten that medical, have you? You're scheduled for five o'clock." Holt came to a stop beside Bryce's desk.

Bryce automatically nodded in response, even though the routine physical at the hospital had completely slipped his mind. He glanced at the clock on the wall of the squad room. He had fifteen minutes to get there.

Collecting his wallet and keys from the top drawer of his desk, he strode toward the exit. On his way, he checked his phone for messages or missed calls, but there was nothing. With his jaw clenched against another surge of apprehension, he left the building.

Traffic down to the harbor was light and he made good time. His phone showed a few minutes to five when he pulled into the hospital car park. Jogging to close the distance between him and the entryway, he threw a brief wave to Marjorie and Dottie on his way to the elevators and punched in Level Two.

The route was a familiar one. It was a requirement for all New South Wales Police officers to undergo a mandatory physical examination every year. Even though he hated to succumb to the poking and prodding he'd inevitably be forced to endure from some trainee doctor, he'd been in the police service long enough to know there was no point protesting.

He pushed open the door that led to the clinic and came up short. Chanel Munro leaned against the counter, her attention fixed on the file in her hands. She looked every bit as fresh and beautiful as she had the first time he'd seen her and it took all that he had not to stare.

"Detective Bryce Sutcliffe?"

She called out his name and looked around the waiting room. The two other occupants shook their heads. Bryce stepped forward.

"I'm Detective Sutcliffe."

She turned to face him. He could tell the exact moment she recognized him. Her eyes widened and her mouth parted ever so slightly. A moment later, she smiled at him and Bryce felt it all the way down to his toes.

"Detective Sutcliffe, I'm Doctor Munro. I'll be doing your physical examination this afternoon. If you wouldn't mind following me, we'll get started."

She turned and headed toward a closed door. Bryce took a moment to collect himself. His reaction to her was ridiculous. She was a doctor, a part of the profession he found very hard to tolerate. After all he'd endured with Angela—first with the endless rounds of IVF and then later, he'd thought he had enough of doctors to last him a lifetime.

"Detective Sutcliffe?"

He looked up. She'd come to a halt a few yards in front of him, her eyebrow raised in silent query. Heat crept up his neck. He felt like a recalcitrant child refusing to take their medicine. With gritted teeth, he picked up his pace and followed her into the room. She closed the door behind him.

"Take a seat," she said and indicated the chair that stood opposite a plain wooden desk, largely free from clutter.

"I'm sure you know how these work. It says in your file you've been employed by the New South Wales Police Service for more than a decade. I'm going to ask you a few questions about your general health and then I'll carry out the physical exam. Is that all right with you?"

Bryce nodded reluctantly. "Sure."

Chanel put his file on the desk and then walked around behind it and took a seat. She opened the file and scanned its contents, every now and then nodding approval.

"You appear to be in good health, Detective. Are you still jogging every day?"

"When time permits."

"Has anything been troubling you since your last visit? Is there anything in particular you'd like me to look at?"

Bryce stared at her and did his best to hold back a grin. In any other circumstances, he might just be tempted to joke with her. Instead, he replied somberly.

"No, Doctor. I do what I can to stay fit and I limit my alcohol intake. I also try and keep my diet in check. My grandmother does her best in that regard."

She smiled and made a note in his file, but the mention of his grandmother reminded him he still hadn't heard from her. With a frown, he pulled out his phone and checked for messages. Misinterpreting his actions, Doctor Munro frowned back at him.

"I promise not to take up too much of your time, Detective Sutcliffe. I understand how busy you are. If you cooperate, I can have you out of here as soon as possible. It's important I conduct a thorough examination. Your employer relies on the information in my report and quite frankly, my employer expects me to do my job. If you don't mind, I'd ask that you refrain from checking your phone and give me your full attention."

There was a new edge to her voice and her cheeks were flushed with anger. He immediately felt contrite. The feeling annoyed him, but he forced himself to apologize.

"I'm sorry, Doctor. I didn't mean to be rude. It's just that—" He broke off, unwilling to say anything more. It wasn't any of her business why he felt the need to check his cell phone.

Her gaze remained pointed. He debated about blowing her off, but decided against it. She was probably one of those doctors who wouldn't let it go until she was satisfied with his answer. Besides, the sooner he gave her what she wanted, the sooner he could get out of there.

"It's my grandmother."

"The one who makes sure you're eating right."

He gave a wry grin. "Yes. I live with her, watch out for her. We... I guess we watch out for each other."

"How lovely."

She sounded so genuine, Bryce couldn't help but believe she meant it.

"I try and check in with her whenever I can. She's eighty-three and her health's not the best. I've been trying to contact her all afternoon. She's not answering her phone."

Understanding filled the doctor's eyes and her expression

turned serious. "Do you think something might have happened to her? Would you like to call an ambulance?"

Bryce shook his head, feeling a little foolish. "No, of course not. She probably just forgot to charge her cell. I shouldn't jump to conclusions just because I can't reach her."

"It's okay for you to be concerned. Elderly people can have sudden health crises that none of us see coming. It happened to my dad a couple of Christmases ago. Scared us all to death. Would you like to try her again?"

The kindness in her eyes hit him like a blow to the gut. He couldn't remember ever feeling kindness from a member of the medical profession and if he had, he'd buried the memory way down deep inside.

"Thank you, I appreciate your offer, but I think I'd rather just get this over with. My shift's almost over. I'll leave for home as soon as we're finished here."

She nodded and returned her attention to his file. "In that case, if there's nothing you're concerned about with regard to your own health, I'll get you to take off your shirt."

Bryce couldn't help it. He blushed. And not just a little heat up the side of his neck. No, this time his whole face flamed. It was ridiculous. He was thirty years old, and married to boot. Being asked by a female doctor, no matter how gorgeous, to remove his shirt shouldn't have him blushing like a teenager. It was beyond embarrassing.

In an effort to avoid looking at her, he pushed back from his chair and turned away. His hands went to his tie and he loosened it and tossed it onto the examination table. As quickly as possible, he undid the buttons on his shirt and tugged it off. It went the same way as the tie. Keeping his gaze directed at some point above the doctor's head, he waited for her next move.

She appeared completely unaware of his discomfort. In silence, she took the stethoscope from around her neck and stepped closer.

"I'll get you to hop up on the examination table so I can listen to your chest."

He did as she asked and a moment later, she pressed the

cold metal disk against his skin. He remained still. The sleeve of her lab coat brushed up against him. It was all he could do not to react.

It had been a long time since he'd been this close to a woman half naked. She might be a doctor, but there were certain parts of his anatomy that didn't give a shit about her profession. He only hoped she didn't ask him to drop his pants. He tried to remember how the exam had gone down last year, but the best he could recall was that the doctor had been a man. The exam hadn't left a lasting impression.

"Take a deep breath for me," she murmured and Bryce did his best to comply.

"And again."

He repeated the effort and wondered if he'd lose points because of his rapidly beating heart. It wasn't like he could hide it from her. She moved the stethoscope around to the back and once again, pressed it up against his skin.

"Cough for me."

He coughed.

"One more time."

He coughed again. She stepped back and nodded, appearing to be satisfied.

"Everything sounds good. Your chest is clear, your heart rate's normal-ish." She grinned. He cursed silently.

"I'm going to check your blood pressure and then I'll give you a form to take to pathology. They're right down the hall. They'll take some blood from you so that we can test your glucose levels, liver function and STD status. They're routine tests and I'm sure you'll have nothing to worry about. As soon as they finish, you'll be free to go."

He nodded. "Can I put my shirt back on?"

She grinned again and her eyes sparkled with good humor. He caught his breath at the sheer beauty of it.

"Shy, Detective?"

He blushed furiously. "Not at all," he managed. "It's just that, the sooner I get out of here, the sooner I can get home and check on my grandmother."

She appeared immediately contrite. "Of course. This won't take a minute. It's easier to fit the cuff around your arm without your shirt, but as soon as we're done, you can go ahead and get dressed. We can do the rest with your clothing on."

Once again, he caught the teasing glint in her eyes and wished he could respond in kind. She was so refreshing, so different to the doctors he'd come into contact with in the past. So unlike the doctors treating Angela.

He frowned at the thought of his wife. He had no right even thinking about returning Chanel's teasing. He was married. For all his failings, adultery wasn't one of them. All of a sudden, he was more eager than ever to get out of there, away from the temptation the young doctor afforded. The minute she loosened the blood pressure cuff from around his arm, he spoke.

"Are we done?"

Surprise flared in her eyes at the shortness in his tone, but she refrained from commenting. Instead, she scribbled something on a form and handed it to him.

"Pathology request. Right around the corner. Then you're done."

"Thanks." He felt a little bad about his gruff attitude, but getting out of there was foremost on his mind. His grandmother might be hurt, or worse. He wished he could believe she was the primary reason for his urgent need to escape.

---

Chanel stared after the detective as he made a hasty retreat. It had taken her a few moments, but she'd finally recognized him as the man she'd collided with at the elevators. He seemed such a mix of emotions, she couldn't work him out. One minute he'd been friendly and open and the next, it was like he couldn't get away from her quickly enough. He was an intriguing mix of contradictions, not the least being his admission that he lived with and cared for his grandmother.

That kind of selflessness scored highly with Chanel. Family was incredibly important to her and she had a great deal of respect for anyone who thought highly of their own, especially the more elderly members of the clan.

It seemed everywhere she turned there was less and less respect for the elders of their society. It saddened and maddened her at the same time, but she didn't know what to do to change it. It was refreshing to find someone who had similar values to her own. Besides that, he was incredibly cute.

She shook her head at the thought. How many times did she have to remind herself, she wasn't on the lookout for a man? Her career was the only thing that mattered. Too bad that couldn't keep her warm at night.

---

Bryce fitted his key in the lock and did his best to slow down the beating of his heart. Night was sneaking up on the day and the dusk around him was heavy with the scent of flowers. The fresh beauty of it reminded him of Chanel and he immediately scowled. Right now, all he should want was reassurance that his grandmother was all right. Taking a fortifying breath, he let himself into the house.

The place was in darkness. Not a single light shone from any of the rooms. His apprehension shot up another notch. He swallowed the lump of fear that threatened to choke him and called out.

"Grandma? Are you home?" His question was met with silence and a fresh wave of fear tightened his chest. *Was this it? Was this the night he'd been dreading? The night he came home to find his grandmother dead?*

He wanted to shout out against the possibility. It was too soon. She wasn't ready to die. He wasn't ready to bury her. Trying hard to hold on to his panic, he called out louder.

"Grandma, it's Bryce. Where are you?"

Once again, he was met with silence. Apart from the hum of an occasional passing car outside and the creak of the floorboards as he moved with increasing urgency from room to room, there was nothing.

He found himself outside the closed door that led to his grandmother's bedroom and braced himself for what he might find. With as much courage as he could muster, he turned the knob and eased open the door.

The light from the corridor illuminated her slight form. She lay still and pale amongst the bedclothes, with the sheet pulled up under her chin. He reached over and switched on the lamp by her nightstand and then almost collapsed with relief. Her chest rose and fell in a steady rhythm of reassurance.

"Grandma!" he breathed, holding back a sob.

Though he'd spoken quietly, her paper-thin eyelids fluttered open. She squinted at him through the dimness.

"Hello, Grandson. You're home early."

He shook his head, unable to speak. "No, Grandma," he finally managed. "It's nearly seven."

She scrunched up her brow and stared at him. "Seven? Are you sure? I only lay down for a few minutes, right after lunch. How could it be seven?"

Bryce smiled down at her, relief at finding her alive still flooding through his pores.

"I don't know, but you scared me half to death. I've been calling you all afternoon. You wouldn't answer your phone."

"I'm sorry; I didn't even hear it ring."

"It's okay." With his world suddenly righted, Bryce leaned down and pressed a soft kiss against the wrinkled skin of her cheek. "I'm just glad to know everything's all right. I was worried about you."

His grandmother opened her mouth as if to remonstrate, but something in his expression must have given her pause. Instead, she nodded and graciously reached for his hand.

"Thank you for caring enough to wonder if I was alive or dead. You're the best grandson an old woman could ever wish for. Have I told you that?"

He grinned and the fear and apprehension of the last few hours melted away. "Yes, Grandma, you've told me that. And right after that I tell you I'm your *only* grandson."

"Cheeky boy," she scolded, but laughter filled her eyes.

He winked at her. "What's for dinner?"

---

It was way past late and Susan would be wondering once again where he was. Leo hated to give her another reason to rant, but there was nothing he could to about it. Duty called.

The ward was quiet and the lights in the rooms had long since been extinguished. Muted conversation came from the direction of the nurses' tea room, but he paid it no heed. Quietly, he made his way to Robyn Evan's bedside.

She lay in the darkness, with her eyes closed. The rise and fall of her chest accompanied by the wheezing of her lungs assured him she was still with this world, despite the fluid in her lungs. Every breath seemed to pain her and he could well understand why. She was slowly drowning.

She drew in another ragged breath and the sound of it took him back decades earlier to the room where his mother had lain. Familiar feelings of helplessness overtook him and his hands began to shake. He clenched his jaw and told himself not to be stupid. He was no longer that helpless and frightened boy. He was a trained physician, skilled beyond measure. Nothing was beyond him.

After awhile, his breathing returned to normal and he leaned over and smoothed away the tangle of hair that was plastered across Robyn's forehead. He frowned. Her skin was damp and hot to the touch. She was burning up with fever. He cursed. The antibiotics weren't doing their job.

Another wave of helplessness surged through him and his hands fisted. His heart thudded so hard he could barely breathe. The woman would die if he didn't do something about it. In sudden urgency, he reached across and punched the button for the emergency call. Footsteps scurried from all directions across the linoleum floor.

"Doctor Baker, what is it?" a wide-eyed nurse called out, panic in her eyes.

"It's Mrs Evan. She's not responding to the antibiotics. We need to try something else. Stat."

As he watched the flurry of activity around him, he couldn't help but wonder if he'd done the right thing. Maybe it would have been better to simply let Robyn Evan die? He could ease her into a death, free from pain and suffering, all the while surrounded by her loved ones. Surely it was a better option than slowly drowning in her body fluids. He couldn't imagine a worse way to die. He should know. He was a doctor.

———————

Bryce stared at the blank screen in front of him and wished he could concentrate. Instead of the routine report he was attempting to file on a recent home invasion, his thoughts kept returning to his wife. It had been two days since the last message from her doctor and Bryce still hadn't returned the call. It wasn't that he didn't know what had to be done. The doctors had told him long ago there was no hope for her recovery. There were zero signs of brain activity. It had been that way from the time she'd been brought in. He had to find the courage to make the decision and let her go.

"Hey, Bryce, did you hear?"

Bryce looked up. His partner, Jett Craigdon, stood in front of him, a grin widening his face. Bryce shook his head.

"The boss just took a call from the prosecutor. Richard Wales is going to plead."

Bryce stared at his partner and tried to focus on what Jett had said. "Richard Wales?"

"Yeah, the prick who held up the Commonwealth Bank. The turd we arrested and threw in an ambulance three weeks ago. His lawyer called the prosecutor. They're going to plead."

"Will the prosecutor reduce the charges in return?"

"No, that's the best part. We caught the asshole red-handed. He's got nowhere else to go. The prosecutor knows it and so does he. For once, the stars have aligned in our favor."

Jett grinned again and Bryce couldn't help but join him. This was good news. With a criminal record an inch thick, it was likely that with a confession, Wales would be out of circulation for a hefty amount of time. Knowing there was one less career criminal on the street should have been cause for celebration—and it was—but the memory of the message from his wife's doctor intruded and put a damper on his glee.

"Hey, we're out of here shortly. How about we go down to the Brewery Hotel and celebrate properly?"

Any other time, Bryce might have been tempted by Jett's offer, but with the knowledge of his upcoming conversation with Angela's doctor on his mind, he couldn't find it within himself to keep up the pretense of joviality.

"Thanks, mate. I appreciate the offer, but I have a few things I have to deal with before the day's done. See if Harry and Joe want to go. Those blokes don't usually need much of an excuse to toss down a beer or two."

When Jett frowned, Bryce was reminded how perceptive his young partner was. "Is everything all right?"

"Yeah, of course. Something's come up. I need to sort it out, sooner rather than later."

"Is there anything I can do?"

Bryce stared at the sincerity in Jett's eyes and wished he could tell him the truth. It would be a relief to share the burden with someone. Apart from his grandmother and a handful of Angela's friends and relatives he'd long ago lost touch with, no one had a clue that his wife had been in a coma for three years, kept alive only by the intervention of men and machine. But he resisted the urge to spill his guts. No use opening that can of worms. He'd be blithering like an idiot. His new partner didn't deserve that. No one did.

He shook his head and responded. "No, mate. But thanks for asking."

"Hey, we're partners. We have each other's backs, right?"

Bryce nodded and forced a smile. "Right. I'll see you tomorrow. Have a good night."

---

Chanel forked another morsel of Beef Vindaloo off her plate and took the time to savor the spicy bite of tender meat on her tongue.

"*Mm*, this is really very good. Maybe even the best curry I've ever eaten."

Tanya giggled at her from across the table. "That's what you said last time. I thought you might be sick of it by now. We've been eating Indian almost every other night since I moved in."

"Are you kidding? I love Indian food."

"I'll ask you in another six months and see whether you feel the same way." Tanya laughed.

"Hey, I'm always up for a challenge. Six months is plenty of time for you to find a few more recipes and expand your repertoire—secret herbs and spices known only to the Singh family." She gave her friend a wink.

Tanya reached across the table and took another crispy, homemade pappadum. The crunch of it filled the small but cosy room and the girls continued to eat in companionable silence. The faint sound of traffic hummed through the open windows that overlooked the street below.

"So, I had a private little tête-a-tête with Doctor Baker today."

Tanya's offhand comment was said with such a casual air, Chanel was sure she'd misheard.

"Excuse me?" she asked around a mouthful of fragrant curry and jasmine rice.

"Doctor Baker. He asked me to wait back after he'd distributed this week's rosters."

Memories of the private meeting she'd had with Doctor Baker bombarded Chanel. Unaware of her silent turmoil, Tanya continued to speak.

"His wife wasn't there this time and just was well." Tanya giggled like a naughty teenager and lowered her gaze.

A sense of foreboding started deep in Chanel's belly and all of a sudden her appetite disappeared. She set down her fork and focused her attention on the woman seated across from her.

"What are you getting at?" she asked, fighting to keep her voice even.

Tanya's grin widened. "Look at you, getting all serious. It was nothing. He propositioned me, that's all."

"He *propositioned* you?" Chanel tried to keep the anger out of her voice, but failed miserably. She nearly groaned aloud when Tanya looked offended.

"Is that so hard for you to believe? We can't all be blond and built like a fashion model. You're not the only kind of woman men find attractive."

Chanel shook her head back and forth with increasing urgency. "No, no, Tanya. I'm sorry. You misunderstood. I didn't mean—"

"To be shocked at the very thought of a man like Doctor Baker making a pass at the likes of me. Is that what you meant to say?"

"No, please. Stop putting words in my mouth. I didn't mean that all!" She tried desperately to make her friend understand. "You took me by surprise, that's all. I-I'm shocked Doctor Baker made a pass, period. It has nothing to do with you. Of course, I can understand his interest. You're gorgeous! You've got what it takes to drive men wild, but Doctor Baker is our *boss*. Our *married* boss. He shouldn't be propositioning *anyone*."

Tanya shrugged, appearing unaffected by the immorality of the doctor's actions. "You've seen his wife. Does she look like she puts out for anyone? She's probably too concerned about getting her perfect hair mussed to get up close and personal with her husband."

Chanel stared at Tanya, aghast. "What did you say to him?" she forced herself to ask.

"I told him I'd think about it."

"You *what?*"

Tanya shrugged, continuing with her insouciant attitude, but Chanel noticed her rooomate wouldn't meet her gaze.

"We find each other attractive. He's looking for a bit of fun. Where's the harm in it?"

"He's our *boss*, Tanya. Okay, if you don't respect the institution of marriage, that's one thing, but sleeping with the boss is a really bad idea."

"I don't know. There could be benefits. He implied I'd be more than compensated for my efforts."

"As in, better grades? Is that what you mean?"

"I don't know. Maybe. If that's the way he does things, I'm happy not to argue. I need all the marks I can get."

"But, like *this?* Is this *really* the way you want to pass the course?"

"A girl's gotta do what a girl's gotta do."

Tanya's attitude infuriated Chanel and her short temper was exacerbated by the knowledge that her suspicions were confirmed: This was *exactly* how Doctor Baker did things. She opened her mouth to tell Tanya about her experience, but then closed it again.

*What good would it do now?* Tanya might not even believe her. After all, it sounded awfully convenient coming clean about the proposition Doctor Baker had made to *her* right on the tail of Tanya's revelation. At best, it would sound petulant. At worst, it could sound contrived to make a point.

No, it was better to keep that awful business to herself. Despite her sister's urging, she didn't intend to do anything about it and it was clear Tanya didn't find the whole thing distasteful. Maybe Chanel was overreacting? Maybe *she* was the one who needed to loosen up?

The fact was, she didn't want to loosen up; she didn't

want to be the type of woman who found that kind of behavior acceptable. She didn't want to think of anyone finding that kind of thing acceptable. And yet, she was sharing an apartment with someone who did.

Picking up the wine glass that stood by her elbow, Chanel took a healthy swallow of Merlot and used the time to calm down and consider what had just happened and what that might mean for them as roommates. Tanya was entitled to her opinion. She wasn't responsible for the way Chanel felt about the doctor making a pass. All in all, Tanya was a lovely girl and was fun to be around and of course, the frequent authentic Indian meals were something else.

Determined to push thoughts of Doctor Baker and his lack of morals well away from her, she leaned across the table and clinked her glass with Tanya's.

"Here's cheers to a successful year, anyway. Whatever Doctor Baker's failings, there's no denying he's an exceptional physician. We'll do well to observe and emulate him, in that regard, if little else."

"Cheers," Tanya replied and repeated the action with her glass. "And you're right about him being an excellent doctor. Have you seen the way he treats his patients? Like they're the most important people in the world? And he's like that with all of them—male or female, young or old—it doesn't seem to matter. They're all special and unique and receive his undivided attention. At least, that's the way it appears."

"Yes, if nothing else, he has an admirable bedside manner. I've never worked with a doctor who's so considerate of his patients. It's good to see. It restores my faith that there's something decent about him, inside that suave and arrogant exterior."

"Well, he has reason to be arrogant. He's at the top of his game, sought after by the elite of the medical world, here and overseas."

"If you count presenting at a couple of conferences in New Zealand," Chanel replied dryly.

Tanya shook her head. "You really don't like him, do you?"

"I didn't say that."

"You didn't have to. I guess I understand your aversion. He treats you worse than he treats any of us. I still can't work out why."

Chanel busied herself emptying her wine glass, determined not to walk down that path again. With a tight smile, she picked up her fork and continued to eat.

# Chapter 6

Leo Baker stared out through the floor-to-ceiling plate glass window of his penthouse at the pedestrians far below him and wondered at their lives. Like little ants scurrying to and fro, intent on their business, it seemed like everyone had a purpose. Unlike him.

He sighed in annoyance, aware that he was being too hard on himself. Of course he had a purpose. He had a career anyone would be proud of, a wife who still turned heads, two children who were high achievers. He had come a long way since the difficulties of his childhood and had much to be thankful for. God had been good to him. It was more than he could have hoped for.

After watching his mother suffer a long and painful death, he'd felt called to become a doctor, driven to heal the sick and ease the suffering of those beyond help. It hadn't been easy and his father had opposed him at every turn, but he'd managed it and here he was, celebrated and lauded in every circle of the medical world. He'd lost count of the number of doctors he'd mentored and helped along the way. He believed in giving back. But he'd never lost sight of the reason he'd joined the medical profession.

This burning conviction that his career had been ordained by God had been with him from the beginning. Even when he'd been studying full time and holding down three part-time jobs to pay for his tuition, he'd remained convinced he was doing the right thing. Whenever he became fatigued or his enthusiasm waned, he remembered his mother and how he'd felt, watching her die. He never wanted to feel that way again.

It was his dedication to the cause that started it, at least, that's what he liked to think. A patient here, a patient there who was never going to improve. Some were young, many were old, but all of them deserved to find peace. It wasn't going to happen for them in this world. It was up to him to give them the means to find it in the next.

He chose the special ones with care. Each one was his gift to God. Patients struggling with terminal cancer, HIV and worse. The stroke patients who would never again speak or even know who the hell they were. The victims of tragic car accidents who wished they were dead. They told him so—and those who were even beyond that showed him with their eyes. He listened and observed and acted.

"It's time to meet your Maker," he'd whisper and a peacefulness would come upon them. With little trouble, it was done and they were soon free of pain forever.

But lately, the urge to ease the suffering of others had gotten out of control. He only had to recall the situation with Robyn Evan. He'd struggled with the decision to press the emergency button. In the end, he'd done it, but it was almost like another being had entered his body and had taken over his mind. More and more, a voice urged him to end the life of this one or that one and often it wasn't for any good reason.

Take poor old Amelia Arncliffe. Okay, she'd been treated abominably by the staff at the nursing home, but her affliction was far from terminal. With proper treatment, she would have made a full recovery. It angered him beyond measure the gross negligence of those who'd been responsible for her day-to-day care and chances that she'd continue to be mistreated were high, but still, she hadn't deserved to die.

He felt bad about it, really bad. Not that he could do anything about it now. He'd sent a sympathy card to her family and he'd meant the heartfelt words. What was done, was done.

It was as simple as that.

———————

Bryce stared at the young doctor with the thick wavy hair who sat across from him and did his best to remain calm. He'd heard it all before, of course. What the doctor had to say about Angela was nothing new.

He could still remember the day it had happened. The emergency room doctor had found him pacing up and down inside the waiting room.

'Detective Sutcliffe, I'm afraid it's bad news.'

The look on the doctor's face told him everything he needed to know. He only caught snatches of the doctor's words, but it was enough. His wife had suffered massive brain injuries. She was lucky to be alive. If it hadn't been for the quick response of the paramedics, she might already be dead. She was on a respirator. As her next of kin, they needed to know what he wanted them to do. Did he want them to turn off life support? The question was as difficult for him to comprehend now as it had been then, but for entirely different reasons.

The doctor across from him cleared his throat and Bryce knew he was waiting for an answer. It was a different doctor from the one who'd brought him the news three years ago, but the gist of what he had to say was much the same: Angela was brain dead. There was no hope of a recovery. Again, they asked him to consider taking her off life support.

The question was stated a little more forcefully than it had been three years ago. The doctor explained that Angela was nothing more than a corpse breathing with the aid of a machine. No machine, no Angela. Of course, he'd put it a little more delicately than that, but his meaning was just the same. Apparently, it was pretty simple how that correlation worked. Switch it off and pull out the plug. Let his wife rest in peace.

*Simple, right?* Hell, who was he kidding? If it were simple, he would have signed the consent three years ago. Simple didn't even come close.

---

Chanel glanced over her patient list and was pleased to see Robyn Evan's name was on it. A week had passed since she'd met the elderly woman and a notation showed the antibiotics had finally done the trick. It was possible Mrs Evan might even be discharged that day.

She entered Ward Three and nodded to the nursing staff. "Good morning, everyone. How are we today?"

"Hi, Chanel," the nursing unit manager responded with a smile. "You're bright and early. Who are you here to see?"

Chanel consulted the list in her hands. Some of the names were familiar—patients who'd been hospitalized over the last few days. A couple others had come in overnight. Chanel read through the list of names and the NUM nodded.

"Good. I'll leave you to it," she said. "If you need me, just give me a yell."

"Will do." Chanel turned away and headed toward the first room.

Mrs Evan looked up when she entered and waved at her. "Doctor Munro, how lovely to see you."

"And how lovely it is to see you, too, Mrs Evan. You're looking so much better today. How are you feeling?"

"I'm feeling great," she declared with a grin that set her double chin wobbling. "When I came in here, I could barely breathe. It was like there was a red-hot knife stabbing right through my chest. Every breath was agonizing. Now look at me," she added. "Almost as good as new."

Her grin was infectious and Chanel found herself smiling

back. "I'm so glad to hear it. It looks like those antibiotics did the trick."

"You can say that again. Whatever Doctor Baker gave me worked like magic. I haven't felt this good since I first took ill."

"Well, you look great." Chanel pulled the stethoscope from around her neck. "Do you mind if I listen to your chest?"

"No, of course not. I bet it sounds better than the last time you checked."

Chanel drew the curtains around the bed and then listened to the old lady's lungs. As she expected, they were clear. Slinging the stethoscope back around her neck, she nodded.

"You sound as good as new. I'll speak to Doctor Baker. I think you might just be well enough to go home today."

Mrs Evan's face lit up with delight. "That's the best news I've heard all week, Doctor Munro. I can't wait to call Lionel."

"Is that your husband?"

Her face softened. "Yes. Married for just on sixty years. We're just as in love now as we were all those years ago. He's been totally lost without me. Hasn't been able to find anything around the house. He's been living on canned soup ever since I was hospitalized. He'll be pleased that I'm on the mend."

Chanel's heart tugged at the tenderness in the elderly lady's voice. It reminded her of her own parents and the way they still talked about each other. They hadn't been married nearly as long as Mrs Evan and her husband, but the sentiment was the same. A touch, a look—it wasn't hard to see the love they shared was as strong as ever.

It gave Chanel hope that one day she'd find what they had. In fact, it inspired her not to settle for anything less. The fact that she was only three years short of thirty and still unmarried was a minor cause of concern for her mom, but her mother would be the last person in the world to encourage her daughter to marry anyone other than her one true love.

As the youngest in a family of seven children, Chanel had been given plenty of time to observe her older siblings. Five older brothers and a sister were all blissfully married to their soul mates and happily raising families. She loved spending time with them, despite the fact it often left her yearning for a special someone of her own.

"Do you know what time you're going to see Doctor Baker?"

Mrs Evan's question intruded into her musings and Chanel blinked and focused on the woman in the bed.

"Um, I assume I'll catch up with him sometime this morning. As soon as I get the okay from him, I'll let you know."

"It's just that I don't want to call Lionel and get his hopes up until I know for sure."

"Of course. I understand. I promise to come and see you as soon as I catch up with Doctor Baker."

After farewelling Mrs Evan, Chanel moved on to the next patient on her list. She was halfway through her rounds when Doctor Baker walked into the ward. Her heart immediately leaped into her throat and nerves fluttered around in her stomach. She might not find him attractive any longer, but he still had the power to disturb her equilibrium. He held her career in his hands. He had the power to destroy her and both of them knew it.

Failing to report him for his earlier behavior had only increased his confidence. He now knew she didn't have the courage to call him out. She could only hope he quickly found someone else to take his bad temper out on. She'd had more than enough.

"Doctor Munro, how pleasant to find you at work so early in the morning. The nurses tell me you're at least halfway through your rounds..."

"Good morning, Doctor Baker. Yes, I've seen eight patients, with another six to go."

Doctor Baker nodded his approval and Chanel couldn't help but wonder why he was being so amendable. Probably because there wasn't an audience. The usual crowd of students hadn't yet materialized. It was just her and him in the corridor outside one of the hospital rooms.

Unsure of how long his good mood would last, she hurriedly filled him in on Mrs Evan's progress. He listened and nodded.

"How are her observations? Has her temperature abated?"

"Yes and her chest sounds perfectly clear. The antibiotics have done their job."

"Good. Does she have any help at home? She's going to feel a little weak after battling such a severe case of pneumonia, despite the magic of the drugs."

"Yes, she has a husband who's very keen to bring her home. I'm sure she'll have plenty of support."

"Well, in that case, I think she can be discharged. I'll leave it up to you to complete the necessary paperwork."

"Great. Thanks. I can't wait to give her the good news."

Doctor Baker stared at her for a few minutes. Heat crawled up Chanel's neck, but she refused to lower her gaze.

"What about the other patients you've seen so far? Is there anything to report?"

As quickly and efficiently as she could, Chanel brought him up to date on the status of his patients. He nodded and commented here and there, and she walked away from him feeling more than satisfied with their encounter.

*Perhaps she'd judged him too harshly? Perhaps he was turning over a new leaf?* She didn't know and could only hope, but she'd take this Doctor Baker over the old one any day.

The smile that lit up Mrs Evan's face when Chanel told her she could go home sent warmth flooding through Chanel's veins. After arranging for an additional supply of antibiotics from the hospital pharmacy and giving the woman a prescription for a repeat course, she completed the necessary paperwork for the woman's discharge. With a fond smile of farewell, Chanel left the room and continued on with her rounds. It was going to be a great day. She was sure of it.

---

"Hey, Chanel, wait up!"

Chanel turned on her way out of the hospital after the end of another tiring shift and saw Tanya hurrying toward her. She acknowledged her friend with a wave and a smile and waited for her roommate to catch up.

"Hey, how are you?" Tanya asked, giving her a quick hug. "It feels like forever since I've spoken to you. We seem to have caught opposite shifts lately. I've been heading off to work and you've been coming home. We've been like ships in the night this week."

Chanel nodded. "You're right. I'm glad it's you and not me who pulled all those nightshifts. I hope I didn't wake you when I got home yesterday afternoon?"

"No, I didn't even hear you come in. I was dead to the world. I didn't even feel Zoe when she jumped on my bed."

"You were tired."

"Yeah, it's been a tough week. Doctor Baker's a hard taskmaster."

"I take it he isn't giving you any special treatment yet?"

"You guess right." Tanya averted her gaze. "I still haven't given him my answer."

"Well, I'm glad you're taking the time to really think about it before you make a decision."

"Right. Let's not get into that again. We all do what we have to do, remember? It's as simple as that. I won't judge you and you won't judge me. Deal?"

Chanel looked at her for a moment and then grudgingly nodded. "Deal."

They began walking in the direction of the train station.

"So, how's your week been?" Tanya asked.

"Good. It started off a little rough with the usual run-ins with Doctor Baker, but on rounds a few days ago, he was almost polite. It threw me off. I'm not used to him being nice."

"See, I told you he wasn't so bad."

"Yeah, well, I'm not sure I'd go that far, but it was a pleasant change, for sure."

"You're lucky you've been off for the last couple of days.

He lost a patient last night and he took it hard. He's been snapping at everyone who comes near him."

Chanel stopped and turned to face Tanya, her heart filling with sadness. The chances she knew the patient were high.

"Who was it?"

"Who?" Tanya asked distractedly, her attention on the traffic.

"The patient. The one that passed away. Who was it?"

"Robyn Evan. It's weird. She was..."

The rest of what Tanya had to say was lost to Chanel. A buzzing sound started in her ears and quickly took control. She watched Tanya's lips moving, and heard nothing but the roar in her head.

*How could Mrs Evan be dead?* She was due to be discharged three days ago. Chanel had done her paperwork. It couldn't be her. It wasn't possible. She clutched at Tanya's arm to make her stop.

"Robyn Evan? You don't mean the lady I diagnosed with pneumonia more than a week ago?"

Tanya's face filled with sympathy. "Oh, that's right. You knew her. I'm sorry, Chanel. She died last night."

Chanel shook her head in confusion and disbelief. "How? Why? I don't understand. She was meant to be discharged. She couldn't wait to go home."

"I'm sorry, Chanel. I don't know all the details. Apparently, she started complaining of pains in her abdomen not long after you left her. By that night, she was suffering from severe vomiting and acute stomach cramps. She couldn't keep anything down. Nobody could work out what was happening. Her blood pressure sky rocketed. And then, it was all over. She died with Doctor Baker by her side."

Chanel pushed her hand against her mouth and tried to hold back a sob. Shock ricocheted through her and left her gasping. It couldn't be true and yet it was. Tanya had no reason to lie. Mrs Evan was dead and Chanel had no idea why.

At the thought of the old woman's husband, tears welled

up in Chanel's eyes. She wondered who'd told him and whether he'd made it to his wife's bedside to say good-bye. She prayed that he'd made it in time and that his wife had known he was there. It was suddenly important for Chanel to believe it had happened that way.

"What did Doctor Baker say? He must have some idea what caused her death?" she asked.

"I think he's as shocked as the rest of us. No doubt there'll be an autopsy."

The mention of an autopsy triggered another memory. She turned to Tanya. "Do you remember a woman by the name of Amelia Arncliffe? She was a patient we saw with Doctor Baker on our very first day, when we were all still together."

Tanya frowned in thought and then shook her head. "I don't think so. Why?"

"She was hospitalized so that she could be treated for a horrible bed sore. It was an abscess the size of my fist. She'd been brought in from a nursing home."

"Oh, that's right. I remember her. She was a tiny little thing with a pile of white hair. You did the diagnosis, right?"

"Yes, that's her."

"What about her?"

"She died a few days after we met her. Doctor Baker told me. I'm sure she died the same way Mrs Evan died—with severe vomiting and stomach cramps."

Tanya frowned again. "What are you saying? Do you think their deaths are related? Could it be a superbug? Are you suggesting—?"

"I don't know what I'm suggesting, but the similarity is a little odd, don't you think?"

Tanya shrugged in bewilderment. "Maybe. I don't know. It could merely be a coincidence. This is a hospital. As much as we hate to admit it, sometimes people die."

Impatience surged through Chanel and she took off toward the train station. Tanya hurried to keep up with her.

"Hey, slow down. I didn't mean to annoy you. I don't know what you want me to say."

Chanel slowed her steps and drew in a deep breath. Letting it out on a heavy sigh, she gazed at Tanya and shook her head.

"I'm sorry. I shouldn't have said anything. I don't know anything for sure. As you said, it could merely be a coincidence. They were both old and according to Doctor Baker, Amelia Arncliffe at least had a number of other health issues."

The girls lapsed into silence, each lost in their own thoughts. Chanel wished she could get rid of the sense of foreboding that had taken hold deep inside her, but right at that moment, that was beyond her.

---

Chanel took another sip from her wineglass. Her heavy sigh wasn't lost on her brother Tom, who refilled his glass with iced tea and then regained his seat across from her. Dinner was over and Tom's teenaged children had drifted away from the table to concentrate on homework—or more likely, to text and talk to their friends. Tom's wife, Lily, was in the living room, on the phone to her mother who was caravanning with her husband somewhere in the far north of Australia.

"What's the matter little sister? That's the third sigh in as many minutes and you were way too quiet over dinner. What's going on?"

Chanel bit back another sigh and glanced at Tom over the rim of her glass. He'd always been able to judge her moods, even when she was a child. As the oldest, he'd grown up observing them all and he had a knack for seeing past the obvious to what was at the heart of the matter. It was one of the things that made him such a good police negotiator.

"Do you mind if we sit outside?"

Tom's eyebrows rose in silent query, but he pushed back his chair and stood. Chanel followed him through the French doors and out onto the paved outdoor area that bordered the inground swimming pool. The air was warm and heavy with the scent of Lily's roses and the star jasmine vine that grew over the fence. Chanel filled her lungs with it and took a seat in a deck chair.

Tom sat next to her and put his glass and a jug half filled with iced tea on the ground beside him. The night had fallen at last and tiny stars bathed them with faint light.

"Talk to me, little sister. I thought you loved your job and being in Sydney."

"I do, Tom. I love everything Sydney has to offer. The rush and noise and excitement; the people, the beach and you guys, of course. It's so nice to be close enough to drop around for dinner when the whim strikes me and not to have to plan days off, travel time and everything else that goes with an interstate excursion. You don't know how much I've enjoyed being this close to you all."

Tom smiled. "The feeling's mutual, honey. We love having you around." He picked up his glass and took another swallow. "So, what's troubling you?"

Chanel sighed. "My job's getting me down. Weird stuff's been happening and it seems like I'm the only one who's concerned. Things keep going round and round in my head and I don't know what's true and what's only imagined. I'm so confused, I sometimes feel like I'm going crazy."

Tom blew out his breath. "Whew! That's what I call a pickle! Why don't you start at the beginning? Tell me about this weird stuff."

"If you want me to start at the beginning, I have to tell you about Doctor Leo Baker."

Tom gazed at her. "So, tell me."

---

Hours later, back in her apartment, Chanel stared at her reflection in the bathroom mirror. It seemed like she'd spent half the night filling Tom in on what had happened, including the improper approach by Doctor Baker.

After managing to convince her brother not to seek out her boss at first light and pummel him into the ground, she'd listened to Tom's advice and in particular, his take on the recent patient deaths under Doctor Baker's care. While Tom had reiterated Tanya's words that it wasn't unusual for patients to die in a hospital, especially elderly ones, he was just as concerned as Chanel by the sudden and unexplained manner of their deaths. With his cop instincts humming, he urged her to take her concerns to the police.

The very thought sent quivers of fear and nerves rushing through her. To give voice to her suspicions to a trusted brother was one thing, even if he was a detective held in high regard. There was no question he'd keep her confidence. But to walk into a police station and talk to a stranger about her misgivings and to have them recorded... That was something else.

*What if she were wrong?* The police would initiate an investigation. Doctor Baker would be interviewed. If her accusations proved groundless, she'd never work in the state again—maybe not even the country. The Australian medical profession wasn't that large, after all. Something of this nature would eventually get out. She'd be forever labeled as the Judas doctor who'd had the audacity to accuse one of their own, and one at the pinnacle of the profession. The betrayal would never be forgotten—or forgiven.

*But what else could she do?* Every time she thought of Amelia Arncliffe and dear old Robyn Evan, fresh pain built up inside. If there were even the slightest chance their deaths hadn't been from natural causes, she owed it to them and their families to search out the truth.

*What was her career in light of something like that?*

Her sense of fairness and justice had always been acute. She guessed it came from being raised by a family intimately involved in law enforcement, including her father who was a retired District Court judge. It must have rubbed off.

The clock in the hallway struck one. Despite her misgivings, she was clear on what she had to do. She'd go to the police and file a report. What they did with it after that was their concern. Whether they chose to pursue it any further or not would be outside her control. Her conscience would be clear.

Maybe then, she could get some sleep.

# CHAPTER 7

Bryce stared at the computer screen in front of him and tried to concentrate on the words in his report. He'd been at it for more than an hour and a half. It was just as well the station was quiet. Every time he tried to focus on the case file, last week's conversation with his wife's doctor kept coming back to him.

No matter how much he wished for things to be different, the truth was, Angela was never going to wake up and talk to him. She wasn't ever going to wake up, period. The weight of his decision rested heavily on his shoulders and filled his heart with dread. Three years might have elapsed, but the guilt was just as fresh.

"Hey, Bryce."

Jett strode toward him. Forcing his dark thoughts aside, Bryce acknowledged his partner with a nod. "What's up?"

"There's a hot-looking woman downstairs who wants to talk to a detective about a suspicious death at the Sydney Harbour Hospital. I'd do the interview myself, but I'm about to go on a break and I have an appointment downtown. You up for it?"

"Sure. Bring her up and put her in one of the interview rooms. I'll be there shortly."

"Will do." Jett turned and walked back the way he'd come.

Turning his attention back to his screen, Bryce saved the work he'd managed to put together and exited the program. A few moments later, he heard Jett's tread on the wooden stairs, followed by the lighter tapping of a woman's heels. He caught a glimpse of a lemon-colored summer dress and the back of a pair of shapely tanned calves before Jett and the woman disappeared around the corner. Collecting his pen and a blank legal pad, Bryce headed after them. He met Jett in the corridor.

"I've left her in Interview Room Two. She's all yours." Jett offered him a wink and disappeared.

The woman stood with her back to him, her arms folded across her chest. She turned upon his entry and with a start, Bryce recognized her. Chanel Munro. *Doctor* Chanel Munro.

In one quick glance, he took in her gilded hair, this time swinging loose in a casual ponytail. It somehow managed to make her look younger than he remembered. The yellow, sleeveless cotton dress he'd glimpsed outside clung to her in all the right places and it took considerable effort to keep his body from reacting. The V-neck offered him a tantalizing glimpse of her cleavage and despite his best efforts to cool his ardor, he was wholly unsuccessful.

In an effort to deflate his hard-on, he fixed his thoughts on something other than the beautiful woman in front of him. She'd come to speak to someone about a purported crime. The least he could do was act professional.

"Doctor Munro, I'm Detective Sergeant Bryce Sutcliffe You might remember me from the clinic last week..." He extended his hand by way of greeting and she shook it firmly. He tried not to think about how small and soft her hand felt in his.

"Of course. I did your physical exam. I should have realized you worked here. How's your grandmother?"

Bryce was quietly impressed that she remembered. "She's fine. She'd fallen asleep in her room and didn't hear the phone. It was nothing."

"I'm glad. She's lucky to have such a caring grandson."

He flushed with pleasure. "Thank you. My grandmother feels the same way, although she's not exactly objective. Now, what can I do for you?"

She lowered her gaze and stared at the charcoal-and-navy patterned carpet. A pulse leaped in the side of her neck. Her arms once again were folded across her middle. He'd seen his fair share of nervous people before and he'd had plenty of practice putting them at ease. It was the least he could do after her earlier comment.

"How about you take a seat and get comfortable, Doctor Munro? Can I get you a coffee or maybe you'd rather a Coke? It's hot out there today."

"A-a Coke would be great. Thank you."

"Diet or regular?"

"Diet, please."

Bryce wasn't surprised. A figure like hers would take some maintenance. Good genes could only take you so far.

"I'll be right back," he murmured and took his leave.

Heading to the drink dispenser further down the corridor, he was relieved to realize his erection had subsided. He wished he could better control his responses, but the truth was, he couldn't. His was a purely physical reaction to a beautiful woman. The last woman he'd made love to was his wife and it had been so long ago, he could barely remember. The strain of his enforced abstinence was taking its toll.

He pushed a few coins into the slot and punched in the Diet Coke code. It fell into the bin and he reached down and pulled it out. He turned and made his way back to the interview room.

"Here you go." He handed her the can and didn't even flinch when their fingers brushed. She murmured her thanks and opened the drink. He busied himself by taking a seat opposite her. Out of the corner of his eye, he saw her take a mouthful of Coke. Her tongue snuck out to lick at a stray droplet on her lip and he dragged his gaze away. With a quick breath, he tugged the notepad toward him and got down to business.

"My partner, Detective Craigdon, said you wanted to report a suspicious death. Is that right?"

The nerves were back, but she took a deep breath that

seemed to give her a level of control. When she spoke, her voice was clear and firm.

"Yes, that's right."

"All right, how about you tell me what you know?"

She made a quick swipe across her lips with a small pink tongue, but nodded. "Okay."

"Right, start at the beginning. How long have you worked at the Sydney Harbour Hospital?"

"A little over a month. I started there in early February. I was accepted into a medical residency program headed by Doctor Leo Baker. It's a twelve-month tenure."

Bryce noted the information and then nodded for her to continue.

"Doctor Baker's known in every medical circle in Australia. He's an excellent physician and demands the best from those doctors who train under him. I was thrilled to be accepted and more than a little surprised. Doctor Baker chooses only the best."

Bryce inclined his head. "So, you're good at your job."

She shrugged and a becoming blush stained her cheeks. Her humility intrigued him. It was unexpected from someone who must know they stood head and shoulders above their peers.

"When I met Doctor Baker, he was everything I expected. He was good-looking, charismatic and a brilliant physician. I had both admiration and respect for him, but it wasn't long before my impression of him was shattered."

Bryce leaned forward. He'd heard of Doctor Leo Baker, of course. You couldn't live in the city of Sydney and not know about one of the country's most eminent doctors. Apart from that, the man treated Bryce's grandmother. Naturally he'd looked into the doctor's credentials.

From what he'd read on the Internet, Leo Baker deserved every one of the numerous accolades. Not only was he an exceptional doctor, he was also a generous philanthropist and had even privately funded a cancer rehabilitation center in the western suburbs for underprivileged women. As much as Bryce disliked the medical profession, he had to concede the man was a saint. Or so it appeared.

"What happened?" he asked, his attention now focused sharply on the woman in front of him.

"He made a pass at me. Actually, it was more than that. He said if I slept with him, my career path would be smoothed out along the way. Any job was mine for the taking. In effect, he promised me the world."

Bryce frowned. "He actually said that? He told you that sleeping with him would be beneficial to your career?"

"Yes, only there was more. If I didn't sleep with him, my career would suffer accordingly. The threat was very clear."

"What did you say?"

"I told him to go to hell."

"What was his response?"

"He didn't take it well. In fact, he made certain I knew he'd do all he could to make my remaining time under his tutelage as difficult as he could."

"And has he?"

"For most of the time, yes."

Bryce jotted down a few more notes and thought about what she'd said. She was beautiful enough to tempt any man, but what she said didn't make sense. Why would a man at the top of his game, and according to the tabloids, happily married to a stunning socialite, jeopardize all of it by making a pass at one of his students? And not only make a pass, but follow through on his threats when she hadn't responded in the way he hoped.

The slightest whiff of scandal and the medical board would string the man up for breakfast. The board prided itself on taking the moral high ground every single time. There was no room for a gray area, even for a favored son.

"How did the medical board react when you reported him?" he asked and glanced up at her.

She studied the backs of her hands where they rested on the desk. "I-I didn't go to the board."

Bryce started in surprise. She was bright and confident and far from a pushover. In fact, she said she'd turned the doctor down flat. It couldn't have been easy if what she'd told him was true. And yet, she hadn't reported the incident.

"Did you tell anyone at all?"

"Yes, but not right away."

"Why not?"

She shook her head again with increasing agitation. "I don't know. I guess I was in shock. I just wanted to forget it happened and concentrate on getting through the program. Then, later, I didn't think anyone would believe me, least of all the medical board. Where else could I go?"

"So, who *did* you tell?"

"First, I called my sister, Josie Barrington. She lives with her husband in northern New South Wales, up near Grafton. She's a psychologist. Well, she treats children, but I needed someone to talk to."

"Okay and how long after the incident with Doctor Baker did you talk to your sister?"

"I don't know—maybe a fortnight later?" I don't really remember. I just knew I had to tell someone."

"What did your sister say?"

"She told me to report him to the medical board."

"But you didn't."

"No."

"What made you come to the police?"

The woman took another deep breath and let it out slowly. When she spoke again, her voice was soft and measured.

"I have five older brothers who are all in law enforcement. My father was a District Court judge. They live and breathe fairness and justice every single day of their lives. Last night, I visited my oldest brother.

"Tom lives in Sydney. He knows me well. He guessed something wasn't right. He urged me to tell him what was troubling me, so I did. He wanted to come with me today and file a report, but I told him no. I needed to do this on my own."

Bryce stared at her. The blueness of her eyes reminded

him of a clear summer day. There wasn't a hint of guile. In his previous dealings with her, she'd come across as genuine and honest and yet, his gut urged him to be cautious.

"Where does your brother work?"

"He's stationed at Chatswood. He's a police negotiator. He's been there for years."

Bryce started in surprise. *Detective Senior Sergeant Tom Munro.* Of course. He was well known in the ranks. A good guy and a highly respected police officer.

"So, Tom was upset to hear a high-profile doctor, old enough to be his sister's father, had hit on her. Is that why he was anxious for you to file a police report?"

The woman looked up from where her hands now lay twisted in her lap and met his gaze straight on.

"No. After I told him about Doctor Baker's sexual harassment, he wanted to tear the man from limb to limb. The reason he insisted I file a report with the police was because I also told him I thought Doctor Baker or someone close to him might have intentionally caused the deaths of some of his patients."

Shock waves ricocheted through Bryce's gut, but he schooled his face into an expressionless mask. No need to alert her to the degree of his surprise.

"That's a pretty serious statement, especially about such an eminent physician."

Her eyes narrowed and he caught a flash of anger. "Do you think I don't know that? Why do you think I've tossed and turned all night trying to decide what to do? It's like the complaint of sexual harassment. Who's going to believe me? But I've now seen two of Doctor Baker's patients die— patients who had no business being dead. I can't stand by and let it happen again."

"I take it you have some proof that these deaths weren't from natural causes?"

Anger flashed in her eyes. "No, I *don't* have any proof. Do you think I would have lain sleepless all night if I had proof? That's your job. All I can tell you is that Amelia Arncliffe and Robyn Evan, both patients under Doctor Baker's care, died in the last month or so of strangely similar symptoms."

She drew in a deep breath and continued. "I've asked around. Nobody can tell me what killed them. Everyone assumes we'll have the answers from their autopsies, but Amelia Arncliffe died a month ago and I haven't yet heard about any autopsy findings."

"She died in a hospital. I take it the death didn't occur within twenty-four hours of surgery?"

"No."

"Well, it's not an automatic coroner's case."

"I understand that, but why can't anyone give me a cause of death?"

She made a noise of frustration at the back of her throat and Bryce looked at her sympathetically.

"Did you know the patients?"

"Yes. They were both lovely women, elderly and not in the best of health, but nowhere near death. It shouldn't have happened."

"And yet it did. Tell me," he said, changing tack, "why do you think Doctor Baker or someone else at the hospital is involved?"

"I don't know for sure that he is, but they were *his* patients. The investigation must start with him."

"If there *is* an investigation."

Her eyes widened in shock and he could see tiny, darker blue flecks in the irises of her eyes.

"What do you mean, *if*? Surely you're going to look into this? I can't be the only one who thinks the deaths of these women are suspicious?"

His non-committal shrug sparked fresh anger. Her eyes narrowed.

"You mean to tell me I've scrounged up the courage to come in here and you can't even reassure me you're going to investigate? What kind of detective are you?"

Her harsh accusation stirred his temper, but he stared at her without flinching.

"If you have a complaint about the doctor and his treatment of you, I suggest you start with the medical board.

As to the other, I'll consider what you've told me and decide whether there's enough to warrant me spending more of my time on it. If there is, you can be assured, I'll give it my utmost attention."

He made a show of gathering his pen and notepad. "Now, if you don't mind, I have a number of pressing matters to attend to. If you'll give me your contact details, I'll be sure to let you know when I decide how to proceed. If I do open an investigation, you'll be notified of the outcome. Will that be all, Doctor Munro?"

She opened her mouth as if to throw more words at him, but then closed it again without speaking. With every taut line of her body shouting her anger, she snatched her handbag off the floor and stalked out of the room. In silence, he caught up and directed her to the stairwell and then turned away before she began to descend. When she brushed past him, he swore he could hear the grinding of her teeth.

———

Chanel couldn't remember the last time she'd felt so furious. Even her ears burned with the harsh disappointment of the last hour. She'd spent so much time guessing and second guessing her decision to go to the police station and now, looking at the outcome, it had all been a waste of her time.

Okay, so the detective had listened to her and plied her with questions, but in the end it seemed he'd decided there wasn't enough evidence to investigate the matter. What irritated her the most was that he was probably right.

No one else at the hospital appeared to be worried about the deaths of those elderly patients. Even Tanya hadn't thought much of it. But after talking it through with Tom, she'd expected the detective to take her concerns a little more seriously. The problem was, unlike her brother, Detective Sutcliffe barely knew her.

It was obvious her failure to complain to the medical board about Doctor Baker's harassment had counted against her. If what she said were true, it was only logical to assume it would have been reported. They were living in the twenty-first century. Nobody tolerated sexual harassment in the workplace.

The fact that she hadn't filed a complaint raised questions about the truth of her claim. That was inevitable. She could tell from the detective's body language that he didn't believe her. And then she'd complicated the harassment matter by claiming two of Doctor Baker's patients had been murdered—okay, she hadn't actually said the "m" word, but she as good as said as much.

It was possible Doctor Baker didn't have anything to do with the deaths. The women were under his care when they died, but he wasn't the only one who had access to those patients during their time in the hospital.

The truth was, the deaths could have been caused by anyone—if it were proved the deaths were suspicious at all. So far, it appeared everyone was treating the deaths as resulting from natural causes. Doctor Baker had certainly intimated as much when he'd spoken to her about Amelia Arncliffe.

Chanel needed to find proof of wrongdoing, tangible proof. *Any* kind of proof would be good. She wondered if her instinctive desire to blame her superior had anything to do with his treatment of her. She wanted to follow that thought with an instant denial—but she couldn't.

If she were fair, she would admit, if only to herself, that if he'd lived up to her expectations of the kindly, brilliant doctor, humbly and generously sharing his wisdom with his dedicated students, her attitude toward him would have been far different. Instead, his lack of integrity, questionable morality and personality flaws made her skin crawl and angered her beyond belief.

Were those the reasons she was so quick to suspect he could be the one behind his patients' deaths? Was it something as simple and humiliating as spite? She didn't think so, but she couldn't say for sure and the knowledge that she could be so vindictive toward a fellow human being left her deeply ashamed.

Her parents had raised her to be a better person than that. She *was* a better person than that. With a deep breath, she crossed the street and headed toward the train station. If the police didn't believe there was anything worth investigating, then so be it. She'd accept that and move on. She'd put her energies into getting through the program and learning as much as she possibly could.

At the end of the day, all she wanted to be was the best doctor she was capable of.

———

Back at his desk, Bryce read over the notes he'd made during his interview with Chanel Munro. He'd Googled her family and confirmed her story that she was indeed part of the reputable Munro family. Five brothers in law enforcement and an older sister who was married to a cop. Her father was the first aboriginal District Court judge appointed to the bench in New South Wales.

It was an impressive lineage and one that also explained her golden-tanned skin, although the Google images of Judge Munro had shown a man as dark as Bryce. Chanel's mother was the fair one. From photos he'd seen on the Internet, it was clear Marguerite Munro was Caucasian.

It was an interesting combination and one that would have garnered its fair share of critics in the past. That Chanel had grown up in a biracial household might explain her confident and forthright attitude. She was used to fighting for what was hers and defending her basic rights. He wondered again why she hadn't filed a complaint against her boss.

The thought that the man might be using his position to solicit sexual favors from his students turned Bryce's stomach and sent a flash of anger burning through his veins. It only added to the already low opinion he had of members of the medical profession.

It was time he had a chat to Doctor Baker. Reaching across his desk, he picked up the phone and dialed the number he'd found on the Internet. It was answered after the second ring by a woman with a throaty voice that called to mind whiskey and sex and late night parties.

"Doctor Baker's office. How can I help you?"

# Chapter 8

Bryce didn't need directions to the location of Doctor Baker's private medical rooms. He'd dropped his grandmother outside the building a month earlier. This time, he was fortunate to score a car park only a few doors down and after a quick ride in the elevator to the tenth floor, he knocked on the door that identified itself as Doctor Leo Baker's.

The same throaty female voice he'd heard on the other end of the phone bade him enter and he opened the door. Behind a high counter sat a well-put-together blonde, somewhere in her mid-fifties. He'd read on the Internet that despite coming from a very wealthy and influential family, Susan Baker liked to divide her time between her many charitable projects and overseeing her husband's busy medical practice. That involved running the office in his private rooms and in his rooms at the Sydney Harbour Hospital. She greeted Bryce with a wide smile,

"You must be Detective Sutcliffe. We spoke on the phone."

Bryce nodded in surprise. "How did you know it was me?"

"When Doctor Baker heard you wanted to see him, he cleared his schedule. You'll have his undivided attention."

Once again, Bryce was filled with surprise. That explained why there were no patients lining the waiting area. Clearing the doctor's afternoon schedule must have involved contacting and rescheduling a significant number of people. Bryce knew, through his grandmother, how difficult it was to obtain an appointment with the busy physician. It seemed half of Sydney wanted him to treat them.

The fact that he'd rearranged his patients to suit Bryce's visit seemed a little odd. After all, Bryce hadn't even told him what he wanted to speak with him about. For all Doctor Baker knew, Bryce's visit could be nothing more than requesting patronage at an upcoming police fundraiser.

Unsure what to make of it, Bryce took a seat in the waiting room and idly selected a glossy sailing magazine from the pile stacked on the coffee table. He was impressed to see it was the latest edition. Most clinics leaned toward magazines that were years old—sometimes even decades.

A door to the left of Bryce opened and he looked up. A man with a thick head of graying hair, wearing a navy suit that looked custom made to fit his impressive physique, appeared in the doorway.

"Detective Sutcliffe?"

"Yes."

"I'm Doctor Leo Baker. Please, come in."

Bryce stood and followed the man into his office. The walls, painted a tasteful pale gray contrasted with crisp white architraves. Prints of brightly colored beach scenes decorated the walls. On closer inspection, Bryce could see they were originals. An Aram lily sporting a profusion of creamy white flowers stood in a large ceramic pot by one corner, its glossy green leaves looking healthy and clean. A gentle gust of cooling breeze came from the vents of the air conditioner.

Doctor Baker closed the door behind them and strode across the room. He took a seat behind a large cedar desk that was scrupulously tidy and clean. Apart from a large computer monitor, a blotter pad and two Montblanc pens, the entire surface was bare.

"Detective, please take a seat." The doctor motioned to one of the two leather chairs opposite the desk.

Bryce seated himself in one of them and pulled out his pen and notebook.

"I must admit, I was surprised to hear of your call, Detective, but you have me intrigued. I assume you're here on police business?" Without giving Bryce a chance to answer, he continued. "What could you possibly want to see me about?"

Bryce held his gaze. "There's been a complaint from one of your students about sexual harassment, among other things. She wants to press charges," he lied smoothly. "Given that the alleged offender is you, a man held in the highest regard, I decided to give you the benefit of the doubt and speak to you first, before the matter went any further."

While Bryce was speaking, the doctor's face went from pale to red. Anger suffused his cheeks and his face puffed up with self-righteous indignation.

"A complaint of sexual harassment? You must be kidding!"

"I'm afraid I'm not, Doctor Baker. Would you care to explain?"

"Explain? There's nothing to explain. The very idea is ludicrous. Which one of my students was it? They'll be cut from my program tomorrow."

"I'm afraid I'm not at liberty to say, Doctor Baker, but I'm curious. Why would one of your students make such an allegation? Surely, they have a lot to lose by spreading lies? You've just told me you'll have them removed from your program—a program I believe is held in very high esteem." Bryce frowned and shook his head. "Why would a student take such a risk? They'd be forever tainted and their career would be in ruins."

"I don't know what you want me to say, Detective. I have no idea what goes on in the minds of some of these girls. It wasn't that long ago when women weren't even allowed to study medicine. Maybe our forefathers were onto something back then..."

The last was said as a bit of an aside, but Bryce couldn't help but respond. "Surely you don't believe that? We have many brilliant female doctors." Bryce recalled another snippet of information he'd found on the Internet and added, "In fact, your own daughter is following in your footsteps, isn't she?"

"Yes, and she's doing very well, I might add. Her mother and I are very proud of her."

"Justifiably so, from what I understand. She's the Head of Neurosurgery at St Vincent's Hospital, just a stone's throw from here."

"Yes, and she's worked hard to get where she is. She deserves everything that comes her way."

Bryce adjusted his weight in the chair. "Getting back to my question, Doctor Baker: Why do you think a student would accuse you of something they can't prove?"

The doctor shrugged and looked toward the window that framed an enviable view of the park Bryce had enjoyed the previous month.

"As I said, I have no idea what goes through the mind of some of these women. Take Chanel Munro, for example."

Bryce stilled. *How had Baker guessed the complainant was Chanel?* Unless what she'd told Bryce was true. He forced another breath in his lungs and drew his notepad closer.

"Tell me about Chanel Munro," he said.

The doctor sighed and pushed back his chair. He stood and made his way over to the window.

"Doctor Chanel Munro appeared to have so much promise. Her application was exemplary. Her references top notch. I personally spoke to all five of her referees and they couldn't praise her enough. She was intelligent, eager to learn, kind and compassionate—all in all, she had the makings of a brilliant doctor. At least, on paper... However the reality was vastly different."

Bryce scribbled notes in shorthand as fast as his fingers would allow. He glanced up. "How so?"

"Well, for a start, she's drop-dead gorgeous. I'm talking model material. Even the lab coat can't disguise her appeal. Now, I'm not against good-looking women at all— hell, have you seen my wife? I enjoy a beautiful woman as much as any man, but there's so much more than beauty that's important. Don't you agree?"

"Of course."

"A beautiful woman has often had an easy run in life. Her beauty smooths the way, makes difficult situations disappear. It's not right, but that's the way it is. When Chanel Munro appeared on my ward, it was obvious she'd never learned how to get to the top the hard way."

Bryce frowned. "What do you mean?"

"From the moment we met, she was all over me. She'd giggle and laugh at everything I said. She'd open her big blue eyes wide and act like she was hanging on my every word. It might have flattered some men, but not me. I'm far too old to fall for that kind of act."

Bryce thought of the Chanel he'd met and tried to reconcile her with the woman the doctor described. It didn't fit. But then again, how could he say with any certainty what she was like? He barely knew her.

"When I quizzed her about a patient, she'd come up with some long-winded excuse as to why she couldn't provide me with a diagnosis. In the end, I stopped asking her. It was just a waste of time and quite frankly, embarrassing."

"Why do you think she came so highly recommended? You said you telephoned all five of her referees."

Doctor Baker turned away from the window and shrugged. "Who knows? Maybe she had them just where she wanted them—where she wanted me."

"And where was that?"

"She made it very clear she wanted to sleep with me, Detective. She thought it would help her get better grades. It was obvious to me it was a tactic she'd employed more than once in the past."

"What did you do?"

"I told her very gently that I wasn't interested. I'm a married man who's still very much in love with his wife. Apart from that, the impropriety of it turned my stomach. She was my student. There was no way I'd betray that bond. I love mentoring other doctors and watching them go from great to out of this world. Do you think I'd do anything to jeopardize that?"

Bryce didn't answer. Instead, he asked a question of his own. "What happened when you turned Doctor Munro down?"

Doctor Baker frowned in disgust. "She reacted as badly as I guessed. There were tears and tantrums and finally threats. She threatened to tell my wife I'd raped her. After that, she was going to the media." He shook his head. "What could I do? She was out of control. All I could hope was that whoever she told would see it for the pathetic ploy that it was and dismiss it out of hand." He shrugged.

"Considering I have yet to see my name splashed across the headlines, I'm guessing that's exactly what happened. Either that, or she changed her mind and came to her senses."

"Did you have her removed from your program?"

He hesitated. "No, I didn't."

"Why not?"

"It seemed better to let sleeping dogs lie, so to speak. The next week after her proposition, she seemed calmer, more agreeable and more willing to just get on with the job. I won't lie and tell you I wasn't relieved. I decided to leave things as they were. I didn't want to risk setting her off again. Who knows? This time, she might have just gone through with her threats."

"Did you tell your wife about it? Write a report? Put a notation in her file?"

"No."

For the first time, the doctor looked uncomfortable. Bryce frowned and sat forward in his seat.

"My wife types all of my correspondence, Detective. She also suffers from bipolar disorder. She's medicated, of course, but she doesn't need any unnecessary emotional stress. I do my best not to contribute to it."

"How long has she worked for you?"

"All of our married life. She likes to...stay close to me. She says it makes her feel safe."

He held Bryce's gaze for a moment or two and then headed back to his seat. "Now, if you don't mind,

Detective, I have to get moving. I have another appointment soon."

Bryce frowned in surprise. "Your wife told me you'd cleared your schedule."

"And she was right. I used your visit as an excuse. What I didn't tell her was that I'm taking the afternoon off so that we can go sailing on the harbor. She loves getting out on the water and it helps with her mood swings."

"Right," Bryce said, secretly impressed at the man's thoughtfulness. Putting off an afternoon's worth of patients to see to his wife's needs ranked way up there with husband of the year.

Bryce collected his notepad and pushed back his chair. "Oh, by the way, I understand there have been at least two patients who have recently died under your care. Would you enlighten me as to the causes of their deaths?"

The doctor shook his head, his expression filling with sadness. "I'm a doctor, Detective. I treat hundreds of patients a year. As much as it saddens me to admit it, occasionally, I lose one."

He leaned back against the soft leather of his chair. "Since you said recently, I assume you're referring to Amelia Arncliffe and Robyn Evan. Amelia Arncliffe was admitted with a grossly infected abscess on her sacrum. Unfortunately, she was also suffering from a number of other unrelated illnesses. It's merely a coincidence she died whilst under my care. She was in her eighties. It could have happened any time."

He cleared his throat and continued. "As for Robyn Evan, she presented with bilateral pneumonia. She was progressing well. She didn't die from pneumonia. About six months ago, we discovered several malignant tumors in her stomach. She was eighty-eight and refused treatment. She didn't want to spend whatever time she had, in and out of hospitals feeling awful." He shrugged. "It was her choice. She was fully informed of the risks of refusing treatment. We can't force a patient to accept treatment, Detective, and I wouldn't, anyway. There should be some right to die with dignity."

Bryce raised his eyebrows in surprise. "Do you support the right of a person to refuse treatment even to their own detriment, Doctor Baker?"

The doctor paused and appeared to think about Bryce's question. At last, he answered. "I support the right of anyone to live with dignity. The right to die with dignity is just as important. Would I assist someone to commit suicide when there was nothing but pain and indignity and ultimate death in front of them?"

He turned and captured Bryce's gaze. The color in the doctor's eyes darkened with the intensity of his thoughts. Bryce's heart picked up its rhythm. Long seconds passed.

"No, Detective. I wouldn't. At the end of the day, I took an oath to help the sick and treat them to the best of my ability. I take that oath very seriously."

He looked down at his desk and then back at Bryce. "I hope I've answered your questions, Detective. If you don't mind, I'll let you see yourself out. I have a couple of letters to dictate before I can leave for the day."

"Of course. Thank you for your time, Doctor. Have a good afternoon."

"I was happy to help, Detective and thank you. I'm sure the weather will be kind. It looks like a beautiful day out."

---

Tanya's fingers shook and stuttered over the letters on her iPhone. She cursed softly. As if it wasn't hard enough to find the words to tell her boss she welcomed his attentions. Why wouldn't her fingers cooperate? She'd mulled over the question long enough and Doctor Baker wanted an answer.

Just that afternoon, he'd found her in the ward and had maneuvered her into the treatment room. He'd closed the door behind them with a decisive click. Tanya's heart went crazy with excitement and nerves, although the frown on his face slightly dimmed her enthusiasm.

"Is something the matter Doctor Baker?" she asked shakily.

"I don't know, Doctor Singh. Is it? I've heard a whisper that there's been a complaint about my...behavior. You wouldn't happen to know anything about that, would you?"

She stared at him in confusion and then frantically shook her head. "No, of course not. I don't know what you're talking about. I'd never do something like that."

He stared at her, his eyes hard. A moment later, he relaxed and a lazy smile tilted up the corners of his mouth.

"So, little Tanya. What's your answer? Are you going to succumb to me and enjoy hours of mindless fun and pleasure and reap the rewards on your tests? Your indecision is driving me mad. I can't concentrate on anything but you."

He moved closer, pressing her against the shelves that were stocked with medical supplies. His cock pressed hard into her stomach. There was no denying his need.

"I want to fuck you, Tanya. I want your sweet lips around my cock. You're wet and hot and tight for me. I can see it in your eyes. Why are you teasing me like this? It's time we ended it."

His crude words both shocked and excited her and heat rushed to her core. He was right. She wanted him in every way he described. She opened her mouth to tell him, but the door to the treatment room opened. A nurse stood in the doorway, surprise flooding her face.

"Oh, I'm sorry. I didn't realize you were in here."

Doctor Baker stepped away smoothly and threw the nurse a practiced smile. "I was showing Doctor Singh where the sutures are kept. We're changing the dressing on the patient in bed four.

Tanya managed a nod that felt mechanical and fled the treatment room without another word. Doctor Baker's quiet, derisive laughter followed her all the way down the ward.

---

Chanel heard the sound of the doorbell and wiped her wet hands on a towel. It was her night to cook and she was in the middle of preparing dinner. She was far from a cordon bleu chef, but she could hold her own in the kitchen. After being wowed for a month by Tanya's Indian dishes, she wanted to serve up something special for her roommate.

Thai pumpkin soup and roast chicken salad were the starters, to be followed by a succulent rack of lamb, finished with baby potatoes and greens. She couldn't wait for Tanya to try it. A caramel and chocolate coconut cheesecake was chilling in the fridge.

The doorbell sounded again and Chanel hurried to answer it. Not bothering to look through the eyehole, she opened the door and then gasped.

"Doctor Baker! W-what are you doing here?"

He was dressed in an impeccable, tailored black suit and a tie that looked like it cost a fortune. In his hand, he held a bouquet of roses, the color of dark blood.

Chanel stared at the roses in confusion and then all of a sudden comprehension struck. With it, came a feeling of dread. Tanya appeared in the hallway, making the final adjustments to her dress.

Black chiffon and lace swirled around her petite figure, clinging to all of her curves. Lipstick as red as the roses glistened on her mouth. She smiled at the doctor and greeted him in a voice that was soft and breathy. He offered her the roses.

"Oh, thank you! Aren't you sweet? Come in a moment while I find a vase to put them in."

Chanel forced her legs to move backwards so Doctor Baker could enter. She couldn't believe he was here, in her apartment, collecting her roommate for a date. It was awful; it was obscene; it was so disgusting she thought she might puke. But she held her ground in the living room, refusing to be intimidated.

Tanya headed toward the kitchen in search of a vase. Chanel felt his eyes on her and wished she hadn't changed into her short summer nightdress so early. It was Friday night and she thought they were having a girls' night in. Tanya hadn't said a word to her about a date. Now she understood why.

The doctor's gaze raked over her chest and continued down the bare length of her legs. Chanel grasped the edges of the nightdress and wished she could tug it lower. Ending mid-thigh, it was far from indecent, but she felt naked beneath his gaze. Desire glinted in the depths of his eyes and a knowing grin turned up the corners of his lips.

"I take it you're staying in?" he murmured and reached out to lift a strand of hair off her face.

Chanel pulled away, but he merely chuckled, unperturbed by her reaction.

"There, that's better. Now I can see you properly."

She could still feel the press of his fingers against her cheek and her stomach clenched in disgust. *How on earth could Tanya bear to go out with him...and more?* Chanel shuddered at the thought.

"There you are!" Tanya said, bouncing back into the room. "All done. And thank you once again. They're absolutely beautiful." She smiled at him.

"Almost as beautiful as you," he replied smoothly and reached for her hand.

Tanya blushed and Chanel had to turn away to prevent herself from retching. She hurried from the room.

"I'll see you tomorrow at the hospital, Doctor Munro," he called after her. "I do hope you have a good night."

"Bye, Chanel. Don't wait up." Tanya giggled.

Chanel didn't unclench her fists until after she'd heard the click of the door as it closed behind them. Anger surged through her and she looked around for something to hit. She wanted to pound something hard until it no longer resembled what it started out to be. Really, she wanted to pummel Doctor Baker's smug face.

*How could Tanya be so stupid? So blind? So desperate?* It was beyond Chanel to understand. Delayed shock set in and she shook until she was forced to find somewhere to sit. Collapsing on the couch in the front room, she drew her knees up to her chest. She couldn't deal with this. She couldn't deal with the thought of her boss having sex with her roommate.

Consensual or not, it was wrong on so many levels. It needed to be stopped. She'd gone to the police and gotten nowhere. Despite the detective's assurances, she hadn't heard from him again. It had been more than a week. By now, he must have made a decision about whether or not to proceed. He'd probably dismissed her as some hysterical female the minute she left the building. She didn't dare report that back to Tom.

No, she'd take her complaint to the medical board and force them to see it for what it was. If need be, she'd take Tanya with her. When the girl found out she wasn't the first one to be propositioned, she might not feel quite so kindly toward their boss. Chanel could only hope.

It was hours later when Chanel heard a noise at the door and woke to find she'd fallen asleep on the couch. The smell of burning meat seared her nostrils. She'd forgotten all about the lamb. She squinted at the illuminated dials of the clock from where it sat up on the dresser. Two fifty-three. Rubbing at her eyes, she looked up in time to see Tanya stumble into the hall.

Chanel frowned and sat up. "Tanya," she called out in the dark.

The girl jumped and then slowly turned around to face her. "Chanel, you frightened me half to death. What are you still doing up?"

"I'm sorry, I didn't mean to scare you. I fell asleep on the couch. I only woke when I heard you at the door."

Tanya looked away. "I didn't mean to wake you. I tried to be as quiet as I could. What's that smell?"

"It's the lamb. I forgot about it." She paused and then said as calmly as she could, "I thought you were spending the night somewhere else?"

Tanya shrugged. "I thought so, too, but Leo changed his mind. He dropped me off here just now."

"Where did you go?"

A smile lit up Tanya's face. "He took me to that swanky new restaurant down at Circular Quay. I've heard you have to book months in advance for a table. We dined on oysters and caviar and drank the most amazing wine. Afterwards, we went for a walk along the wharf."

"I'm surprised he took the risk he might be recognized. He's married, after all."

Tanya's expression turned petulant. "Why do you have to go and spoil things? We had a lovely night."

"So, did you sleep with him?"

Tanya gasped at Chanel's bluntness, but Chanel didn't care. Sex was what Doctor Baker was after. Chanel couldn't believe he'd put out for such an expensive meal and not get what he wanted in return.

"Not that it's any of your business," Tanya replied in a voice breathy with excitement, "but yes, we did. In a hotel room down near the harbor. On sheets that were as soft as silk. For an older man, he's got what it takes, if you know what I mean." She giggled and Chanel turned away in disgust.

*How could Tanya be so blind?* It wasn't like she was a teenager, unwise to the ways of the world. She was thirty years of age. Old enough to have experienced the *modus operandi* of sleazes like Doctor Baker. Or so Chanel would have thought.

Tanya came from a strict Hindu background. Whilst loving, her father was very protective of his only child. Perhaps he'd shielded her from the worst men had to offer? Was it possible she really was that naïve? Was it up to Chanel to save Tanya from herself?

Unable to listen to another minute of Tanya's praises of their boss, Chanel pulled herself off the couch, turned off the oven, switched on the fan and strode toward the door to her room.

"Hey, where are you going? Don't you want to hear how we—?"

Chanel spun on her heel. With her hands on her hips, she glared at her friend. "No, Tanya. I don't. It's almost three in the morning. I'm tired and I'm going to bed. Goodnight."

And with that, Chanel turned and left the room.

# CHAPTER 9

The early morning sun beamed in through Chanel's opened blinds and hit her straight in the face. She groaned and flung her arm up to cover her face, but the damage had been done. She was awake and far from happy to be facing the day. She looked at the clock on her nightstand and groaned again, but this time for an entirely different reason. She had less than an hour to shower and get to work.

Noises coming from the direction of the kitchen told her that Tanya was already up. They were both rostered on the morning shift. It would serve Tanya right if she were as tired and out of sorts as Chanel was.

Knowing there was nothing to do but get on with it, she sighed and climbed out of bed. Padding to the bathroom down the hall, she turned on the water in the shower and did a quick scrub. With no time for the luxury of shampooing her hair, she quickly stepped out and dried off. Another five minutes and she was dressed and ready to go. With a fortifying breath, she strode into the kitchen.

Zoe was eating breakfast from her cat bowl near the door. Tanya sat at the small kitchen table chewing on a piece of toast. Fresh coffee percolated on the stove. The smell of it was almost enough to soothe Chanel's disgruntled mood.

"I made coffee. There's toast in the toaster. I even saved you the crust."

As far as peace offerings went, it was huge. Both of them

loved to toast the crust and smother it in butter and honey. Chanel threw Tanya a small smile, acknowledging her kind gesture.

"Listen, about last night, I'm really sorry," Tanya started.

Chanel sat down across from her. "No, please, I'm the one who's sorry. I had no right snapping at you like that. What you do with your life is your business. It's not my place to judge."

"You're right, it's not. You don't know how important it is for me to get through this program. I'm the first Singh in my family to go to college, let alone be accepted into something as prestigious as this course. It means everything to me. My dad's so proud he could burst."

She shook her head, pleading with her eyes for Chanel to understand. "I can't disappoint him. If sleeping with Leo...I mean, Doctor Baker means I don't have to worry about passing anymore, I'm prepared to do it. Besides, it's not exactly a hardship. He'd give men half his age a run for their money."

She smiled, but Chanel couldn't find it within herself to return it. She shook her head. "You shouldn't be put in this position, Tanya. He's taking advantage of you. It's not right."

"Oh, Chanel! Nobody cares about what's right! Haven't you learned that yet? Look at Doctor Baker! Do you think he knows he's doing the wrong thing? Of course he does! Does he care? Of course he doesn't. It's just the way it is."

"Would it make any difference to you if you knew you're not the first student he's hit upon?"

Tanya frowned. "What do you mean?"

"Surely, you can't think he's never done this type of thing before? Men like Doctor Baker thrive on exercising their power and what better way than to get a young student to sleep with him?"

"You don't know that for sure," Tanya replied, uncertainty clouding her voice. "You're just guessing."

"That's where you're wrong. I *do* know for sure. He propositioned me back in February, a few days after starting the program."

Shock, followed quickly by disbelief and anger spread across Tanya's face. "I don't believe you," she stated.

Chanel shrugged. "Believe me or not, it doesn't matter, but I'm telling you the truth. Why do you think he turned on me? Everyone noticed it, even you. He propositioned me for sex, probably the same way he propositioned you. He promised me an easy ride through the program and a boost to my career. All I had to do was sleep with him. He didn't take it well when I turned him down."

Tanya stared at her in increasing horror, her eyes wide. "No, no! You're lying! There's no way he made a pass at you! You just can't stand the thought that he might prefer me over you. That's all it is! You're jealous!"

"No, Tanya! Oh, hell. How can I make you understand? He's a sleaze of the highest order. He's using you for his own pleasure. It's nothing more than that."

"No, you're wrong! He told me I was beautiful!" She gasped. "And last night... Last night he told me that he loved me. He said he'd been trying to fight it since the moment he laid eyes on me. He didn't want to fall in love with me, but...but he did!"

Chanel stared at her, aghast. She couldn't believe how easily her friend had fallen for his lies. Knowing Tanya wasn't in the mood to hear anything more against their boss, she clenched her jaw and moved over to the counter. She poured herself a cup of coffee and took refuge in the caffeine. Tanya returned to her toast.

Chanel looked at the clock on the wall and then over at Tanya. "We're due at the hospital in fifteen minutes. We need to get moving."

Tanya's head snapped up. "I can't go to work today! What will I do if I run into him? I love him, just like he loves me. How will I stop from throwing myself into his arms? It would be the worst possible thing I could do! He told me last night we have to be discreet. I promised it would be our little secret. I promised I wouldn't breathe a word about what we'd done and yet, I've broken it already!"

She pushed away from the table and clutched at

Chanel's blouse. "You won't tell him I told you, will you? Please, Chanel! I'm begging you! Please don't tell him you know!"

Chanel closed her eyes against the wild desperation in her friend's expression. She couldn't bear to witness the madness a minute longer.

"Tanya! Stop it! You need to get a hold of yourself. You're a grown woman, not a silly teenager. Besides, I was here when he turned up with those roses last night. I watched you both walk out the door. He knows I know at least that much. Now, I'm going to work and you're coming with me. If you're mature enough to carry on a relationship with your married boss, you're mature enough to face the consequences if and when it all heads south. Do you understand?"

Tanya blinked at Chanel as if trying to make sense of what she was saying.

"Tanya, we need to get to work, okay?"

"Okay."

"Go and finish what you need to do. We're leaving in five minutes."

With a gentle push, Chanel sent Tanya in the direction of the bathroom and then hurried to finish her coffee. After being woken at three in the morning, the last thing she'd needed was a confrontation with her roommate, but that's the way it went. She could only hope Tanya would think about what she'd said and reconsider her relationship with their boss. It would make life much easier for both of them if Tanya ended it, although from what Chanel had seen so far, she didn't hold out much hope.

---

Bryce stared at the papers on his desk and tried to make sense of the statements made by Chanel Munro and Leo Baker. On the one hand, there was a young woman who freely admitted she was feeling justifiably wronged and angry after her boss had made a pass at her. It wasn't too much of a stretch to imagine she might even be feeling vindictive. It would explain why she thought the object of her anger could be responsible for the deaths of two of his patients.

On the other hand, there was the doctor. The fact that he was older, rich and good-looking wasn't his fault. Bryce had no right to hold those things against him and he didn't. The man was a successful, highly regarded doctor. His healthy ego didn't make him a sleaze.

There was nothing illegal about coming on to a work colleague—unethical, yes; distasteful, certainly; but very much within the law when the alleged victim was an adult, provided it wasn't actual sexual harassment. Even if the doctor was guilty of such behavior, it didn't make him a murderer. The leap from one to the other was absurd. *So what was behind Chanel Munro's accusation?*

It had been a week since he'd met with the beauty and he still wasn't sure what to make of it all. She'd appeared genuine in her complaint about Leo Baker and had come across as far from hysterical. In order to get a better sense of her, he'd done a little more digging into her background. In addition to her impeccable family credentials, she didn't have a criminal record. Not so much as a parking ticket.

She'd attended college at the prestigious Brisbane University and had graduated with honors. He'd managed to track down a couple of her professors and at least one of her former bosses and all of them spoke highly of the lovely Chanel Munro. Without exception, they were sad to see her leave Brisbane and wished her all the best in her new endeavors.

No matter where he turned, he couldn't find anyone who had a bad thing to say about her, apart from Doctor Baker. Certainly, there wasn't even a sniff of a scandal in her past. This didn't gel with Baker's certainty that she'd slept her way to the top, but it could well explain her discomfort at coming forward with a complaint.

Baker would be publicly outed, but her reputation would also be scrutinized and laid bare for all to see. Bryce could understand how a decent woman with a reputation to protect might be reluctant to risk having it tarnished.

Tugging the phone out of his pocket, he dialed his grandmother's number. She'd been a patient of Baker's for years. Not only that, she was a good judge of character. He wanted to get her take on the situation.

"Bryce, how nice of you to call. What's the matter?"

"Nothing, Grandma. I just wanted to see how you were doing. Did you take your medication at lunch time?"

"Of course I did, like always. I keep telling you, it's not necessary to check up on me. I might be old, but I haven't yet lost my marbles."

"I'm not checking up on you," Bryce protested. "I'm checking *in* with you. There's a difference. In fact, I called to ask for your opinion."

"Really?"

Bryce grinned at the pleasure in her voice. "Yes, Grandma, really."

"What do you want to know? Are you trying to decide what color tie will go with that new suit you bought last week?"

Bryce laughed and shook his head. "No, although now you mention it, I probably do need to get a new tie."

"It's such a smart suit, Bryce. I'm so glad you splashed out on it. Every man needs a decent suit."

"So you've told me, maybe a hundred times before."

She made a sound of mock annoyance and pretended to be upset. "All right, I promise you won't hear a word out of me about your wardrobe again. I was only trying to help, but who am I to—?"

"Okay, Grandma, enough with the theatrics," he said dryly. "We both know you don't mean it. Now, are you going to listen to the reason for my call?"

"You wanted my opinion."

"Yes."

"I'm not sure that I want to give it."

Now it was Bryce's turn to make a sound of irritation in the back of his throat. "Grandma," he said, warning thick in his voice.

She laughed. "I'm just having fun with you, Grandson. What is it you'd like to ask?"

Bryce cleared his throat and readjusted his thoughts. "I wanted to talk to you about Doctor Baker."

"Doctor Baker?" He heard the confusion in her voice. "Why would you want to talk to me about Doctor Baker?"

"Something's come up at work and I just wanted to know what you thought about him."

"At work? You mean, like something *criminal*?"

"I can't say anything more, Grandma, but I'd appreciate it if you'd answer a couple of questions."

"On the record?"

Bryce groaned in frustration. "On the record, off the record... What difference does it make? I'm not going to use it against you."

"Okay, just checking. A lady can never be too sure."

"Okay, are you finished? I want to know how you find Doctor Baker. What kind of man he is."

"Well, he's been treating my diabetes for years. I keep going back. That ought to tell you something. Besides, I enjoy my visits with him. He's polite and charming and good-looking. I'm not too old to appreciate a little eye candy, Grandson."

Bryce suppressed another groan and forged on. "Has he ever done anything or said anything inappropriate?"

"No, of course not. He treats me with the utmost care and respect. Why do you ask?"

Bryce debated in silence about how much to tell her. Her confidentiality was guaranteed, but he didn't want to upset her by putting thoughts in her head about her doctor that might be totally unfounded. On the other hand, he valued her insight and opinion.

"A young doctor came to me recently with concerns about the level of Doctor Baker's care. A couple of his patients have died recently. The young doctor's concerned they might not have died from natural causes."

"That's ridiculous! What did Doctor Baker say? I assume you've spoken to him?"

"Yes. He denied any wrongdoing. He said the female doctor in question was struggling with the demands of his program. She'd approached him with a view to trading grades for...er...certain sexual favors."

Bryce felt the heat rush up his neck and spread across his face. He might have turned thirty last birthday, but that didn't mean he was comfortable talking about sex with his eighty-three-year-old grandmother.

"What did he say?"

Bryce's cheeks got hotter at the open curiosity in his grandmother's tone. "He rebuffed her, of course," he said, and hurried on. "He says her accusations of his wrongdoing are probably her way of getting back at him for turning her down."

"Doctor Baker's a much-sought-after physician, Bryce. He must treat hundreds of patients over the course of a year. It's not beyond reason he might lose one or two along the way."

"Yeah, you're right. The more I think about it, the more it makes sense this woman was only trying to stir up trouble, no matter how genuine she appeared. Some people just know how to turn it on for the cameras, don't they?"

After final good-byes and assurances he'd be home as soon as his shift was over, Bryce ended the call. He blew out his breath on a sigh. *So, that was it.* According to his grandmother, Doctor Baker was the epitome of virtue—a godlike figure who could do no wrong—apart from losing a patient or two here or there... And that was to be expected, wasn't it?

So where did that leave his investigation? *Was* there an investigation? With Baker such a public figure, Bryce wanted to be sure before he took things any further by making contact with the hospital. If the media got wind of it and it all turned out to be nothing more than a young woman hellbent on revenge, he'd be a laughing stock. Not to mention the negative publicity the police service and the hospital would suffer.

He cursed under his breath and shook his head. He was

getting nowhere. He needed to go over everything with his boss and get his take on all of this. As if conjuring him up, Detective Superintendent Holt Denman strode out of his office and headed toward Bryce, his expression grim. Sitting up straighter in his chair, Bryce waited until his boss came to a stop a few feet away from Bryce's desk.

"Bryce, what are you up to?"

Bryce looked down at the statements on his desk and gave a noncommittal shrug. "This and that, boss. I'm just trying to work through something. What can I do for you?"

Holt's frown darkened and he stared down at the papers in his hand. "I've just had a call from Senator Jeremy Green."

"You mean...?"

"Yes, from the state legislature."

"What's he lobbying for this time? Don't tell me he's still going on about the bail laws?"

"No, not this time." Holt tightened his lips. "This time it's personal."

Bryce leaned back in his chair. "Okay."

"The senator's wife was admitted to the Sydney Harbour Hospital three days ago suffering an acute asthma attack. The attack was brought under control and all was good, but before Eileen Green could be discharged, she started complaining of severe stomach cramps. She began vomiting quite violently. By midday today, she was dead. The senator's convinced she was murdered."

A shiver of dread ran down Bryce's spine. "Shit."

"Yes, it gets worse. The senator's called a press conference. It will take place in an hour. He's taking his accusations public."

"Who's the doctor?"

Holt grimaced. "As if this thing couldn't get any worse, Eileen Green was admitted under Sydney Harbour's poster boy: Doctor Leo Baker."

The dread in Bryce's gut intensified. He shook his head slowly back and forth, unable to believe what he'd heard and yet from the moment his boss had started talking, a part of him had known what the man was going to say. He looked up at Holt.

"You're not going to believe this, but a week ago I interviewed a junior doctor from the Sydney Harbour Hospital. She came forward with two similar, unrelated complaints."

"You're kidding me!" Holt sounded as shocked as he looked.

"No, I'm afraid not. I've been sitting on it because... Well, it's complicated. During the same interview, she also accused Doctor Baker of sexual harassment. I spoke to the doctor and his explanations seemed reasonable. It appeared that the woman was merely causing trouble. Now, I'm not so sure."

"Give me everything you have. I want to be kept fully informed. Have you looked into the deaths of these others?"

"No, as I said, I was still trying to determine the legitimacy of the woman's claims. It's quite possible her complaints are nothing more than sour grapes."

"Except now we have a third death and an independent claim of wrongdoing."

"You and I know full well how easy it is to blame the doctor when a loved one dies unexpectedly. Some people find it difficult to let go. They need someone to take responsibility."

"Of course and who knows, this might turn out to be that, after all, but we don't have the freedom to investigate it at our leisure. By four o'clock this afternoon, everyone with access to a media outlet will have heard about it. We need to act fast. You can bet your bottom dollar I'll be expected to front the press shortly afterward and I'll need to be prepared."

"Right. "I'll call the hospital now. See when the autopsy's scheduled."

"*If* there's an autopsy scheduled. It's not necessarily automatic."

"I'm sure they'd have knowledge of the senator's claims. He wouldn't have gone straight to the police. They'll have to do an autopsy, if only just to cover their asses."

"Yes, you're right. Find out about the others while you're at it. Do you have names?"

"Yes. I'll look into it. Both of these deaths occurred nearly six weeks ago. If there wasn't an autopsy, we want to hope the women weren't cremated or else it's going to be tough proving any cause of death other than as stated on the death certificate."

"Let's cross that bridge when we come to it."

"You got it."

"Take Jett with you. Keep me in the loop."

Bryce nodded and pushed back his chair, ready to do battle with whatever came his way. A part of him was filled with anticipation at the thought that he might have an excuse to once again speak with Chanel Munro.

# CHAPTER 10

Chanel dodged the barrage of news cameras and cameramen that lined the walkway to the entrance of the hospital. It had been that way for hours, ever since the senator had gone public with his accusations.

Hurrying past them, she covered the side of her face with her hand and averted her gaze. She couldn't believe another one of her patients had died a mysterious death.

Not *her* patients, she quickly corrected. *Doctor Baker's patients*. Though technically, his patients were her patients, including the recently deceased Eileen Green. The senator had a right to be suspicious and as far as she knew, he wasn't aware of the others. Chanel had a sick feeling in her stomach every time she thought about those women.

She wondered if the detective she'd spoken to had heard about the latest patient death. She'd heard nothing to indicate his take on her revelations, one way or the other. She could only hope that when the third death hit his radar, it would be taken seriously and something would be done.

She still had no proof that Doctor Baker was responsible and the only thing tying him to all three of the deaths was that they had been patients under his care. The police would need to investigate all of the staff members who had access to those patients during the relevant time. With a start, she realized one of those staffers would be her.

While Amelia Arncliffe had died only a few days after Chanel had started at the hospital, she'd still had contact with the woman shortly before her death. It was the same for Robyn Evan and Eileen Green. They were all patients allocated to Chanel. They were all on her list. And she'd attended every one of them, listened to their complaints, suggested treatment, and overseen their recovery. That was all under the guidance of Doctor Baker, but he hadn't been present every time she'd seen them. Could she be held responsible…?

No, she was sure she had nothing to be worried about. She certainly hadn't done anything to cause their deaths. She just hoped the police would find who was responsible, before others met what she believed were untimely ends.

Reaching the bank of elevators, she pressed the button and waited for one to arrive, glancing over her list of patients as she did so. She'd already seen most of them earlier that morning. There was a new patient on Ward Three who'd been admitted right after lunch. Doctor Baker had requested she attend upon Yvonne Latham for the purposes of an examination. He wanted Chanel to report back to him with her diagnosis and a prescribed plan of treatment.

Flipping over the page, she continued to scan her list. Most of the names were from patients she'd known over the past few days who were all progressing well. She'd check on each of them again before she finished for the day.

"Doctor Munro, I'm glad I caught you. Are you on your way to see Yvonne Latham?"

Chanel tensed at the sound of Doctor Baker's voice, but forced herself to respond with a courtesy she was far from feeling.

"Good afternoon, Doctor Baker. Yes, as a matter of fact, I am."

"Good. I'll accompany you. It will save you from having to report back to me later. I'm going to be a little busy this afternoon. The general manager wants to see me."

Chanel spared him a glance. "Is this about the press conference held by the senator?"

Doctor Baker's mouth twisted into a grimace. "Yes. Have you ever heard a more absurd allegation? The idiot's accusing someone in this hospital of foul play. His wife died of a heart attack. I'm sorry to say it, but there it is. She was at least ninety pounds overweight. She had chronic heart disease. Okay, so she was hospitalized with an asthma attack. But how long did she think her heart was going to put up with that kind of treatment? It's probably best that she went when she did."

Chanel gasped in shock. She shook her head, unable to believe she'd heard right. "Doctor Baker, you can't mean that. Mrs Green was a lovely lady, so kind and funny. She had the wickedest sense of humor. So what if she was overweight? She was enjoying life and living it to the fullest."

Doctor Baker clicked his tongue and looked at her with an expression of such condescension it was all Chanel could do not to shout at him. Instead, she clenched her jaw and silently counted to ten. The final number had just rolled into her head when the elevator arrived. She breathed a sigh of relief.

The elevator quickly filled with other staff members and Chanel was thankful it prevented further conversation with her boss. Too soon, they arrived at their destination and stepped out of the elevator at Level Three. Doctor Baker kept pace with her and they entered the ward together amidst cheerful greetings from the nursing staff.

"We're just checking in on Yvonne Latham," Doctor Baker explained to the nurses with a smile.

"She's down in room six, Doctor Baker. She's been admitted to the ward and is resting peacefully. Would you like one of us to accompany you?"

"No, that's fine, nurse. Doctor Munro is going to wow me with her diagnostic skills. I'm keen to discover what she's learned this past month and a half."

Chanel gritted her teeth over the nurse's tittering and continued in the direction of room six. She heard Doctor Baker's measured tread behind her.

Room six was a four-bed room. Only one bed was occupied. The nameplate above the bed identified the patient as Yvonne Latham, but Chanel was nothing if not thorough.

"Mrs Latham?" she enquired, smiling at the elderly woman in the bed.

"That's me, but call me Yvonne, honey. And my, don't you have pretty hair."

Chanel touched her ponytail reflexively. "I'm Doctor Munro, but you can call me Chanel. I'm one of Doctor Baker's residents. He's asked me to come and take a look at you."

"Oh, my, that Doctor Baker's something, isn't he?" Pale blue eyes twinkled up at Chanel with such cheeky abandonment, she couldn't help but laugh. Aware of the doctor's presence behind her, she pitched her voice down low.

"Oh, yes, he's something all right."

"He fair gets my old heart racing," Yvonne replied. She winked at Chanel. "What I wouldn't give to be a decade or two younger."

Her giggle turned into a hacking cough and she began to struggle for breath. Chanel stepped forward and reached for the oxygen mask attached to the equipment behind the bed. Turning the oxygen on low, she adjusted the mask over Yvonne's mouth and nose. "Big, slow breaths, Yvonne. Take it easy. That's it. There you go."

Despite the fact there were no other patients in the room, as a matter of courtesy, Chanel turned to draw the curtains around the woman's bed. Doctor Baker stepped forward. He stood so close she was forced to brush past him in order to complete the job. With gritted teeth, she returned her attention to the patient, who was breathing normally again.

"How long have you had that cough?"

"Oh, too long, honey. Must be going on five or six years. It's gotten to the point that I can hardly walk down to the bus stop without gasping for breath and that sets off another bout of coughing. I thought it was asthma, but it turns out it's not."

"Do you mind if I listen to your chest?"

"Honey, you listen to whatever you want." She leaned forward and Chanel used her stethoscope to listen to the air as the woman labored to breathe.

"Are you a smoker, Yvonne?"

"Was, honey. I quit about six months ago. Just couldn't seem to catch my breath. The ciggies made it worse."

"How long did you smoke?"

"Well, I started when I was fourteen and I turned seventy-three last month. A lot of years, honey. Too many."

"I'd like you to have a lung function test; is that all right?"

"I guess so. Why do I need to have one of those?"

Chanel drew in a deep breath and then eased it out. It was never easy delivering bad news.

"I think you might have emphysema, Yvonne. It's a disease related to long-term smoking. It could also be chronic bronchitis. A spirometer test will tell us for sure."

"I guess I should have known my smoking would catch up with me eventually. That's what the ads on the TV say. Too bad they were right."

The light from her eyes had all but disappeared and there was no mistaking the sadness and regret that turned down her mouth. Chanel's heart went out to her, but there was nothing she could do. If it was emphysema, the damage had already been done.

"Is there a cure, Doctor Munro?"

Chanel glanced in Doctor Baker's direction. His expression was stern, but he nodded for her to continue.

"We can't cure it, Yvonne, but we can offer treatment. There are certain medications that can work to widen your airways and reduce the amount of phlegm in your lungs. We also have what we call pulmonary rehabilitation, which involves a lot of respiratory exercises that help to maximise your lung capacity. In the very worst cases, we can offer you portable oxygen, so you have it with you whenever you need it."

"Is this emphysema going to kill me?"

Chanel compressed her lips against a sudden surge of emotion and nodded. "It might not be the emphysema directly, but it will be a disease associated with it. Emphysema is only one of a host of chronic obstructive pulmonary diseases or COPD illnesses associated with the effects of smoking. I wish I had better news to tell you."

The woman was silent for a while and then murmured, "How long have I got?"

"The fact that you've given up smoking is the best thing you could have done for your health. It really is the best way to treat a COPD, so you're already on the way to helping yourself. As for life expectancy, who knows? Will the disease cut your life short? Probably. But there's no guarantee you wouldn't have succumbed to some other disease." She shrugged. "It's impossible to tell."

Tears glinted in the elderly lady's eyes. "Thanks for being upfront with me, honey. I appreciate that," she murmured, her voice little more than a husky whisper.

A lump formed in Chanel's throat. She reached for Yvonne's hand and gave it a squeeze. "Doctor Baker will prescribe a drug regime that will help you to get on top of that cough. Once you're well enough to go home, I'll arrange for you to attend pulmonary rehab. You'll get a lot of information about pulmonary diseases there, as well as ways to improve your health through breathing exercises and that kind of thing. You'll also meet other people affected by similar diseases. It will become a 'go to' place for information and a sharing of experiences."

"Thank you, Doctor Munro. You're very kind. When will I see you again?"

Doctor Baker moved closer to the bed and smiled down at the patient. "She'll be in to see you every day, Yvonne. I'll make sure of it. Doctor Munro is a second year resident. She's part of my medical team. I'm pleased with her diagnosis and suggested treatment. It's exactly what I would have done. She'll make a fine doctor one day."

"What do you mean, one day?" Yvonne demanded. "She already is a fine doctor." Another bout of coughing took hold of the woman. Her shoulders shook with the effort. Doctor Baker reached for the oxygen mask and once again, it was gently fitted it over the woman's face.

"Thank you, Doctor," she gasped.

"Breathe," Yvonne," Doctor Baker murmured. "Breathe."

Chanel watched and was struck anew by the kindness and tenderness employed by her boss toward his patients. At times like this it seemed ludicrous to contemplate for even a second that he could be responsible for murdering some of these dear people. She watched while he patted the woman's hand until the coughing bout ceased and her breathing returned to normal.

"It's all right, Yvonne. It's all right. There, there, you're going to be all right. Catch your breath; that's the way."

The woman stared up at him with gratitude and relief. "Sometimes it gets so bad, I feel like I'm suffocating. I can't breathe and it scares the life out of me."

"I'm sure it does. I can't imagine what it must feel like. Don't worry, we're going to do all we can to make you more comfortable. I promise you." He turned to encompass Chanel in his glance.

"Doctor Munro will be here whenever you need her. Just get the nurse to page her and she'll come and sort you out. Okay?"

"Yes, thank you, Doctor. I appreciate your time."

Doctor Baker smiled. "It's my pleasure, Yvonne. That's what I'm here for."

---

Bryce pushed the food around his plate and wished he had the appetite to do it justice. His grandmother had gone all out, cooking a lamb roast and baked vegetables. The gravy was smooth and fragrant, just as he liked it, but he couldn't bring himself to eat more than a bite or two.

"What is it, Grandson? You've been quiet all evening. Did you have a tough day at work?"

Bryce put down his fork and sat back in his chair. He rubbed a hand tiredly through his hair and sighed.

"Yeah, work's been tough the last few days, but that's not what's got me twisted up in knots."

"Then, what is it?"

He sighed again and then decided on the truth. "It's Angela. Or more accurately, it's her doctors. I met with one of them a fortnight ago. They're coming under pressure to free up the bed. They can't do anything for her. They're urging me to switch off her machine."

His grandmother looked stricken. "Oh, Bryce! That's awful! Why didn't you tell me? You shouldn't have had to bear this alone!"

He shrugged, but just the same, appreciated that she cared. "They weren't telling me anything new, Grandma. If it hadn't been for the baby—"

"But there wasn't a baby, Bryce. You have to stop thinking like that!"

"We didn't know that at the time, Grandma! She was driving home from the fertility clinic. She'd just undergone another IVF treatment. They'd only just implanted her. When she was T-boned by that drunk driver, there was a real chance she was already pregnant."

He pushed away from the table, unable to sit still a moment longer. With his hands clenched, he paced the confines of the kitchen.

"We'd wanted a baby for so long! You don't know how many nights we dreamed about it happening. The hormone treatments, the mood swings, the continual disappointments—all of it put a terrible strain on our marriage. But we weren't prepared to give up. We both wanted a baby so badly. I couldn't turn off the machine that night or even the day after. I couldn't take the risk that she was pregnant. I couldn't kill our baby, too."

His grandmother watched him, a sad expression filling her timeworn face. Tears slid slowly down her cheeks, glinting in the light.

"I understand, honey. But she *wasn't* pregnant. The IVF attempt failed. It's been three years." She paused. When she spoke again, her voice was low. "I've said it before, Bryce. As difficult as it is, it's time to let her go."

Anger and frustration surged through him. He squeezed his eyes shut against it. "You don't understand, Grandma! At the time of the accident, I felt so guilty at the thought of possibly killing our baby, I couldn't turn off the machine. When I found out Angela wasn't pregnant, I still couldn't bring myself to do it!"

A ragged breath caught in the back of his throat and he struggled to breathe through the tumult of emotion that twisted up his insides. He had to make her see.

"I kept Angela alive for the sake of our baby. By the time I knew there was no baby, it seemed cruel and heartless to even consider letting her go. I'd kept her on life support in the hope that if she was pregnant, our baby would live. How could I switch off the machine so callously once I found out that hope had died? We'd promised each other we were in it for the long haul, no matter what life threw at us..."

He shook his head, the familiar darkness and despair washing over him. "I didn't want to think I'd only kept my wife alive to incubate our child. It seemed wrong, so wrong to even contemplate turning off the life support after that. It seemed like somehow I was punishing her for not being pregnant. Like, now that there was no baby, she wasn't wanted anymore."

"No one who knew you thought like that, Bryce and they don't think like that now," his grandmother said gently. "You loved Angela as much as anyone and gave her all you had."

She shook her head sadly. "You mention the strain your marriage was under, but marriages are tested every day. It doesn't mean you no longer love and care for one another or that divorce is on its way. It's just life, with all its ups and downs. We get through it and come out the other side.

"Only, in your case, you weren't given the chance. Your wife was so badly injured, you were left with little more than a shell. She looks like the woman you married, but it's all an illusion. She's had no signs of brain activity since the time she was brought into the ER. If the emergency services hadn't responded so quickly, she probably would have died at the scene. I hate to say it, but there have been many times when I wished she had. It would have spared you so much pain. It would have allowed you to grieve in the normal way and finally move on with your life."

Bryce wanted to block out his grandmother's words and howl out his agony against the injustice of it. He wanted to scream and shout and pull things off the walls. He wanted to hit something. Hard. It was like it was happening all over again—the confusion, the panic, the fear. And along with it, the questions nobody wanted to hear.

'Are you Angela Sutcliffe's next of kin?' 'Is your wife an organ donor?' 'Is there anyone else you'd like us to call?' 'Do you want to switch off her machine?'

The nightmare of it washed over him and bombarded him from every side. He'd managed to avoid thinking about it for three years, but now he'd run out of time. He had to make a decision. The knowledge sat like concrete in his gut.

With a heavy sigh, his anger left him and he dragged himself back to his chair. His grandmother wiped at the tears on her cheeks and delicately blew her nose. He sat with his head in his hands and tried to make sense of his thoughts.

Deep down, he knew what he had to do. Had always known. It was like his grandmother said: Angela had been dead from the moment it happened. Advanced technology and quick medical intervention were the only things keeping her alive. If he didn't feel so damned guilty every time he thought about why he hadn't made the decision to end things in the first place, it would be a hell of a lot easier now.

Not that anything to do with making such a decision was easy. In fact, it was the hardest thing he'd had to do. But, he owed it to his wife to let her go; to let her find her peace.

He lifted his head and looked at his grandmother, his heart stuttering at the love and kindness in her eyes.

"I'll support your decision, no matter what, Grandson. Like I always have. I love you, Bryce and it doesn't come with conditions. Don't forget that."

Tears burned behind his eyes and he blinked hard to keep them back. Reaching across the table, he took her soft, worn hands in his.

"I love you, too, Grandma and I'm so glad you took me in. I don't know what the hell would have become of me if you'd turned me away. I'll be forever grateful for everything that you've done."

Fresh tears sparkled in her old eyes. "You're my family, Bryce Sutcliffe, my flesh and blood. How could I turn you away?"

Bryce shrugged and swallowed the lump in his throat. She knew how important she was to him. He'd told her more than once. He couldn't bear the thought of losing her, but he knew one day, he must. Life was tough. And hard decisions sometimes had to be made. Like the one about Angela.

He hated the very thought of it, but his grandmother was right. It had to be done. He had to stop living with his guilt every day and do what was best for his wife. She could lie there in a bed for another sixty years on a machine that did the living for her. The woman he loved and had made his wife was gone and was never coming back. End of story.

---

The sun still had a bite to it, even though the afternoon was nearly done. A cooling breeze that blew in from the ocean brought a modicum of relief. It had been four long days since Bryce had given his wife's doctors permission to switch off the life support. Now, he stood with his grandmother and Angela's parents on the cliffs high above Bondi Beach. Seagulls squawked in the distance and waves rolled in far below. The gray shadows of hulking freighters hugged the horizon as they made their way to far off shores, laden with cargo. It had been one of Angela's favorite places.

In his hands, Bryce held the urn that contained his wife's ashes. She'd wanted her ashes to be scattered over the cliffs of the eastern coastline she loved so much. It saddened him that she'd had to wait three years to have her wish granted and he was determined that at last, she'd rest in peace.

Her parents read a couple of passages out of the bible. They stumbled over the words, but the soothing psalms appeared to bring them comfort. Without accompaniment, his grandmother began to sing *Amazing Grace*. Her voice, though weak with age, still held a pleasant tune and the simple, but powerful words brought tears to Bryce's eyes.

When it was over, he glanced across at his parents-in-law. They clung to one another, sobbing quietly. Only the gentle rush of the ocean and the occasional call of a bird disturbed the stillness. With a deep breath, Bryce lifted the lid of the urn and held it high up in the air. Tilting it sideways, he shook it slightly and waited for the breeze to catch his offering. Within moments, Angela's remains were taken by the wind. One second she was there, the next, she was not. Just as it had been in life.

At least they hadn't argued the morning she'd been injured. He could be grateful for that. He'd kissed her good-bye like he usually did and wished her luck with her day. He might have stopped attending the IVF appointments, but that didn't mean he'd stopped caring. He'd wanted a baby as much as she did, but when they came away disappointed time after time, he'd learned to accept it wasn't meant to be. Eventually he'd focussed his energies elsewhere.

After the accident, he'd worked like a madman and made had detective sergeant in no time at all. Now, he was in line for another promotion. If he managed to solve the case involving the deaths at the Sydney Harbour Hospital, it would almost be guaranteed.

A light touch on his arm gave him a start and brought him back to the present. His grandmother gave him a reassuring squeeze and he offered her a sad smile. Putting his arm around her thin shoulders, he drew her in against his side. Together, they stared out across the mesmerizing blue of the ocean. Bryce breathed in a lungful of warm, salty air and eased it out again.

"You did the right thing, Grandson. She's at peace now."

"Thanks, Grandma. I think so, too." He leaned down and pressed a kiss against the softness of her wrinkled cheek and tightened his hold around her shoulders. She barely came halfway up his chest and yet she was a pillar of strength, of solidness, of love.

She'd given him a good life when his had been torn apart. She'd given him comfort and stability when he was floundering in a world of fear and confusion. She'd raised him with love and discipline so that he became the man he was today. He owed her everything. He owed her his life.

"What are you going to do now?" she asked and he knew she meant right now.

"I need to get back to work. We're investigating a death at the Sydney Harbour Hospital. We're under pressure to put someone behind bars. I need to pull my weight."

His grandmother patted his hand. "Yes, the Senator's wife. I saw it on the news. You go and do what you have to do. I'll find my own way home."

"Don't be silly. I have time to drop you back home. Or anywhere, if there's somewhere else you might like to go."

"Thank you, Grandson, but Angela's parents have offered to have us over for tea. I accepted on behalf of both of us."

Bryce bit his lip. The last thing he wanted to do was spend another hour or two remembering his late wife. It was entirely selfish, but what he needed was to get busy and returning to the station was the best place for him to be. He realized he'd been unconsciously mourning her death for three long years and as well as tossing her ashes to the wind today, he also had to move forward.

"I'm sorry, Grandma. I really need to get back to work. I'll go and see them now and offer my apologies."

He walked over to where Angela's parents were huddled against the wind and offered them his sympathy and his apologies for having to return to work. After bidding them a somber farewell, he turned and headed toward his car.

# CHAPTER 11

Bryce hesitated outside the Glebe morgue and braced himself for what lay behind the closed steel doors. He'd attended autopsies before and those memories now gave him pause. Apart from the distinctive, peculiar smell, the place just flat out gave him the creeps. He didn't know how people could work there day after day.

Aware that he was wasting time, he swallowed a curse and pushed open the door. Having taken pity on Jett who'd never witnessed an autopsy, he'd sent his young partner back to the station. There was no need for both of them to spend the rest of the day erasing the unsettling memories viewing a post mortem could bring.

During the course of his enquires, he'd been relieved to discover both Amelia Arncliffe and Robyn Evan had undergone autopsies. Although it wasn't legally required, the hospital had opted to do them, and for that, Bryce was grateful. He was eager to discover the official causes of death.

He nodded a greeting to a couple of female assistants who were in the ante chamber counting and recording supplies. They acknowledged him with waves and friendly greetings. He didn't attend the city morgue often enough to be on a first name basis with either of them, but he was far from a stranger.

"Detective Sutcliffe, we heard you were stopping by. It's nice to see you again."

He tried hard to think of the brunette's name, but came up empty. Fortunately, the other woman spoke, saving him from responding.

"Doctor Wolfe's already in there. She's waiting for you."

"Thanks," he managed and quickly pulled protective garments over his clothes and donned a pair of gloves. He imagined doing this ritual was similar to scrubbing up for surgery—except no one would be saved that day. But perhaps they would reveal some badly needed answers? He could only hope. Covered from head to toe, he pushed through the door that led to the main room.

Two rows of at least ten tables each lined the room. Four or five of them were occupied with forensic pathologists bent over bodies that were pale and stiff. The temperature was at least ten degrees cooler than the antechamber. Bryce scanned the room until he found the doctor he sought.

Forensic pathologist, Doctor Samantha Wolfe, was the head of the city morgue. Bryce shuddered to think how many people she'd cut open and examined to determine the cause of death. He couldn't believe such an attractive and normal-looking woman would want to bury herself among the dead, but there was no accounting for what drove some people. There had to be a reason she preferred to spend her time with corpses.

"Detective Sutcliffe, good morning. I'm sorry it's taken us so long to get to this. We've been flat out dealing with that house fire a few days ago. There were five victims. Three of them were children."

Bryce nodded. He'd heard about it. Thank God it had been out of his jurisdiction. "I understand and I'm sorry I'm late. I was caught in traffic. Thanks for waiting."

"No problem. My patients don't have the greatest interaction skills. I'm glad for the company."

He inclined his head by way of reply and forced himself to move closer to the stainless steel gurney. On it lay an elderly woman who he presumed was Eileen Green. A cloud of blue-gray hair stuck out from all sides of her large head. It wasn't the only thing that was large. He wondered what had killed her.

"All set?"

The doctor looked at him over her plastic face shield and gave him a wink. In another environment, he might have returned the smile he saw in her eyes, but something about the creepiness of the morgue held him back. He wished he could treat the whole thing as light heartedly as Doctor Wolfe, but the truth was, he was way outside his comfort zone. As if understanding his reticence, Samantha reached for a scalpel and made the first incision.

With quiet efficiency, she cut through Eileen Green's chest. After using the Stryker saw to cut through the ribs, she prised open the woman's chest. What followed was an examination of one organ after another. Each was removed, examined, weighed, sliced for pathological testing and then placed in a large, blue plastic bag to be eventually returned to the chest cavity. It was a macabre, yet fascinating process and Bryce watched in silence, both awed and revolted.

"She has an enlarged heart and serious clogging of her arteries, which isn't surprising given the size of her, but I don't think she had a heart attack."

"What killed her, then?"

Samantha's dark brows came together in a frown over the top of her face shield. "From what I read in the hospital notes, it sounds to me that she suffered some kind of poisoning. She was seen vomiting repeatedly and complained of severe stomach cramps. I want to pay particular attention to her stomach contents and I intend to test some of her tissues for known poisons."

"You think she might have been poisoned?"

"Either that, or she had an acute reaction to something she ingested. The lining of her stomach is severely abraded. I need to ascertain what caused it."

Bryce nodded and then conversation ceased when the doctor once again picked up the Stryker saw and cut through the woman's skull. He wanted to look away when she peeled back Eileen Green's face, but forced himself to hold his gaze steady.

It was simply part of the procedure, a necessary part of the autopsy. He had to stop thinking of the body as a person. She'd never feel anything again. It was important to determine the cause of death. It might mean the difference between a murderer being captured or remaining free.

An hour later it was over. Bryce was more than relieved when Samantha put down her scalpel and peeled off her gloves.

"It's done. I'll send these samples off to pathology. Hopefully, we'll have an answer in the next day or two. From what I've seen, I'm almost certain she was poisoned. There's no other reason for her death."

Bryce nodded and took a moment to absorb the doctor's words. It appeared Chanel might have been onto something. If Eileen Green were poisoned, it was possible the other two patients had been, too. He was reminded of the need to obtain a copy of their autopsy reports and ascertain their causes of death.

"I'm also looking into the deaths of two other women who were patients at the same hospital," he said. "Amelia Arncliffe and Robyn Evan. They died within the last couple of months."

"If you can provide me with their full names and dates of birth, I'll look them up for you."

"I'm not sure I have that much information at hand, but I'll do my best. I have first and last names and can get a pretty close date of death."

"I'll see what I can do. It's been a little quieter than usual around here the past month or so. You never know your luck."

Samantha led the way back into the antechamber and after disposing of her gloves and stripping off her protective clothing, she began to wash her hands thoroughly.

"What are you looking for, anyway?" she threw over her shoulder, curiosity plain on her face.

"I'm not sure. I guess I want to rule out the possibility of any other suspicious deaths. The two came to my attention a couple of weeks ago through an unrelated source. Now we have a third linked to the same hospital. I'm just being thorough."

Samantha smiled and winked at him. "No harm in that."

He stared at her. She was even more attractive now that she'd removed the standard-issue hospital scrubs and protective face shield. She looked like she was somewhere in her early thirties, probably not much older than him, but working so often with the dead had taken its toll. It was barely past eleven in the morning and yet lines of fatigue were etched into her face. He guessed they were permanent fixtures on her otherwise clear complexion.

Still, for all her attractiveness, he didn't feel the slightest physical reaction to her. Apart from being able to appreciate a pretty, intelligent woman, she did nothing for him.

He frowned at the thought. He hadn't had sex with a woman for three years. He ought to be more excited when an attractive woman winked at him. Okay, it wasn't exactly a come on, but there was more than a little interest in her sparkling, brown eyes.

Averting his gaze, he busied himself by removing the protective clothing that covered him. He tossed them into the laundry skip that stood in one corner. As if sensing his withdrawal, Samantha turned away and gathered her things.

"I'll let you know when I have the results back from the lab."

"Great. If we have a rogue staff member on the loose killing patients, we need to act fast, before he can strike again."

She raised a delicately curved eyebrow. "He? So you already have a suspect in mind?"

Bryce shrugged, unwilling to speculate in front of the doctor. She was a member of the medical fraternity, after all. Not that Bryce anticipated she'd do anything untoward, but the sensitive nature of his information dictated he proceed with caution.

"He. She. We're not sure of anything at this stage. We'll have to wait and see."

"Who alerted you?"

"A doctor working at the hospital."

She stared at him a moment longer, as if weighing what he'd said. In an effort to avoid further conversation about the ins and outs of his case, Bryce turned away and pulled on his jacket.

"How long before you can get me a copy of those reports?" he asked.

"I have a little time before I start my next PM, so I'll go back to my office now and see what I can find. Do you have the information handy?"

Bryce pulled out a sheet of paper from his jacket pocket. It was a copy of the details he'd taken down in Chanel's statement. He handed it to the doctor.

"This is all I have."

She reached over and took it from him. Their fingers touched and again, he felt nothing.

"I'll see what I can find. Do you have time to wait?"

"Yes, of course."

He followed her through a labyrinth of offices divided by glass-walled partitions. Some were occupied, but most of them were empty. At last, they came to hers. It was larger than the others, but despite the fact it commanded a corner of the room, it was without a window.

"You guys aren't big on looking out onto the outside world, are you?" he joked. He had yet to see a window in the whole building.

"We spend so much time with the dead, I guess it would feel a little weird looking out into the sunshine. Besides, it helps the cooling system to work more efficiently without hot air coming through the windows."

"I guess."

Samantha sat down at her desk and shoved aside a pile of files so that she could draw her keyboard closer. Her fingers clicked over the keys. It hardly seemed like any time at all before she announced she'd found what he was after.

The printer whirred beside her desk. He watched while the tray filled with paper. When it stopped, she picked up the sheets and separated them into two piles which she secured with staples.

"There you go. Two autopsy reports."

Bryce scanned them quickly. Neither of them listed poisoning as the cause of death. He didn't know whether to be grateful or not.

"So, do they help or hinder you?" Samantha asked with a smile.

"Would you still have blood and tissue samples from these women on file?"

"Sure, those autopsies were done seven weeks ago."

"Is it possible to test them for poisons?"

"Of course. Do you think there's a connection with the PM we did today?"

Bryce pursed his lips. "I don't know, but my gut's telling me we need to look into the possibility. Would you mind?"

"No. I tell you what, I'll run the same tests on them that I've ordered for Eileen Green. It'll take at least a day or two, though."

"I can live with that."

He stuck out his hand and she shook it. "Thank you for your time today, Doctor Wolfe. I really appreciate it," he said and meant it.

"You're welcome to join me over a PM anytime, Detective," she replied with a smile. "It's been fun."

Bryce tried not to grimace at what he assumed was a joke. He managed a nod and then made his way out of the room, past the other offices and out the exit, grateful to be heading into the fresh air and sunshine.

Once outside, he filled his lungs. Even the pollution from the passing cars was better than the unsettling smell of death and formaldehyde. He headed back to where he'd parked the unmarked police car and opened the door. The heat of the car was a welcome change from the chilly conditions in the morgue. He climbed into the driver's seat, tugged out his phone and called Holt.

"Bryce, how are you doing?"

"Good, boss. I'm outside the morgue. I just got done with the Green autopsy."

"Yeah, Jett told me you'd taken it easy on him. That was kind of you, but he's got to learn sooner or later. It's not easy for any of us and I don't think it matters how many you watch."

Bryce let the reprimand wash over him. Holt wasn't mad. Not really. He just didn't want anyone taking it easy on his men. Jett had only transferred to their station a few months earlier. As far as Holt was concerned, he needed to earn his keep. Bryce, on the other hand, was prepared to cut his new partner a little slack and if that meant letting him play hooky from a post mortem, he didn't see the harm in it.

"How did it go, anyway?" Holt continued, his voice a little less gruff.

Bryce drew in another deep breath and let it out slowly. "Samantha Wolfe did the post mortem. She's waiting for the lab results, but she thinks the senator's wife was poisoned."

"Shit. That's just what we need."

"Yeah. It'll take a day or so to know what kind of poison did the damage, but she's almost certain poisoning is the cause of death."

"So the senator was right. His wife was murdered."

"It sure appears that way."

"What do we know about the other two?"

"Nothing helpful, as yet. I got hold of the autopsy reports. Neither of them list poisoning as the cause of death. I explained to Samantha there might be a connection with the senator's wife and the good doctor agreed to test their tissue and blood samples for poisons."

"Who did those autopsies?"

"Doctor Harry Wiseman. I've dealt with him in the past. He's been there forever and unfortunately, has a reputation for delivering less than stellar performances. Too bad it wasn't Samantha. We wouldn't have to guess how accurate the reports are."

"I thought she was out at Westmead? What's she doing at Glebe?"

"She transferred about six months ago. I'm not sure what prompted it. I remember someone saying she wanted to be closer to the city."

"Well, I'm just grateful we got her this time around. We have every media outlet in the city watching our every move, not to mention the calls I've taken from the police commissioner and the State premier this morning. Both of them are concerned about where this might be heading. We need to dot the I's and cross every T. You can be assured every aspect of this investigation will be scrutinized from top to bottom."

"I understand, boss. Don't worry, I won't do anything rash. We've got a day or two before the official cause of death will be known. Until then, I'll do my best to keep a lid on it."

"Talk to the hospital. Impress upon them that it's in everyone's best interests for them to cooperate with us in a discreet manner. Get a hold of the medical records of all three women. We want to be prepared if something shows up in the lab results. Let me know as soon as you hear anything."

"Will do."

Bryce ended the call. The first thing on his list was another visit to the hospital. He waited for the usual feeling of dread to manifest itself in his gut, but it didn't happen. Instead, his heart leaped with anticipation. He refused to acknowledge it had anything to do with a certain blond doctor who went by the name of Chanel Munro.

---

Armed with copies of the autopsies of all three women, Bryce and Jett made their way through the main building of the hospital. They waved to Marjorie and Dottie as they passed the information booth and headed up the stairs to the administration area that housed the office of the general manager. They were met by a stylish, middle-aged receptionist who asked them to take a seat. The waiting area was small, but tidy with a dark leather sofa against one wall.

"Ms Healy will be with you in a moment," the receptionist advised. "Can I get you something to drink? Coffee or tea? Or maybe something cooler? The weather's warmed up out there today."

Bryce glanced at Jett and answered for both of them. "No, thanks. We're fine."

The woman nodded and returned to her seat behind the counter. A moment later, a door to their left opened and a tall, thin woman wearing a tailored, charcoal-gray suit and pale blue blouse strode into the waiting room. Without pause, she came straight up to where they were sitting and put out her hand.

"Detectives, I'm Deborah Healy. Sorry to keep you waiting."

Bryce stood and shook the proffered hand. Jett followed suit.

"Come in, Detectives."

The woman turned on her four-inch, shiny black leather heels and headed back the way she'd come. Bryce noticed how Jett checked out her shapely butt. She must have been edging fifty, but she was still very well put together and despite her slenderness, she had curves and bumps in all the right places. More athletic looking than skinny, it was obvious she was a woman who took pride in her appearance.

They followed her into a corner office that overlooked the front entryway of the hospital a floor below. Mid-afternoon sunshine poured through the tall windows that graced the wall behind her desk, flooding the room with natural light. Healthy plants grew in small, colorful ceramic pots along the window ledge. Soft classical music played from an iPod docked a little further along the ledge. The overriding mood was one of peace and tranquillity and was a surprise find in a hospital. All that was missing was a water feature.

"Please, take a seat."

Bryce and Jett took the only two chairs available, opposite her large wooden desk. Unlike Doctor Baker's, this desk look well used. Its pale, scarred surface was covered with files and loose papers. A handful of medical reference books sat in a pile on one end. Pens were scattered haphazardly across the desk, along with paperclips and highlighters. A large computer monitor and keyboard stood on the other corner, angled toward the general manager.

Deborah Healy took a seat behind the desk and drew her chair in close. Sitting tall, she folded her hands together in front of her and addressed them again.

"Now, Detectives, I assume this isn't a social call. What can I do for you?"

Bryce raised his eyebrows in surprise. Okay, so the media presence had disappeared from outside the front of the hospital, but it had only been five days since the senator's accusations had aired across the state. Surely it wasn't too hard to deduce what they were there for?

Bryce stared at her with narrowed eyes. She didn't look stupid. In fact, the intelligence in her light brown eyes was plain to see. So what game was she playing?

"Ms Healy, we're investigating the suspicious death of Eileen Green, wife of Senator Jeremy Green."

"A very sad circumstance and on behalf of the hospital and all of the staff, I've extended my deepest sympathies to the senator and his family, but I'm afraid it's only the senator who believes it's suspicious. Preliminary examinations conducted by our doctors found otherwise."

"I hate to be the bearer of bad news, Ms Healy, but this morning I went down to the city morgue. Doctor Samantha Wolfe conducted the autopsy on Eileen Green and she's determined the woman was poisoned."

The general manager gasped and then quickly covered her mouth, as if to hold the offending emotion back. Color leached from her cheeks and a little of her confidence diminished. A frown creased the skin between her eyes.

"Poisoned? How can that be?"

"The forensic pathologist is still waiting for lab results to determine the particular substance used, but yes, she's very certain poison was involved."

Deborah shook her head slowly back and forth. "Oh, dear God, how dreadful. That poor woman."

After taking a moment to compose herself, she turned back to them and asked, "Who else knows about the preliminary findings?"

"I've informed our superintendent. He's aware of what's happening. I'm not sure who he's spoken to. It's possible that it's still contained within the police service. As a matter of courtesy, we wanted to bring this to your attention before the media got wind of it. If you think yesterday was a media circus, you haven't seen anything yet."

The woman nodded, her expression grim. "I'm afraid you're right, Detective and I appreciate you coming as quickly as you have, but there's no hiding from it. If a patient in this hospital has been murdered, I'll let nothing and no one stand in the way of finding the person or persons responsible." She hesitated and her expression turned hopeful.

"There isn't a chance it was an accident, is there? Like food poisoning, or something? Or perhaps it was an allergic reaction?"

"Doctor Wolfe was certain it was a poisoning, but until we know what the poisonous substance is, we can't rule anything out. We'll proceed with open minds until we know what we're dealing with."

"Of course, I'm sure you will, and thank you for coming to me with this. I can assure you I'll cooperate fully with your investigation, as will the members of my staff. Let me know how we can be of assistance."

"I should tell you we're investigating the deaths of two other patients in your hospital. Their autopsy reports don't show death by poisoning, but we have reason to suspect otherwise. Tissue samples retained on file have also been sent to the lab for testing."

What little color that was left in the general manager's cheeks disappeared. Her eyes went wide with shock.

"Two *other* deaths? Are you certain? How do you know?"

Bryce eyed her solemnly, almost feeling sorry for her. It wasn't her fault a member of her staff could be out of control.

"These deaths took place more nearly two months ago. They weren't immediately reported as suspicious, but in light of what Doctor Wolfe found with Eileen Green, we have reason to suspect otherwise. We'll know for sure once the lab results are in."

Deborah shook her head again, looking dazed. "Two more... What...? What do you want me to do?"

Jett slid a piece of paper across the desk. It contained the full names of Amelia Arncliffe, Robyn Evan and Eileen Green, along with their dates of birth.

"These women were all patients admitted under Doctor Leo Baker. We're going to need copies of their hospital records during their stay, including clinical notes, medication schedules and anything else that was recorded while they were here," Jett said.

"We're also going to need a copy of all staff rosters, including nursing, medical, kitchen and cleaning staff for the time these women were patients. We need to know exactly who had access to them and when."

Fear and concern now darkened the general manager's eyes and her lips were pinched and pale. She reached for the piece of paper and held it closer. Her hand shook.

"W-when do you need it?"

"As soon as possible and we'd appreciate your discretion," Bryce responded grimly. It would take a mammoth amount of manpower to collate the rosters of the thousands of staff members employed by the Sydney Harbour Hospital. The sooner they started, the better.

"I-I'll get on it right away." She picked up the phone near her elbow and dialed a number and then looked back at them, her expression grim.

"If you don't mind, Detectives, I'd appreciate it if you could please see yourselves out."

Bryce nodded. "We'll be in touch. Call as soon as you have that paperwork."

# CHAPTER 12

Bryce tried to make sense of the rosters spread out across the large tables in the major incident room at the station. A couple of other officers had done some preliminary groundwork, highlighting the names of staff members who had direct access to all three women during their stay at the hospital. Thankfully, none of the deceased had been a patient for longer than a fortnight prior to their deaths.

It had been three days since the autopsy. He was still waiting to hear from Samantha, but his gut was telling him the deaths were related. As if on cue, his phone rang. The Caller ID of the city morgue came up on his screen. His gut clenched.

"Detective Sutcliffe," he announced.

"Detective, it's Samantha Wolfe. Sorry it's taken me so long to get back to you. The labs are more backed up than I expected."

"That's fine, I understand. What do you have?"

"Eileen Green was poisoned with ricin. We also found large traces of it in Amelia Arncliffe and Robyn Evan. It looks like you have a serial killer on the loose in Sydney Harbour Hospital."

"Fuck." Bryce whispered the expletive in deference to the forensic pathologist, but she heard him just the same.

"That's one way of putting it. Do you know what ricin is?"

"Yeah, it comes from castor beans, doesn't it?"

"That's right. It's extracted from inside the castor bean by a process of filtration. It sounds complicated, but it isn't. Anyone with half a brain could do it in their kitchen."

"Are castor beans readily available?"

"It's illegal to import castor bean seeds into Australia, but there are plenty of nurseries around Sydney where you can buy the plants. An easy search on the Internet would point you in the right direction."

"I take it this poison was ingested by the women?"

"Yes, although even inhaling it can be fatal. It was found in both the blood and tissues of our victims, which leads me to believe it was swallowed."

"So someone tampered with their food?"

"That would be my guess. If the ricin's been reduced to a powder form, it would be simple enough for someone to mix it in with the yoghurt or mashed potato."

Bryce's jaw clenched. This was even more difficult than he imagined. When he'd included the kitchen staff in the people he wanted to look at, it was more from the point of view of being thorough, rather than any real belief they were involved. What could a member of the kitchen staff have against the women, unless the victims selected at random? The endless thoughts chased themselves around his head until he gritted his teeth in frustration. A sound escaped his tightly clenched jaws.

"Excuse me?" she asked.

He was snapped back to reality by the doctor's question and he hurriedly focused his thoughts once more on their conversation.

"What time frame are we talking between ingestion and death, Doctor Wolfe?"

"It depends on a number of factors. Usually, we'd say it takes between one to three days for a person to die once they've been exposed, but if they ingested a large amount of ricin or were otherwise susceptible, it could happen sooner. For example, children or the elderly will generally die faster from ricin poisoning than an otherwise healthy adult."

Bryce mulled over her answer. "So, in this case, where we

have three ailing, elderly women, it could have taken less time for them to die?"

"Correct. And although we don't know the dosage they were given, significant amounts were found in all three. Enough to kill them, for sure."

"One final question, Doctor Wolfe. How long would it take after ingestion for our victims to begin showing symptoms?"

"Generally, when ricin is ingested, you'll start seeing signs of poisoning within ten hours, often sooner if the dosage is high and the patient is small. Signs such as severe abdominal pain, vomiting and diarrhoea are all classic indicators of poisoning."

Bryce thanked the doctor and ended the call with a heavy sigh. At least they'd done some preliminaries. Now all he had to do was compile a list of all staff members who had come into direct contact with their victims ten or twelve hours prior to them showing symptoms of poisoning. He looked down at the piles of scattered papers and sighed again. A moment later, he threw back his shoulders and headed toward the door, determination surging through him. He called out to Holt on his way across the squad room.

"Boss, I just heard from Samantha Wolfe. We need to talk about putting together a task force."

---

Chanel took a sip from her Styrofoam coffee cup and did her best to concentrate on the excited chatter coming from her roommate. They were both on a break and had agreed to meet in the hospital cafeteria. The conversation had been going fine until Tanya mentioned Doctor Baker. Chanel was certain if Tanya mentioned Doctor Baker's name in that breathy, girly voice one more time, she'd puke.

She couldn't believe the woman was still so hung up on him. Twice more, he'd dropped by their apartment and collected Tanya for a date. Both times, she'd gone with him, giggling and blushing like a teenager. The last time, she hadn't returned home until midway through the next morning.

Chanel swallowed a sigh and determined to tune out her roommate's chatter. Then she heard the words 'meeting with the police' and snapped to attention.

"Can you believe it? It's so exciting! It's just like something from *Criminal Minds*."

Chanel blinked hard and frowned. "I'm sorry, Tanya. What did you say about the police?"

Her roommate rolled her eyes in exasperation. "Haven't you been *listening*? We're being interviewed by the police. They're investigating the death of three patients. Can you believe it? Not just the senator's wife, but two others!"

Chanel's heart thumped so hard she was afraid it would drown out the rest of Tanya's words and all of a sudden, she was desperate to hear what her friend had to say.

"What are you talking about, two others? Do you have their names?"

Tanya leaned forward across the cafeteria table and lowered her voice although the place was so crowded with lunchtime diners, Chanel didn't think anyone would overhear. *She* could barely hear.

"The word on the street is that they're also looking into the deaths of Amelia Arncliffe and Robyn Evan."

Tanya's eyes were wide with excitement. Chanel felt a growing sense of hope. *Amelia Arncliffe and Robyn Evan.* The women she'd mentioned to the police. Were their deaths finally being investigated? Perhaps her theory that the women had died suspiciously wasn't as farfetched as some people had thought? Perhaps Detective Sutcliffe had listened to her, after all?

At the thought of the darkly attractive police officer, warmth suffused her body. Even her cheeks felt hot. It had been nearly three weeks since she'd seen him and yet she remembered him like it had been yesterday.

The shade of his hair, so dark it was almost black, with eyes to match. The impressive height and width of him...

She was tall for a woman, but she'd felt dwarfed beside

him. Even in high heels, she'd had to look up and that was no mean feat for any man to achieve. The knowledge that he might have started an investigation into the deaths of Mrs Arncliffe and Mrs Evan warmed her through, even if it didn't have anything to do with her.

Rumor had it the senator's wife had died in a manner similar to the other two. Chanel was more and more certain there was something very wrong. Patients were dying on Ward Three and she had a terrible feeling the reasons behind it were pure evil.

"When are the police conducting the interviews?" she asked as casually as she could manage.

"I've heard they've already interviewed the kitchen staff. They're supposed to interview the doctors today."

*Today...* Chanel was gratified to learn the police weren't wasting time. She picked up her coffee cup and tilted it to her lips. Out of the corner of her eye, she spied a tall dark figure who looked very familiar. In fact, he'd been in her thoughts only moments earlier.

Detective Sutcliffe stood in the crowded cafeteria line with a tray in his hand. Another dark-suited man stood behind him, looking similarly stern and authoritative. She recognized him as the officer who'd brought her upstairs the time she'd gone to the police station. As if sensing her scrutiny, Detective Sutcliffe turned his head in her direction.

His gaze clashed with hers and Chanel's heart skipped a beat. A second later, it pounded against her ribs. His dark eyes flared with an emotion she was scared to define. The intensity of his gaze seared her from across the room. A flush crept up her neck and spread across her face. Her pulse leaped wildly. He excited her like no other man had and she didn't have a clue what to do about it.

For a start, the timing was all wrong. He was likely investigating the suspicious deaths of three of her former patients. While she knew she had nothing to do with them, he didn't know that. She wasn't stupid. Anyone who'd had contact with the dead women would be a potential suspect and that included her.

Dragging her gaze away, Chanel tried hard to get her erratic breathing under control. With determination, she focused on her roommate who was still talking animatedly across the table, in between taking bites from her sandwich.

Chanel was pleased for the distraction. She was acutely aware of the detective in front of her. There was nothing she could do to relieve the pressure his presence had put on her stress levels.

"Ooh, do you think they're officers?" Tanya whispered loudly and turned and pointed in the direction of Detective Sutcliffe and his colleague. "They have that look about them, don't you think? I wouldn't mind being interviewed by either of them. They are H-O-T. Oh my God! Don't look now, but they're coming this way!"

Chanel's stomach dropped to her feet and simultaneously clenched with a rush of nerves. As much as she wanted to see the detective again, the thought of him speaking to her sent her into a panic.

*What would she do if he acknowledged her? How would she explain to Tanya how she knew him? She could pretend she'd met him at the clinic. It was the truth, if not the whole truth. Would Tanya buy it?* Her thoughts spun frantically back and forth, but her concern was unwarranted.

With equal parts relief and disappointment, she realized the men were leaving the cafeteria. Neither man spared them a glance, despite the fact they passed within two or three yards of their table.

Chanel frowned, more than a little peeved. *What the hell game was he playing?* First he sends her a look that could melt ice cream from thirty paces and then he ignores her completely. Conveniently forgetting her panic of mere moments before, she compressed her lips indignantly and did her best to bolster her dented pride.

———————

Bryce strode out of the cafeteria and did his best not to think about the woman he'd just passed by and ignored—a woman who'd filled far too many of his dreams. She looked as beautiful as he remembered, but different to the girl who'd come to the police station.

She looked like the doctor he'd met in the clinic. Her navy suit and pale pink blouse were mostly obscured by a white lab coat. Her blond hair was as thick and vibrant as it had been in his dreams, only rather than hanging loose and flowing, it was pulled back into a plait, like it had been the last time he'd seen her.

His cock hardened at the thought of tugging out the elastic hair band and loosening the thick waves with his fingers. The urge to do that was so strong, he clenched his fists and cursed under his breath.

*What was it about this woman that turned him into a quivering mess of want and need?* He'd been around beautiful women before. Only a week earlier, he'd been unaffected in the company of Samantha Wolfe. It was clear his reaction to Chanel couldn't be in response to the fact he'd been celibate for so long. There was something about her that touched him way deep inside and he yearned to discover more.

*Was she as aware of him as he was of her? Or was his interest totally one-sided?* That possibility filled him with disappointment, but still, he looked forward to them reconnecting. He'd get his chance when he interviewed her.

The task force had spent hours analyzing the hospital staff rosters and had narrowed down the list to fifty potential suspects. Most of them were kitchen staff. It stood to reason, if the poison had been ingested, it had originated in the kitchen.

Bryce and his other colleagues had spent two days interviewing the kitchen staff who'd come to their attention. Most of them were eliminated right away. The chefs merely prepared the food each day. They had no contact with the patient list or any idea of what meal had been ordered by whom.

The handful of people who tagged each meal with the name of the patient had also been interviewed at length. None of them knew the victims personally. It seemed none of them had a reason to want the women dead.

Bryce then turned his attention to the nursing and medical staff. Out of the nineteen nurses who worked on Ward Three, none of them had the care of all three patients during the relevant time. Of course, it was possible the murderer slipped into the patient's rooms with some excuse, but like the kitchen staff, none of the nurses knew the women personally and none of them had a motive for seeing them dead.

Jett had compiled the list of the medical staff who'd come into contact with the victims. When he showed it to Bryce, two of the names immediately stood out: Doctor Leo Baker and Doctor Chanel Munro. Out of the seven doctors who had patients admitted to Ward Three, along with their students, only Chanel Munro had been assigned the care of all three victims. That knowledge was disturbing. Even more so, because to consider her a viable suspect didn't make sense.

Chanel was the one who'd brought the first two deaths to his attention. She'd attended upon him at the police station of her own volition at least a week before the senator's accusations. It was absurd to think the killer would draw attention to her crimes, particularly then, when no one even knew a crime had been committed.

He and Jett arrived at the bank of elevators and waited for one to arrive. The general manager had set up the task force in vacant and adjoining clinic rooms on the fifth floor. A steady stream of staff members had been coming in and out for the past two days. Now, it was the doctors' turn.

Jett had elected to interview Doctor Baker and this suited Bryce fine. He'd already interviewed the man and had come away with a favorable impression. It was important an objective observer deal with the man this time around. Besides, Bryce was curious to hear Jett's assessment of the doctor.

Bryce made sure, however, that Chanel was put on his list. She intrigued him and not just on a professional level. He yearned to spend more time with her, to get to know her outside of work, find out what made her tick. He knew, in a different life, she was a woman he could fall in love with. In fact, much to his chagrin, he was already in lust.

He was drawn to her on so many levels, he couldn't even describe it. He'd never felt this way about any woman, not even his wife, and yet, as it stood now, he barely knew the woman who had stirred up so many emotions. It was like they'd met in a previous life; there was a connection so tangible he was sure she felt it, too.

There was no way he was giving up the opportunity to see her and talk to her again, even if that was in a police interview. Although his hormones were dictating otherwise, he was sure he could maintain a professional distance when it mattered. Besides, he refused to believe for an instant she was guilty.

Objective? Hell, no. But this was his investigation and he wasn't having it any other way.

---

Chanel took a deep breath and tried to steady her nerves. She didn't know what she was worried about. She didn't have anything to do with the deaths of the women. It wasn't as if she was any more a suspect than every other staff member who'd attended upon them. Besides, if it weren't for her, the police wouldn't even know about Amelia Arncliffe and Robyn Evan.

She reached the door to the clinic where she'd been told the police interviews were being held. The staff had been briefed by the general manager and told in a no-nonsense tone to cooperate with the investigating officers. Knowing it was best to get it over with, she took another deep breath, squared her shoulders and opened the clinic door.

She should have guessed he'd be the one to conduct the

interview. Memories of the way he'd stared at her in the cafeteria came back to her in a rush. His gaze was as intense now as it had been then. He nodded in a polite, businesslike way, but the fire in his eyes remained.

Her pulse stuttered and her heart took a dip. The fluttering of nerves in her stomach intensified. She didn't need to be told they had nothing to do with the impending interview and everything to do with the man who stood in front of her, still and silent and assessing.

He was every bit as good-looking as she remembered and her body reacted just as strongly. With all five of her brothers in law enforcement, she'd never been afraid of the police, in fact, she'd been just the opposite. There was something so solid about this officer, an air of safety and security that drew her. She wanted to take shelter against his broad chest. He cared for his ailing grandmother. With him at her back, Chanel would never fear anything again.

But all of this was nonsense. She barely knew the man. It was ridiculous imagining him in her life. That kind of instant attraction only happened in the movies. For most people, attraction was a gradual thing. Not that she had any experience. She'd yet to discover what it felt like to be in love.

Apart from her teenage crush on the star of the Grafton High School football team, her life had been too full of college and exams and internships to devote any time to her social life. A drink with friends on odd occasions after classes, a rare date with a persistent colleague and dinner out with her sister every now and then was the sum total of her social life.

Not that she regretted shunning the traditional college life. Less time at parties meant more time to study and she'd graduated top of her class. Her academic success had opened doors for her at the best hospital in Brisbane and she didn't doubt it had also had some bearing on her acceptance into Doctor Baker's prestigious residency program.

At the reminder of her boss and the reason for her

presence in the clinic, she grimaced. Mistaking her reticence, the detective hurried to reassure her.

"Thank you for coming, Doctor Munro. I appreciate you taking the time to speak with me."

"Of course, Detective Sutcliffe. I understand you're speaking to staff about the deaths of Amelia Arncliffe, Robyn Evan and Eileen Green. If you recall, I was the one who approached you with my concerns regarding the first two women."

A little color crept up his neck. "You're right and as it turns out, you had just cause to be concerned. Recent tests indicate all three of the women were poisoned."

Surprise shot through her. It was one thing to have suspicions about the way the women had died, but to have those suspicions confirmed was heartbreaking and more than a little upsetting.

"I assume you believe the offender is employed by the hospital?"

He nodded, his expression grim. "Yes, that's the theory we're working on. The poison was ingested. In particular, we're looking at everyone who came into reasonably close physical contact with the victims, including you."

His gaze didn't shift from her face. She stared back at him. She had nothing to hide. "Am I a suspect, Detective?"

"Everyone's a suspect, Doctor Munro. Given that you came to me with your concerns about at least two of our victims prior to anyone else becoming aware of it leads me to think you're innocent of their deaths. Then again, maybe you're a brilliant sociopathic killer masquerading as a healer and it was a clever ploy to put us off the scent? It wouldn't be the first time."

Chanel narrowed her eyes and her heart rate picked up its pace. *Surely he didn't believe that?* It was ludicrous beyond words. Still, something about the seriousness of his expression gave her pause. She needed to know his thoughts.

"You don't believe that."

He stared at her a few moments in silence, as if debating

what to tell her. She held her breath and waited, unable to believe that he was seriously contemplating the last statement.

"I don't know what to believe," he stated finally, his voice harsh. He turned and strode across the small room and sat behind the hospital desk. A single chair sat opposite.

"Take a seat and let me explain," he added with a little less gruffness.

A tiny trickle of fear crept through Chanel's veins. He couldn't possibly think she had anything to do with it and yet, from the grim expression on his face, that was exactly what he was thinking.

Stepping forward, she sat down and did her best to focus on the man across from her. He opened a file and took out a sheet of paper. His shoulders slumped on a sigh and her disquiet spread into a cold feeling of dread.

He met her gaze, his eyes troubled. "We've analyzed the staff rosters. We've gone through hundreds of names. How many people do you think had contact with the victims?"

Chanel frowned and tried to think where he was going with his question. She assumed there were a decent number of people who'd been in close proximity to the patients. The obvious ones were the nursing and medical staff, but of course there were the cleaners, kitchen staff, people who filled the water jugs, brought the tea trolley around... The list was almost endless.

Aware that he was waiting for an answer, she shrugged and said, "I imagine there were quite a few. Hospitals are busy places. It takes a lot of people to keep them functioning."

"How many?" he asked again.

"I don't know. Maybe fifty or sixty."

"You're close. According to the rosters, there were fifty-seven members of the hospital staff who had reason to be in contact with the victims and that doesn't count the people who happened to be nearby without a specific reason." He sat back in his chair. "We have no way of quantifying that.

We're working on the theory the killer wouldn't have wanted to draw unnecessary attention. A staff member with a reason to be there would go unnoticed and in fact, *did* go unnoticed."

Chanel nodded. His reasoning was sound. "Is that why you're not sure whether I'm a suspect?"

The detective blew out his breath on another sigh and scrubbed his hands through his hair. It left the short, dark ends standing mussed upon his head. His hair looked clean and soft and Chanel itched to run her fingers through it, until she gave herself a mental shake at the inappropriateness of her thoughts.

"Tell me, Doctor Munro, how many staff members do you think had access to all three victims?"

Chanel frowned. "I thought I just answered that?"

"No, the fifty-seven staff members had access to one or another of the victims. How many do you think had access to all three?"

The expression in his eyes grew intense and the air around them hummed. The tension in Chanel's stomach increased tenfold. She had a sudden feeling life as she'd known it was about to end.

"I-I don't know."

"Guess."

"I have no idea."

"Guess." His tone brooked no argument.

Chanel's mind spun. The tightness in her chest increased, making it difficult to breathe. She gripped the desk with both hands and did her best to slow her pulse. She looked up at the detective and found his gaze still on her. A single dark eyebrow rose in silent query.

She shook her head. "What do you want me to say? I don't know! At least four or five. Doctors, nurses, cleaners..."

"I'll tell you how many people had access to all three patients: one. Out of all the names we analyzed, only one staff member had contact with all three patients on the mornings before they were taken ill. The timing's important because the poison that was used is slow acting. It can be eight to ten hours, sometimes even more, before a person will display symptoms."

Chanel's heart pumped so fast she was sure she was suffering from a heart attack. With her hand held tightly against her chest she snatched breaths and tried to calm down. She knew where this was heading. All three women were her patients. She'd made a point of seeing both Robyn Evan and Eileen Green every morning she'd been rostered on during their stay. She wanted both women to feel like she cared—and she had. She'd also met with Amelia Arncliffe in the hours before she'd fallen ill, even though Chanel hadn't known it at the time.

"It's me, isn't it?" she whispered, her voice hoarse.

He leaned forward, his face mere inches from hers. His gaze softened, almost as if he dreaded being the one to confirm her fears.

"Yes."

She gasped with shock, even though she'd known what was coming. She shook her head, wanting to shout her denial, but it was no good. She didn't need to pore over the rosters to know he spoke the truth.

The victims were all under Doctor Baker's care. She was a resident under Doctor Baker's supervision. Every day, he supplied each of his students with a list of patients. No one's list was the same. It was only during ward rounds with their boss that several of them were present at the same time and it would be a confident killer indeed who carried out his work in the presence of his peers. She'd had personal contact with all three of the victims. The only other thing she knew was that she hadn't been the one to kill them.

"It wasn't me."

He stared at her, his face impassive. Panic tightened its grip. She grabbed hold of his arm and shook him.

"You have to believe me. It wasn't me."

"I want to believe you. I do. It doesn't make sense that you'd kill two patients and then alert the police to their deaths. If the senator hadn't come forward with his accusations, no one would have been the wiser."

He shifted away from her and held his hands palm upwards, looking almost as bewildered as she felt.

"But the facts don't lie. You were the only one assigned to treat all three women in the days before their deaths."

"What about Doctor Baker? He doesn't have a roster, but he attends all of his patients every day."

"You're right and he'll be interviewed, but from what I understand, he's usually in the company of other staff when he's conducting his ward rounds. It would be unusual for him to attend upon a patient without one of his students or a nurse around. Is that correct?"

Chanel nodded, downcast. "Yes, you're right. I guess it's possible he might pop in and see a patient spontaneously, but it's usually during a scheduled ward round with two or three nurses and a couple of students in tow. I've been part of that myself."

"I don't believe you're a killer, Doctor Munro, but at the moment, I have very little to go on. My partner's in the process of interviewing Doctor Baker. It'll be interesting to hear Jett's take on your boss. I wonder if he forms the same opinion I did when I met with him nearly three weeks ago."

Chanel frowned. "You interviewed Doctor Baker three weeks ago?"

"Yes, you might have forgotten my assurances that I'd investigate the matters you raised if I thought they warranted it. The fact is, I attended upon Doctor Baker the same day you came to me with your concerns. He provided me with what I thought at the time was a satisfactory explanation. Now, I'm not so sure."

"What do you mean?"

"I told Doctor Baker a student wanted to file charges against him for sexual harassment."

His words sunk in. She shook her head back and forth. "You had no right—"

"I didn't provide him with any names. I found it interesting that he gave me your name without prompting. I was intrigued that you came to mind when I mentioned sexual harassment. Anyway, he told me you'd propositioned him;

he'd turned you down; and any claims of sexual harassment were nothing more than sour grapes. At the time, I didn't have reason to disbelieve him."

Anger surged through Chanel. Her cheeks burned. "I *told* you the truth about what happened! Why would you believe him over me?"

"You're a very attractive woman and he told a very convincing story of how you'd used your looks to pave your way—first through medical school and then later, into Brisbane's most prestigious hospital. Apparently it wasn't the first time you'd used sex as a way to get better grades."

Chanel gasped with shock and this time, her anger found its head. "That's a *lie!* A filthy lie! As if I'd ever stoop so low! As if I *had* to! I've never been so insulted in all my life and I don't think I've ever been so angry. How *dare* he!"

Her chest heaved and her breath came fast. She glared at the officer who sat across from her, calmly surveying her through his dark, dark eyelashes.

"I was surprised when he told me those things. His portrayal of you just didn't sit right. At the time, I had nothing more to base it on but a feeling and I'm sure you can appreciate, in my line of work, feelings only go so far. I needed facts, evidence to support or dismiss his claim."

"What did you do?" she asked, her temper marginally less volatile.

"I made contact with your former employers and work colleagues. I even spoke to a couple of your college professors. They all say hello, by the way."

She frowned and wished he'd just get the hell on with it.

"After more than a dozen conversations, I was convinced Doctor Baker had got it wrong. His story didn't add up. You were every bit as deserving of the accolades as he said, but not for the reasons he gave. Once I'd cast doubt on the way he'd explained your alleged complaint of sexual harassment, I couldn't help but wonder what else he'd lied about."

"You spoke to him about Amelia Arncliffe and Robyn Evan?"

"Yes, I addressed their deaths in the same conversation, but only in a cursory way. You have to remember, this was three weeks ago. We've only recently received proof of criminal behavior. Doctor Baker explained your concerns away in the same manner as your sexual harassment complaint: That it was nothing more than the work of a woman scorned who was hell-bent on revenge. As I said, at the time, I bought it. Now, not for a second."

Chanel mulled over his words, but they offered her very little reassurance. "Where do we go from here?"

"It's no accident you're the only doctor rostered on for those three patients during the relevant times. Someone's setting you up. It's my job to find out who."

"Doctor Baker organizes the rosters," Chanel whispered.

The detective's expression grew grim, but a gleam of anticipation glinted in his eyes. "Yes."

# Chapter 13

Leo poured the powder into the second medicine bottle that stood on the counter near his elbow. Despite his best efforts, his hand trembled. Apart from the bare bulb that hung above his work space, the basement was dark. It was just the way he liked it. A man could get away with a lot of things in the dark.

He worked quickly and efficiently. He had the routine down pat. He ought to. He'd done it often enough. The deaths that had come to light in the media weren't even the half of it.

Knowing that the police were investigating the most recent deaths added a heightened degree of risk...and anticipation. It should have been enough to stop him, but it wasn't. He didn't think anything could stop him. The knowledge both scared him and set him free.

At first, his purpose had been good and noble. God had watched him suffer as a boy, helpless and afraid, while his mother died in agony. God had whispered a promise that had helped him on his way. He finished medical school knowing he had a higher purpose: He was to heal the sick and ease the suffering of God's people.

And he'd been good at it. His patients returned to health faster and better than expected. Word soon got around. In no time at all, he scaled the heights of the medical world and people came from all over to have him treat them.

Of course, there were always the ones who were better

off dead and God was quick to let him know when it was time for a member of His flock to meet their Maker. It was up to Leo to ensure their passage to the afterlife was as smooth as possible.

It hadn't been painless and it saddened him to think of their final hours spent writhing in agony, but God had assured him their sacrifice would be worth it. Soon, they'd have eternal life and all the glories of heaven would be theirs. It was up to him to make it happen.

But lately, God's messages had left him mixed up and confused. He no longer knew the Maker's will. Was it Him who told Leo who was ready to go or was it someone else? The voice in his head was different. Rougher and more demanding and his victims were less and less unwell. He was supposed to be God's earthly instrument to alleviate the suffering. Now, he wasn't so sure.

Still, he continued to obey its urgings. *What else was he to do?* A part of him wanted to resist, especially when he could see the patient wasn't terminal. Take Amelia Arncliffe, Robyn Evan and Eileen Green. They were all on their way back to better health when the voice ordered him from up above.

Still, he believed in the Almighty and would bow to His greater wisdom. Besides, the women had gone to a better place. There was no denying it.

He only hoped he'd said the right things when the police interviewed him. He'd prayed for hours beforehand, seeking God's words of wisdom. God would tell him what to say. God would protect him and keep him safe. Who would be left to carry on His work if he were sent to jail? No, God wouldn't abandon him. Leo was certain of it.

He emptied the final collection of ricin powder into the medicine bottle and carefully sealed the lid. In the dim light, he glanced at his watch and frowned. Time had slipped away. His wife would be wondering where he was, badgering him with endless questions and pinning him with angry frowns.

She thought he had a mistress. She'd discovered the deed to the house in Mount Druitt by accident and had accused him of all sorts of nasty things. She was wrong about the mistress. That wasn't his purpose for acquiring the house so far out in the suburbs. No, it was used for a much higher purpose than mere pleasures of the flesh.

Not that he hadn't enjoyed a dalliance here and there with pretty, young things along the way, but they were casual flings that never lasted and didn't mean a thing—and they never took precedence over his work ordained by God.

Clearing his work space, he returned his equipment to the shelf above the counter. Carefully scraping the residue powder into a dustpan, he emptied it into the trash nearby. He picked up both medicine bottles and wiped them clean before dropping them into the pocket of his jacket.

Satisfied, he tugged off his surgical mask and scrubs and tossed them into the trash can, too. They were followed by his tight-fitting surgical gloves. He always took plenty of precautions. With one last look around to ensure nothing was out of place, he climbed the old wooden stairs that led from the basement into the house.

At the top of the stairs, he switched off the basement light and pulled the door closed behind him. A snap of the padlock and the room was once more secure. He wasn't sure why he went to so much trouble to keep the room locked. It wasn't like the house was occupied.

He'd bought it on the pretext it was an investment property. He'd even gone through the motions of contacting realtors and advising them the property was available to rent. He'd had a few enquires, but had turned them all down, telling them that unfortunately, the property had just been tenanted.

It worked like a charm and had been his little secret for more than a decade—his and God's. It was only recently, when his wife found out, that his secret had been discovered.

He'd tried the rental thing on her, too, and had even produced a fake lease document. She'd scrutinized it in such detail, he was sure she'd see through it. But after what seemed like a lifetime, she'd tossed the papers back to him and had stormed off toward her room. He was grateful he hadn't heard anything about the house since.

The place in Mount Druitt was more important to him than he cared to admit. It had been his private getaway for so long. It was where he went to escape the daily pressures of his life and more importantly, it gave him the freedom to come and go as he pleased, to plan and to carry out his work. No, not just *his* work—God's work.

It was God who had chosen Chanel Munro.

At the thought of her, he broke into a smile. So beautiful, so perfect, so distant. She was one of God's angels. Beauty such as hers had to come directly from the Almighty. It was why He'd chosen her to take the fall. She was His gift to Leo.

Leo had made sure the police knew all about her and had given them plenty of reasons to look at her for the crimes. He'd even managed to secure a little extra insurance by befriending her roommate.

Okay, so they'd become a little more than friends, but the girl had been willing and had gone out of her way to please. She was more than happy to accept his gift a couple of nights ago and do with it as he directed. The confusion was plain on her face when he gave it to her, but he soon alleviated her concerns. Besides, she was so enamored of him, he knew she'd never ask questions.

Yes, little Tanya Singh had proved quite useful and she wasn't a bad fuck at all. Her eagerness to try new things in the bedroom made life just that little bit more pleasant. Of course, it wouldn't last forever. The year would soon be up. She'd graduate from the program with honors and go on to achieve greatness in her career. Or something like that.

Reaching his car, parked in the driveway beside the house, he unlocked the door and slid into the seat. Taking the medicine bottles from his pocket, he slipped them inside a Ziplock bag and sealed it before depositing it carefully in the glove compartment. He never knew what might happen on his hour or more commute back into the city and he didn't want to risk the bottles breaking in his pocket and spilling their precious contents. He had enough to last at least three or four months. Even longer, depending upon the orders from up above.

———————————

Susan Baker pressed back against the side of the house, making use of the shadows cast by the overgrown hibiscus bush to conceal her presence. She watched her husband seated in his car and wondered what he was thinking. It seemed like forever before he started the ignition and eventually sped away.

She'd followed him to the house in Mount Druitt in an effort to discover its secrets. He'd thought he'd fooled her with his story of a rental property and tenants and it had suited her to let him think that way. It gave her time to deliberate upon the latest development and wonder whether the existence of a secret dwelling was cause for concern.

The mere fact that he'd kept it from her caused alarm. If it was as innocent as he proclaimed, he would have told her about it. They owned several investments around the city. It wasn't like they hadn't bought property before.

At first, she'd suspected he was using the house as a place of assignation with whatever slut he was seeing at the time, but she'd been wrong. Not about the slut. She'd seen him with the exotic-looking, dark-skinned girl. But the purpose of the house had come as a surprise and now that she knew the truth, she was mystified.

She'd snuck in behind him, barely breathing and watched him make his way down the darkened hall. He'd paused outside a door and unlocked it and had simply disappeared. When she finally found the courage to follow him, she realized he'd descended into a basement where a single faint light cast eerie shadows across the walls.

Creeping to the edge of the stairs, she'd watched him working at a counter. Something that looked like a coffee pot stood near his elbow. He muttered aloud and shuffled around in the gloom. She could barely make out what he was doing and what she did see didn't make sense. At least it had nothing to do with another woman. For that, she was grateful.

Now, drawing her light coat around her, she picked her way over the uneven ground that led from the house to the street. She'd parked half a block away. She didn't want him to know she was following him. It was far better to keep him at ease. As long as he thought her stupid enough to accept his explanations, it was easier to discover his hidden truths.

It hadn't always been that way. She sighed inwardly at the memory of the way things used to be. He'd been a dashing third-year resident doctor when they'd met at a black-tie hospital fundraiser. Tall and charismatic, he'd blown her away with his charm. They were married within the year and babies soon followed after.

If there were dark times when he retreated from the world and her and the children suffered, she told herself the good times far outweighed the bad and nobody was happy all the time. He worked long hours at a stressful job. It was understandable that every now and then he'd turn on his family in anger. She understood that was his way of dealing with the pressures of his job.

Like the way he felt the need to diagnose her with all sorts of weird and wacky things. His latest conclusion was that she was suffering from bipolar disorder. *What utter nonsense was that?* He even insisted on prescribing her medication. Not that she'd ever filled the scripts. It was ludicrous, but she didn't resist, knowing that somehow, it made him feel needed. There was no harm in it, after all and if it made him feel better about himself and their relationship, she was willing to let it go on.

Now, she wasn't quite so sure. His behavior had become more and more erratic and his explanations more and more bizarre. She no longer cared about his affairs with other women, but it was almost laughable how he felt the need to concoct stories explaining away their existence.

His inability to stay faithful was the reason she'd come with him to work. It was easier to keep an eye on him when she spent eight or nine hours by his side. She also fielded his phone calls. Well, up until the advent of cell phones, at least. Now she didn't know who he called or who called him.

Her friends wondered why she stayed with him, but they didn't understand. She'd been Mrs Leo Baker, the wife of Sydney's eminent doctor for so long, she couldn't imagine being anyone else. Somewhere along the way, she'd lost her identity and now even the thought of trying to get it back exhausted her. Besides, she relished the life she led.

Money had never been a problem and by and large, she and Leo kept out of each other's way. She still came into the office every morning and made sure the filing was up to date, but she did it more out of habit than the need to keep him under watch. She'd stopped caring about how he spent his time a long time ago.

But the discovery of the house in Mount Druitt had sparked her interest and she couldn't really say why. Now, she was even more confused. The house was dark and gloomy. What little furniture in the place was coated with a layer of dust. It was obvious it wasn't a place where he took his female friends and after witnessing his behavior in the basement, she didn't know what to think.

With a sigh, she unlocked her car and climbed back in behind the wheel. She filed the information away, to be pondered over some other time.

# CHAPTER 14

Chanel approached the door that led into the offices of the hospital's general manager with a feeling akin to trepidation. Less than half an hour earlier, she'd received the summons to present herself to Deborah Healy without delay. She'd been part way through her afternoon rounds and had excused herself as soon as they were over.

The police had finished interviewing the staff a few days earlier. Rumors were flying thick and fast around the hospital: A member of the kitchen staff had confessed; a nurse with mental health issues was the culprit; another patient had taken it upon himself to suffocate the women with a pillow...

They were ridiculous and totally baseless and Chanel had done her best to ignore them, but knowing that on paper, other than Doctor Baker, she was the only person who'd had access to all three victims played heavily on her mind. She'd wanted to deny Bryce's suggestion that someone was setting her up, but the more she thought about it, the more likely that seemed.

Surely, it wasn't just a coincidence that all three patients were on her daily list? Doctor Baker had vowed to make her regret rebuffing him, but would his need for revenge extend to the murder of innocent people? The very idea was preposterous. He was a kind and dedicated physician. He truly cared about his patients. Besides, Amelia Arncliffe had died before Doctor Baker had made his tasteless proposition. He couldn't have known beforehand that Chanel would turn him down.

No, as much as she wanted to shift the suspicion from her shoulders, she didn't believe Doctor Baker was at fault either. She just had to hope and pray Bryce would discover another truth.

Bryce. His name rolled off her tongue so easily. She recalled the dream she'd had of him the night before and blushed.

*He was bare from the waist up, beckoning to her through the mist. His muscled chest was displayed to full advantage. When she finally found the courage to stumble through the dark toward him, she reached out a hand to touch him and found the image was no lie.*

*His skin was firm and warm and flexed beneath her fingers. A light scattering of dark hair covered the edges of his nipples. She stepped closer and her breasts brushed against his chest. It was only then she noticed she was naked.*

*He bent his head to nuzzle her neck and his breath whispered past her ear. She shivered from the delight of it and tilted her head away. He kissed and teased his way from her neck to her shoulder, all the way down to her chest. His hands cupped her breasts.*

*When he suckled her, she cried out from the delicious sensations. Need spiraled deep within her and she pressed herself against him, wanting more.*

*His erection strained against her stomach, thick and hard and hot. She moved against him, aching and wet and begged him to give her what she sought. He stared down at her with eyes so dark they were nearly black. When he spoke, his voice was rough with the strain of holding back.*

*"Tell me what you want," he demanded and pressed his cock against her skin.*

*"You!" she gasped. "I want you!"*

*"Are you sure?" he said, his eyes fixed on hers.*

*She stood on tiptoes and did her best to press his cock against her clit. It throbbed and burned and tingled.*

*"I need you," she breathed and stared into his eyes. "Now."*

*His eyes flared with emotion and his grip tightened around her shoulders. He lifted her up easily and spread her legs around his hips. With one hand, he worked the zipper on his jeans and a moment later, his thick, hard cock sprang free.*

*Fire sizzled her nerve endings and raged through every vein. She clung to him and begged him to take her, right there and then. He turned her around and held her close. She felt a wall against her back.*

*"Are you sure you still want me?" he rasped, his cock straining against her wet slit.*

*"Yes! Take me before I explode."*

*The urgency behind her words should have shocked her. She'd never before gotten so carried away. But she'd never been caught up in a need so great that she couldn't think of anything beyond seeking fulfilment. She was burning from the inside out. She needed him hard and fast. She spread her legs even wider and begged him with her eyes.*

*He didn't need any more encouragement. With a slight shift of his hips, he plunged upward and inward and impaled her on his shaft. She screamed from the sheer ecstasy of it and moved frantically against his heat. His cock stretched her wide apart, she was being split in two. She screamed and sobbed and clung to him. He pounded and pounded and pounded...*

She'd woken with a gasp, the sheets twisted around her limbs. Her heart was beating double time and her core still ached with need. She'd woken before she'd climaxed and her body was still strung taut. She couldn't believe she'd dreamed about the detective, or how real it had seemed.

Now, the thought of it made her blush and sent heat rushing to her cheeks. She wasn't one for hot, hard sex. She wasn't one for sex, period. The two casual experiences she'd had in college had been less than satisfactory, but she didn't have time to search for or put the effort into a more long-term relationship. She'd relegated the notion of hot and steamy sex to the pages of racy romance novels or Hollywood movies. She never imagined such a thing could happen in real life.

*Well, not exactly real life.* She'd been dreaming, after all. But a part of her couldn't help but wonder what it would be like to get down and dirty with the hot detective. Not that she had time to contemplate that at the moment. The general manager's door loomed before her. It was time to face the lions.

Chanel's firm knock was met with an equally firm command for her to enter. Pushing open the door, she was surprised to find herself in a bright and cheery reception area that was flooded with natural light. It was so different from the dim and subdued corridors of the hospital, she was slightly taken aback. The well-put-together older woman who sat behind the counter nodded a greeting.

"Hi, I'm Doctor Munro. I received a message that the general manager wants to see me."

"Hi, Doctor Munro. Please, take a seat. Ms Healy won't be long. Can I get you something to drink?"

"No, thank you." Chanel turned and took a seat on a comfortable leather couch, taking in the brightly colored prints that decorated the walls. Their black frames matched the window architraves and the color of the couch. It was clear someone had a clever eye for design.

The door to an inner office opened and a woman appeared in the opening. Chanel was hit with a fresh wave of nerves. She'd seen pictures of Deborah Healy around the hospital, but none of them did her justice. Chanel knew from the woman's bio that she was forty-nine, but she looked a decade younger. Her red hair was in the latest style and framed a face that belied its age. Make-up had been applied with an expert hand, concealing all but the faintest of lines. The knee-length skirt of the woman's tailored gray suit displayed a pair of sculpted calves that only came from hours devoted to the gym.

"Doctor Munro, I'm Deborah Healy. Come in."

Like the reception area on the other side of the door, the general manager's office was also filled with natural light. Plants adorned two corners of the room and despite her unease, Chanel couldn't help but smile at the row of hand painted ceramic pots that lined the window ledge, each pot bursting with color.

The woman took a seat behind her desk and Chanel took one of the chairs opposite. There were no preliminaries. Deborah Healy got straight down to business.

"I'm sure you're aware we're in the middle of a police investigation into the deaths of three of our patients."

"Yes, Ms Healy. I was interviewed by the police earlier this week."

"Then you know you're their prime suspect."

Chanel gasped, even though the news didn't come as a surprise. Having it stated so baldly was difficult to take.

"I'm aware all three patients were under my care, yes. I understand how the police might view me as a suspect, but I can assure you, I've done nothing wrong. I had nothing to do with the deaths of those poor women."

The general manager stared at Chanel, her expression grim and assessing. "I'm sure you know it's not up to me to decide. We're leaving that to the police. The reason I summoned you was because I've had a meeting with the board. Under the circumstances, we've decided to relieve you of your duties at this hospital, effective immediately."

Shockwaves ricocheted through Chanel and she gasped in disbelief. "Ms Healy, please! You can't do this! It wasn't me! I did nothing wrong!"

The woman remained unmoved. "I acknowledge your protest of innocence, but you must understand, we cannot condone any risk that could put our patients in harm's way. We'll be lucky if the imminent lawsuits from the three known victims don't bankrupt us. We can't risk another."

"But, Ms Healy, it isn't fair! My job means everything to

me! I've worked so hard to get here. I can't have it all taken away. Not when I've done nothing wrong. Please, you have to—"

"That will be all, Doctor Munro. You'll be suspended on full pay until such time as an arrest has been made. If you're found to be innocent of any wrongdoing, then naturally, your position in this hospital will be reinstated."

Chanel shook her head, dazed at what had just happened. She pushed away from her chair and stumbled to the door. She couldn't remember making it across the reception room and down the stairs to the ground floor, but suddenly she was in front of the information desk where a familiar face smiled down at her.

"If it isn't Doctor Munro!" Marjorie said. "How are things going, honey? You look like you've had a tough day."

Chanel stared up at the kindly old woman who'd been so friendly to her on her first day. The same kindness and gentleness still shone from the woman's eyes and all of a sudden, Chanel found herself blinking back tears.

"I-I'm fine, Marjorie. Thanks for asking." Her voice cracked on the last word and the tears she'd tried so hard to hold back flooded her eyes. Before she knew it, she was sobbing beyond control.

Marjorie's expression turned to concern and she struggled out of the information booth and came around to offer Chanel comfort.

"Oh, honey! It can't be as bad as that? There, there. You'll be all right. Stop crying, now. You'll make those pretty eyes red."

The woman held Chanel against her soft bosom and patted her on the back. Chanel did her best to get herself under control and at last, managed to draw in a deep breath and heave a heavy sigh. She wiped at the tears with the back of her hand and offered Marjorie a shaky smile.

"I'm okay, Marjorie."

"Are you sure? Would you like to talk about it?"

"Yes, I'm sure. And thanks for your kind offer, but I can't talk about it."

"You have a tough job, being a doctor, and we're glad to have you on board. If it weren't for you and those like you, where would the rest of us be?"

Chanel managed another weak smile of gratitude and slowly turned away.

"You take care of yourself, honey. You hear? If you ever need a shoulder to cry on, you just give me a holler."

Without turning around, Chanel nodded and continued on her way out the door. She couldn't help but wonder if she'd ever be allowed to return. The minute she reached her apartment, she tugged out her phone and dialed Bryce's number. He'd given it to her after the interview and had urged her to call him whenever she needed.

"Detective Sutcliffe."

The familiar, deep voice sent a surge of longing rushing through her but this time it had nothing to do with her dream. After the devastating way she'd been treated by her employer, she needed reassurance from someone she hoped would understand.

"Detective... Bryce... It's me. Chanel Munro. I-I need you. I need to talk to you. Will you come over?" Her breath hitched, but she forced herself to continue without waiting for him to reply. "I've been fired."

# CHAPTER 15

Bryce stared down at the phone in his hand and tried hard to slow his racing pulse. The call from Chanel was unexpected. He hadn't seen her since the day he'd taken her statement at the hospital and even though he was sure she felt the same connection he did, he was in the middle of an investigation with her as the primary suspect.

It didn't come as a surprise to hear that she'd been fired from her job. The hospital's executive had been kept up to date with the investigation, including the fact the police had narrowed down the list of staff members with access to the victims. Chanel's name was at the top of that list.

He was still of the opinion she wasn't responsible for the deaths. Apart from the fact she'd been the one to draw attention to the earlier deaths, she didn't have a motive. In fact, they had yet to uncover a motive for any of the staff on their list and it was frustrating the task force to no end.

Bryce checked the time. His shift had ended an hour ago, but he couldn't bring himself to leave the station. He'd been poring over statements, searching for clues that might have been overlooked, but so far, his extra efforts had come to nothing. The fact that all signs pointed toward Chanel's guilt seemed a little too convenient, as did the fact that Doctor Baker had insisted during his interview with Jett that the only time he'd visited any of the victims was in the company of at least two or three of his students.

Bryce had quizzed Jett about how he'd found the

eminent doctor and his partner admitted he felt the way Bryce had three weeks earlier—the man had been polite and cooperative and had exhibited none of the usual signs of deceit. He'd answered all of Jett's questions without hesitation and appeared for all intents and purposes as a man saddened by the loss of three patients and anxious to find the person responsible.

When Jett had asked him if any of his students were ever alone with his patients, the doctor had said it was likely.

"Of course. They're students. The best way to learn is to be hands-on. I encourage them to check on their patients as often as time permits. Being a good doctor is just as much about establishing a rapport with a patient as it is about choices of treatment. If a patient doesn't have faith in your ability to heal them, it makes your job twice as difficult."

His explanation made sense to Jett, just as it had to Bryce and they were no further ahead in ascertaining the killer, despite all of the man hours that had been spent on just that. He thought of Chanel and how lost and bewildered she'd sounded when she'd told him she'd been asked to step down. He'd expected anger, but maybe that was yet to come.

Despite her distress, he couldn't deny the lift in his spirits when she'd called. The sound of her voice was the best thing he'd heard all day. She was upset and she'd called him. *She'd called him.*

Suddenly clear on what he wanted, he sat forward, shut down his computer, tidied his files and then headed for the lockers. He already had her address from her statement. He could be outside her door in ten minutes.

The thought sent a burst of adrenaline and excitement surging through him and all of a sudden, he couldn't get to North Sydney quickly enough.

---

The sound of the doorbell sent a flurry of nerves cascading through Chanel's stomach. Now that the moment was upon her, she didn't know what she'd been thinking, making the SOS call to Bryce. She'd turned to a man she barely knew and invited him to her apartment. She'd practically begged him to come. She was just thankful Tanya had texted her to say she'd be staying at her father's that night. Chanel didn't want to have to answer questions about why the lead detective in the hospital investigation was getting cosy in their living room.

The doorbell rang again and Chanel blushed. How rude of her to leave him standing out there when she'd specifically asked him around. He must be wondering what the hell was going on. Drawing in a deep breath, she hurriedly patted down a few loose strands of hair that had escaped her ponytail then strode to the door and opened it.

He was leaning against the door frame and looked just as sexy as he had the other times she'd seen him. Dressed in navy suit pants and a business shirt and tie, his suit jacket hung casually from his finger. Despite the late hour, he looked fresh and alluring, like he'd stepped from the pages of GQ.

Heat blossomed in her face and then quickly spread across her stomach to center low in her core. A shiver of awareness coursed through her and her nipples tightened in response. His gaze swept over her from head to toe, further inflaming her senses. Emotion flared in his eyes.

"H-hi," she stammered, tripping over her tongue. "Thanks for coming."

"You needed me."

It was a statement more than a question and once again, she was tongue-tied. He was right. She'd been at a loss about what to do and who to speak to. She could have turned to her family. They'd always come to her rescue, but the shock of being fired was too fresh to share with her loved ones.

They'd commiserate and sympathize and get angry on her behalf. Her brothers might even try to call the general manager and demand an explanation. Her father would immediately contact his lawyers. It was all too much for her to deal with right then. She'd acted on instinct when she'd called Bryce, but she was now certain it was the best thing she could have done.

"Please, come in," she murmured and stepped back to make way for him to enter.

He brushed past her and headed into the living room. She took a moment to steady her breathing and then followed him.

"Let me take your jacket."

He turned and handed it to her. Their fingers touched and her pulse leaped from the contact. Once again, his gaze found hers and the solemnness in his eyes caught at her heart. He'd taken her plea for help seriously. He was there because she needed him. The knowledge warmed her all the way through.

Flustered, she turned away and hung up his jacket on the coat rack that stood in the corner, right by the door.

"You have a nice place here. A great view of the harbor."

"Yes," she smiled, pleased to have something normal to focus on. "I got lucky in the apartment stakes. It's a little out of my budget, but I have a roommate. Together, we manage to meet the expenses."

His lips twitched. "I bet it doesn't leave much for partying."

"I'm not much for partying," she admitted.

A single dark eyebrow was raised in question. "No?"

"No. I spend most of my time at work. At least, I did until today." She grimaced at the reminder. "I guess I'll have to find another way to fill my days."

He shook his head and his expression turned somber once again. "I'm sorry to hear about what happened. They're in damage control. They know you're at the top of the suspect list and even though we've been careful about pointing the finger at anyone, they'd want to take precautions, just in case."

"Just in case I'm charged, you mean."

He stared at her, his gaze intense. "We both know that's not going to happen."

"Do we?" she asked, fear nipping at the edges of her consciousness. "I had nothing to do with the deaths of those women, but I have no way to prove it. All I have is my word."

"You're forgetting that you don't have to prove it. We live in a country that believes in innocence until proven guilty, remember? We, as in the police, have to prove you're the murderer and if there's no evidence of that, then you have nothing to worry about."

Chanel stared at him and tried to believe him. Her thoughts were in turmoil. He made it sound as if innocence always triumphed over guilt, but she was sure he knew as well as she did that sometimes the law got it wrong. Very wrong.

As if sensing her disquiet, he stepped forward and reached out to brush a strand of hair out of her eyes. His touch was gentle, almost tender. She froze a moment before he did. He dropped his hand and turned away.

"I-I'm sorry, I shouldn't have done that."

"Um..." Heat exploded across Chanel's cheeks. She didn't know what to say. It was obvious they both felt a connection, but it seemed impossible to hope that they might fan it to life under these circumstances.

He was investigating her for murder. Okay, in his eyes, she wasn't a suspect, but the truth of it was her employer had fired her because it was a possibility. Though Bryce wasn't the only officer behind the investigation, getting involved with her would be foolhardy for him, too. If someone discovered he was with her, it might not only be her career on the line.

"You shouldn't be here." She blurted the words out without thinking.

His shoulders tensed. When he finally turned back toward her, his face was closed. "You're right."

He did a good job of concealing his hurt, but she caught a glimpse of it in his eyes. She hurried to set him straight.

"You misunderstood me. I didn't mean... That is, I'm glad

you came. I was scared and confused and lost. I didn't know what to do. You're the first person I wanted to call. I...I really wanted to see you."

His expression remained guarded. "Does that mean you want me to stay or go?"

She blushed and lowered her gaze and cursed her inexperience. She was sure other girls would know what to say to keep a man like Bryce from walking out their door.

"I...I like you, Bryce. There's something about you... I don't know how to explain it. I hardly know you and yet, it feels like I've known you forever. You make me feel safe. I'm not doing a very good job of this, but the truth of it is...I want you to stay."

"But you just told me to go."

Chanel bit back a sigh. He wasn't going to make this easy for her. She tried again.

"What I meant was, *your* job could be in jeopardy, too. I'm a suspect and you're the lead investigator. There's bound to be someone in your office who'll take exception to your after hours' visit."

"I couldn't care less what they think. I'm off the clock. My conscience is clear. I'm certain we'll find the killer and I'm just as sure it won't be you."

He drew in a breath. The room was so quiet, she could hear the soft hum of traffic from the street below and the occasional shouts from a passersby. The blast from a train horn sounded in the distance.

"Your voice on the other end of the phone was the best thing I'd heard all day," he said quietly. "Even though I was upset about how you'd been treated, I couldn't help but feel glad when you called. The last little while... Let's just say, life's been tough and hearing your voice...even your forlorn and desperate voice, brightened my day."

He looked away, as if embarrassed. Color tinged his cheekbones. Chanel's heart melted at the sadness in his eyes.

"Are you talking about the investigation?"

He sighed and shook his head. "No, the investigation's the

least of it. There's been so much other stuff going on. Believe me, you don't want to know."

"I wouldn't have asked if I didn't want to know." She paused and then said, "How about I get us a drink and you can tell me about it? Of course, you'll have to change the names to protect the innocent..." She smiled, but he didn't respond to her lame attempt at a joke. Embarrassed, she fled to the kitchen.

She was only an occasional drinker, but she had a couple of bottles of Merlot in the cupboard. After taking one down, she collected two wine glasses and carried everything back to the living room. Bryce had taken a seat on the couch and was resting his elbows on his knees, deep in thought.

The night had settled in around them and after placing the bottle and glasses down on the coffee table, she moved over to the corner and switched on the lamp. Soft, yellow light bathed the room and chased away the shadows.

In silence, she opened the wine and poured them each a glass. She handed one to Bryce and he accepted it with a murmur of thanks. Grateful to have something else to distract her from her melancholy thoughts, she urged him once again to open up to her.

"Talk to me. That is, if you don't mind," she added.

He blew out his breath on a heavy sigh and reached for his glass. After taking a healthy swallow, he set it back down on the table in front of him. His voice was a low rumble when he finally began to speak.

"You're right when you say you feel a connection. I feel it, too. But I don't have any right to feel anything for you. The truth is, up until a fortnight ago, I was married. I shouldn't even be thinking about another woman, let alone longing to get closer to you."

Chanel gaped in shock. "Okay, I...I guess that's fair enough," she said finally. "Did you sign the divorce papers two weeks ago or did the court order come through?"

He shook his head and his expression turned grim. "Neither. My wife's been in a coma for three years. Fourteen days ago, I gave permission to switch off her life support. I spread her ashes over Bondi Beach."

If Chanel needed something to distract her from the events of her day, he'd just blown every other thought out of the ball park. She chased around in her head for something to say, but came up with nothing.

She hadn't given any thought to his marital status, apart from assuming he was single. He certainly hadn't given out any "off the market" vibes. Hell, the night before, she'd been having erotic fantasies about him. Her subconscious had already claimed him as hers. Now she discovered he was married. Well, not anymore, but only because he'd switched off his wife's life support. It was too much.

She stood abruptly. Wine sloshed over her hand. She cursed and looked around for a cloth. Bryce stared up at her with a resigned expression on his face.

"I understand your reaction, Chanel. You're right to feel stunned. It's not everyday someone drops a bombshell like this, but I wanted to be honest with you. There's something between us. We've both acknowledged it. You have a right to know I come with…complications."

He dropped his head and stared at the carpet beneath his feet. "The decision I made to switch off my wife's life support was the hardest I've ever had to make. For three years there wasn't a single day that I didn't think about her and yearn for things to be different."

"Why now? It's been three years. What changed for you?"

He looked up at her and met her gaze. His eyes were bleak. "I'm not sure. Her doctors had been increasing the pressure on me for weeks." His lips twisted into a cynical smile. "They needed the bed. I'm sure you can understand."

Chanel twisted her lips into a grimace and nodded. She knew all about bed shortages and the strain they put on the system.

"It's a sad fact of life that no one wants to talk about, least of all our politicians," she murmured, doing her best to process all that he'd told her. Her head still reeled from the overload of information and then she remembered what else he'd said.

"Do you really feel something between us?"

"Don't you?"

"I already told you how I feel. I need to hear it from you. If I'm going to risk entangling my heart in a complicated situation, I need to know you feel just as strongly as I do."

He stood and came to his full height. Slowly, he came closer until there was nothing but a heartbeat between them. His shirt front brushed hers and she shivered from the impact. Heat flooded to her core.

"From the moment I saw you, my heart wanted you for my own. You bowled me over with your beauty, your vitality and the goodness that shone from your eyes. You were like an angel, a beautiful, untouchable gift from above. And then you were gone. I wondered if I'd ever see you again and then I thought about Angela and felt guilty. I didn't have the right to feel anything for you at all."

"Is Angela your wife?"

"Yes."

"Tell me about her."

He frowned. "You want to hear about my wife?"

"She was an important part of your life. I'd like to know more about her."

He stared at her a moment longer and then slowly nodded. "All right, but let's sit down. This could take awhile."

They returned to the couch. It was small enough that every now and then their legs brushed the other's when one of them moved. Despite the energy passing between them, Chanel did her best to concentrate on his words.

"We met when we were teenagers. She was from a big Italian family. My mother's family was Italian. We had a lot in common and our parents were thrilled when we fell in love. We were married straight out of college."

He leaned over and picked up his glass and took a drink before continuing. "Angela graduated as a nurse. She worked at the local hospital. We were living in the suburbs, near Strathfield. I was a police officer in nearby Croydon. We were young and just scraping by from week to week on our pay cheques, but we were happy. We had our whole lives before us."

He drew in a breath and then took another swallow from his glass. "Of course, we had our arguments, like any couple does, but we also knew how to make up. We'd been married for two years when we decided to try for a baby."

He smiled sadly and Chanel's fingers tightened on her glass. He hadn't mentioned children. She could only guess there weren't any.

"For the first twelve months, we tried the normal way. We were both twenty-four, fit and healthy. We had no reason to believe it wouldn't happen. A lot of our friends were getting pregnant. It didn't seem that hard to do. Because we'd spent years trying not to have a baby, we figured getting pregnant would be easy." He closed his eyes briefly. When he opened them again, his expression was filled with grim resignation.

"Only, it didn't work out that way. By the time the second year of trying rolled around, we'd become a little despondent. Angela probably more so than I. I'd finished my time in general duties and had applied for the detective's course. I was busy and involved with my career. I wanted a baby, but I had plenty of other things to concentrate on. For Angela, it wasn't quite so easy."

He sighed and scrubbed his free hand through his short hair. "The longer it took for us to get pregnant, the more upset and depressed she became. When she suggested we see a doctor, I was happy to oblige. Anything to bring the smile back to her face and give her the baby that she craved. In her mind, having a baby seemed the only way to signify her worthiness as a wife."

He looked up at Chanel and shook his head. "It was crazy, I know, but she'd come from a large, traditional Italian family. Being surrounded by children was a natural and expected progression in life. By this time, we'd been married more than three years and we still didn't have a baby."

He tilted his glass to his lips and emptied it. With another quiet sigh, he set the glass back on the coffee table and then leaned back into the couch. His hard thigh connected with hers and her heart skipped a beat. She surreptitiously drew in a steadying breath and urged him to continue.

"What happened after you visited with the doctor?"

"I was given the all clear. Angela wasn't so fortunate. She had a condition which meant that her ovaries didn't always release an egg. In fact, she could go months without having an egg released, even though she was getting regular periods. It meant that our chances of conceiving naturally were slimmer than most, despite the fact we were young and otherwise healthy."

"Did you look into IVF?"

"Of course. It was the first thing we discussed. Angela was given medication to stimulate her ovaries and several eggs were harvested. It sounds easy, but it was tough on both of us. No one goes through IVF without being affected by it. But, we were hopeful it would work and we were prepared to do whatever it took."

He bent forward to pick up his wine glass and then stopped midway when he realized it was empty. Chanel hurriedly picked up the bottle and refilled it. He murmured his thanks and took a mouthful before continuing.

"Our first four attempts were unsuccessful. We were gutted. Her eggs were healthy and so were my sperm. We'd fully expected it to work. Even the doctors were a little nonplussed to explain why we hadn't succeeded. They told us to give it a break, that both of us could do with a rest. They suggested we get on with living our lives, reconnect with the things we loved."

A quiet sigh escaped him. "We tried, we really did. I think it was easier for me than Angela. While my career was coming ahead in leaps and bounds, she'd lost interest in being a nurse. She gave up her job and spent the time lying around the house, immersed in baby books and crappy TV. I begged her to get out and find something to do. Not only to take her mind off things, but we needed the extra cash. IVF treatment doesn't come cheap and the government subsidies only go so far. I was earning good money on my detective's pay, but it was still a stretch, especially when Angela up and quit hers."

"So, what happened?" Chanel murmured, keen to hear more. It seemed strange to be talking to a man she was interested in about his wife, but that's the way it was.

"Angela begged me to start IVF again. Having a baby had become an obsession. I was prepared to accept that it just wasn't meant to be, but she wouldn't even hear of it. Over the next couple of years, we tried on and off, whenever we could afford it, but the strain of it was taking its toll. Our fights became more vindictive. It took longer for us to reconcile. I felt I'd been relegated to nothing more than a bank account with the added bonus of being able to donate sperm."

He shook his head and blew out his breath on a sigh heavy with sadness and regret. "We let it happen to us. We let it tear us apart. When she was hit by a drunk driver who ran a red light, she was returning home from yet another IVF treatment."

Chanel's hand flew to her mouth and she gasped in shock and surprise. "Oh, no, Bryce! How terrible."

"I'd stopped going to the appointments with her long before that. I couldn't bear the whole buildup, everything she went through, only to discover it had failed. I was at work when I got the call that she'd been involved in an accident."

"How awful for you!"

"Thankfully, it wasn't in my patrol area. I didn't attend the scene. By the time I'd been notified, she was in an ambulance on her way to the hospital."

Over the rest of the bottle of wine and most of the next, he told her of his hope that this time, the IVF treatment might have worked. How he'd felt guilty for maintaining the life support until they knew for sure. When it was clear she wasn't pregnant, he'd been riddled with guilt once more. This time, because he couldn't bring himself to switch off his wife's connection to life just because the treatment had failed them yet again.

It was a sad story and one for which Chanel had no words of comfort. "How did your families feel?" she asked quietly.

"There's only my grandmother on my side. My parents are dead and I'm an only child. Angela's relatives were very sad, but I guess like me, they've had a lot of time to come to terms with the idea that she was never going to wake."

"Wait, you're an only child? I thought you came from a big Italian family?"

"My mother's family is Italian. She came from a family of eight. My dad was Australian. Hence my very un-Italian surname."

She smiled. "I was wondering about that."

"My mom and dad weren't your typical couple. Dad fell in love with a pretty Italian girl who worked in the family café. His parents took some convincing. They were wealthy business people who had made their money in freight. My grandfather was the head of a large and expansive trucking empire he'd built up from the ground. They weren't exactly thrilled when he declared his love for a pretty, but mostly poor, Italian girl."

"And yet they married."

"Love conquers all," he murmured and his eyes captured hers.

Her heart started a slow, heavy pound and the air around them grew charged. She snatched a breath, but it was a struggle. Oxygen was in short supply.

His leg was hard up against hers on the couch and the heat of him burned her skin. As if in a trance, she watched as he drew closer until his mouth was inches from hers. His breath feathered across her lips.

He turned and faced her and one hand fell to her thigh. Her short skirt had ridden high, and a moment later, his fingers caressed her bare skin. At the same time, his other hand came around to cup the back of her head. Slowly, surely, he drew her toward him until their lips touched.

His lips were full and soft and he tasted of warm, sweet wine. She kissed him hesitantly, unsure of the path, feeling way out of her depth. Her limited experience with men hadn't involved a lot of tender kisses and the few she'd experienced hadn't felt anything like this.

His mouth moved slowly, gently across her lips, as if savoring every sensation. It was a kiss of discovery, of new beginnings, of familiarity and wonder. It was strange how right it felt.

He shifted on the couch and angled her head. His tongue pressed against her lips and she parted them, wordlessly giving him entry. When he swept inside and fused their mouths her heart pounded in her chest.

"You're so beautiful, inside and out. I've wanted you from the moment I saw you."

His words flowed over her, warming her all the way through. She lifted her arms and drew him closer. He maneuvered them down until they lay on the couch and still the kiss continued. His erection pressed into her stomach through the fabric of his pants and she was reminded of the graphic dream she'd had the night before.

The memory of it sent a surge of heat flooding to her core. She stirred against him, needing to get close, as close as she could get. He stared down at her, his face in shadow, his eyes burning with intent.

"I want you to know the decision I made a fortnight ago was a long time in coming. It had nothing to do with you. Just in case you're wondering."

Somewhere in the back of her mind, she had wondered if his decision to switch off his wife's life support had something to do with the two of them, but she hadn't wanted to think about that. His reassurance that she hadn't factored into his decision was a relief.

She reached up and loosened his tie and then worked on his shirt buttons. Both articles of clothing were discarded to the floor. She gazed at his chest, all bronzed and hewn, like the fantasy from her dream. Her fingers grazed over his skin and she gloried in the feel of him.

Her hand moved lower and skimmed the dark hair that ran in a thin line from his navel into his pants. Like his chest hair, it was silky and soft and perfect. Her hand moved lower and came to a rest around his impressive erection. She caressed him through the fabric of his suit pants and was gratified to see his eyes flare with heat.

"Can you feel how much I want you? You drive me wild," he murmured and fixed his gaze on hers.

"I've never felt this way, either," she admitted quietly. "You turn me inside out. My heart's pounding so hard, it feels like I could die. I'm hot and aching and I...I need you."

He growled low in his throat and his kisses became more frantic. He ground his hips against hers. Her arms tightened around his shoulders and she held him as close as he could get. Her breasts were crushed against his muscled chest and ached for his touch.

He nuzzled his way down her neck and across her tailored blouse. "You have way too many clothes on, Doctor Munro."

She giggled and he shifted so she could sit up. Making short work of the buttons and clips, the blouse and bra soon joined his shirt and tie.

Chanel lay back down and enjoyed the way his gaze lingered on her body. He reached out with a hand and softly cupped one breast.

"You're even more beautiful than I imagined."

His thumb stroked her nipple and it hardened beneath his touch. He turned his attention to the other one and treated it to more of the same. Her breathing quickened in time with his and she moved restlessly beneath him.

"Make love to me, Bryce," she whispered.

His guttural sound of need reverberated all the way to her core. Quickly and efficiently, he shed his trousers and underwear before returning his attention to her. He slid his hands around her waist and found the button to her skirt. She heard the zip slide down and then lifted her hips so that he could tug the clothing down. Her panties came down with it and within moments, she was as naked as he.

They stared at each other in the glow of the lamplight and took each other in. He was as magnificent as he'd been in her dream—all dark, manly flesh and eyes that burned with desire.

He joined her on the couch once more and she moaned aloud when their skin came into contact. Flush from cheek to toes, they couldn't get any closer. His thick cock nudged against her entrance.

"Do you have a condom?" she whispered.

"No, do you?"

She blushed, but nodded. "I have some I took from the supply the hospital leaves out in the common room for the staff."

Bryce pulled a little way back and looked at her. "Really? You mean they just hand them out?"

She shrugged. "I guess they see it as the responsible thing to do, the prevention of disease and that kind of thing. You work for the government, you know how it is."

He shook his head and smiled. "Well, who am I to argue?"

She smiled back at him. "Particularly when you've come here empty handed." She wriggled underneath him. "You're going to have to let me up. They're in the bathroom cabinet."

He stood and she slipped past him. A moment later, she returned and gave him a condom.

"Only one?" he teased.

"Hey, I didn't want to put the pressure on you or appear too presumptuous." She gave him a wink. "There's plenty more in the cabinet."

"Good, because I intend to love you all night."

His eyes darkened with need and she shivered under the heat of his gaze. "How about we relocate to the bedroom? It'll be more comfortable there."

The words were barely out of her mouth when he bent and scooped her up in his arms. "You won't get any argument from me," he murmured.

His lips found hers and he kissed her hot and hard and fast. His tongue sought entry and she opened her mouth, groaning when he thrust his tongue inside. With her arms around his neck, she clung to him and returned kiss for kiss.

"No, not that room. That's Tanya's," she murmured against his neck.

He halted and raised his head. A slight frown marred his forehead. "Tanya?"

"My roommate. Don't worry. She's away for the night."

He relaxed and continued forward until he came to the other bedroom. Chanel peered around his shoulder and was relieved to see that the bed was made. Sometimes she overslept and left it too late to do a tidy.

He lowered her gently to the bed and joined her a moment later. His mouth found hers again and all thoughts of the state of her bedroom scattered. He loved her with his mouth and tongue and caressed her until every nerve ending was on fire. She moved beneath him, restless, searching, needing even more.

As if sensing her impatience, he pulled away. With quick movements, he sheathed his cock and then returned to drag her close. He kissed her on the mouth and then worked down over her chest. He tugged at her nipples with his lips and at the same time, kneaded the softness of her breasts.

She moaned and his hand slipped lower until his fingers tangled in the curls between her legs. Lower still, his finger slid across her silky skin and delved between her aching lips. He parted her folds with his finger and a moment later, slipped inside. First one, then two. He stroked her until she couldn't bear it a moment longer.

"I need you inside me, Bryce," she murmured and urged him with her hips. She kissed him long and deeply, until both of them were breathing hard.

At last, he pulled away and positioned himself between her legs. His cock, hard and hot, probed her entrance, and a moment later, thrust inside her.

She gasped from the feel of him stretching her wide. He was every bit as wonderful as he'd been in her dream, only this time, it was real. The need inside her raged like a bushfire and she glorified in the knowledge that this time, it wouldn't end until she was replete.

He moved inside her, strong and fast, his face a study in

concentration. She loved every dark and rigid plane of his face, every nuance of emotion that played across his features. His thrusts came harder and faster still and she clung to him with all she had. The ache in her core intensified, got hotter, tighter until with a gasp, she reached the summit.

Sliding, falling, slipping down, with relief she found her release. A few seconds later, Bryce tensec and then collapsed on top of her, his breath harsh in her ear.

"Hell," he gasped, "that was... I'm not sure I can describe it. It felt so good. You felt so good. You felt more than good. You felt absolutely fantastic." He smothered her face with kisses and she smiled in satisfaction.

"You were pretty good yourself."

He propped himself up on an elbow and looked down at her. "Really?"

She marveled that he could doubt it. "Of course. You must know how fabulous that was."

His teasing smile lit up his eyes. "You liked it?"

"I liked it."

"Good. Now, how many condoms do we have?"

# CHAPTER 16

Bryce wasn't sure how many times he'd made love to the woman who lay beside him, but when his phone rang, waking him from a deep sleep, it felt like he'd barely closed his eyes. At some point, he'd sent a text to his grandmother to let her know he wouldn't be home. The phone continued to ring and he stumbled from the bed and padded down the corridor into the living room. He glanced at the Caller ID and frowned.

"Jett, how are you doing?" he said by way of greeting, pitching his voice low in deference to Chanel who was still asleep.

"Bryce, where are you? It's after eight."

Bryce glanced at his watch and cursed. He had no idea he'd slept so late. He was supposed to be at work.

"I'm sorry, mate. I was up all night. Some kind of...stomach bug. I overslept."

"No worries. Do you feel well enough to come in? We've had a development overnight. We received an anonymous tip. The boss has approved a search warrant."

"An anonymous tip? A search warrant? Great. Whose property?"

"It's an address in North Sydney. An apartment rented by Doctor Chanel Munro. The boss—"

The rest of what Jett said was drowned out by the roar of noise in Bryce's ears. His heart thudded and blood rushed through his veins. He sucked in a breath and then another and did his best to find his tongue.

"Chanel Munro? Why the hell would the boss approve a search warrant of her apartment? She didn't have anything to do with the murders. Has he forgotten it was Doctor Munro who came to me in the first place? Who's the so-called anonymous tipster you're talking about? What did he have to say?"

"I'm not sure. The boss didn't divulge any details, only that we needed to search the apartment rented by Doctor Munro."

Bryce shook his head in frustration and cursed again. "I don't believe it. I fucking don't believe it."

"Well, anyway, the boss obviously thinks there's enough to go on. We'll have to toss the place and see."

Bryce opened his mouth to utter another instinctive protest, but then closed it. If Jett had called and given him similar news about any other suspect, he would have accepted it without a murmur. If the boss had okayed a search warrant, that was good enough for Bryce. Usually. It was completely different when the suspect was a woman he believed was innocent. Even more so when he'd just climbed from her bed.

After assuring Jett he would be at work shortly and telling him not to do anything until he got there, Bryce bid his partner a hasty good-bye and headed back to Chanel's bedroom. Her arm was flung out across his pillow and her hair was spread every which way. She was still asleep and he reluctantly leaned across the bed and gently shook her awake.

"Chanel. Come on, honey. You need to wake up."

"*Mm*, no, go away; it's too early." She rolled over, away from him and took the covers with her.

He smiled before he could stop himself and then remembered the phone call. "Chanel, I mean it. We need to get up. The police are on their way."

That seemed to get her attention. She tensed and then a second later, flung the covers out of the way and sat up. She stared at him in surprise and alarm.

"The *police*? Here? What are you talking about?"

He drew in a breath and eased it out. "I just had a call from Jett, my partner. The task force are getting ready to execute a search warrant on your apartment."

She frowned and her face flooded with confusion. "Why would they be doing that? I've done nothing wrong."

"I know that. I'm not sure what changed overnight. Jett said something about receiving an anonymous tip. Apparently, whatever was said was enough for my boss to approve a warrant."

His words seemed to finally sink in. Color leached from her cheeks. Her hand came up to her mouth and covered a gasp. She shook her head back and forth with increasing vehemence.

"No, there must be some mistake. You must have misunderstood. They couldn't be coming here. I didn't do anything. I had nothing to do with those deaths."

Bryce reached out and drew her close, pressing her head against his chest. Her arms went around his waist and she clung to him. Her breath came fast and he did his best to calm her down. Hysteria was the last thing she needed.

"It's all right, honey. I'll look after you. Trust me, this is my thing. If you did nothing wrong, sooner or later, the task force will realize that. They'll execute the warrant, find nothing and then leave."

"Will they make a mess? Cut up the cushions of my couch?"

Bryce allowed himself a small smile. "No, sweetheart. That only happens on TV. Although it does depend a little on what they're looking for. If it was a stash of heroin, maybe your couch would take a hit."

She pulled away from him, not taking kindly to his joke and stood and left the bed. Seemingly unaware of her nakedness, with her arms crossed defensively over her chest, she paced the confines of the bedroom.

"I don't do drugs. I've never even had a parking ticket. This whole thing is entirely ludicrous!"

Bryce went to her. With his hands on her shoulders, he

halted her progress. "Chanel, listen to me. You're right. It *is* ludicrous, but the fact is, it's happening. Why, I don't know. I'll find out, but right now, I need you to get dressed and prepare yourself for the arrival of the police. I'm not sure what time they'll be here, but you need to be ready when they do."

His words seemed to penetrate her fog of confusion and anger. She stared at him, her eyes wide and then she blinked. She looked down at herself and blushed red to the roots of her hair.

"Oh, my God, I'm naked. I need to find my clothes." She hurried around the room and at last, settled on the bedsheet that half-hung onto the floor. Wrapping it around herself, she tucked the ends into her breasts. When she was completely covered and secure, she looked back at him.

"Will you be here, with them, when they come?"

He compressed his lips and told her the truth. "Yes."

She nodded once and dropped her gaze. A moment later, she looked at him again. "You need to get some clothes on. Maybe a towel? What happened to your shirt? I could give you a—"

"Chanel, we've spent the night together. I've touched and kissed every inch of you. There's no need to be embarrassed just because it's morning."

He stepped closer and pressed a quick kiss to her lips. "Although, you're kind of cute when you blush."

She batted him away and grabbed the towel that hung on a hook behind her door. A moment later, it landed on his head. "Quit standing there and go and get some clothes on," she said.

---

Given the choice, Bryce would have opted to remain at the station during the execution of the search warrant on Chanel's apartment, but as the leader of the task force and one of the senior detectives on the case, it would have raised questions and he was far from willing to provide answers.

Not that he had anything to hide, of course, and he was certain she was innocent. They'd execute the warrant, go through the motions, clear Chanel of any wrongdoing and go back to the drawing board. In the meantime, he and Chanel would be free to explore wherever their feelings took them.

He thought of Angela and how he'd held her hand in the final moments before she'd passed away. The machines that had kept her alive for three long years were switched off and wheeled away. Her family and his grandmother had come in and said their good-byes.

In the end, it had been just the two of them in the silent room. He didn't know how long it would take, but it seemed no time at all before the nurses came in and told him she'd gone. Her passing had been quiet and peaceful—and for that, he was grateful. He'd done the right thing. His wife had finally been laid to rest and though he hadn't given it any thought until that moment, he realized he'd also come to terms with the past. For the first time in a long time, he felt hope in his heart when he thought of the future.

"You ready?"

Jett posed the question and Bryce nodded in response. "How about the others?" he asked.

"Yep, all ready and accounted for. We'll go in whenever you give the go ahead."

Half a dozen officers waited on the curb behind him. With little danger of finding an armed suspect, they'd left their combat gear at the station, but the sheer number of them attracted attention.

Bryce couldn't help but wince at the rumors that would circulate around the apartment block. Chanel would be forced to withstand the whispers and pointed looks that would surely come her way. He wished he could do something about that, but it was out of his control.

The anonymous tip had hinted that she was storing the ricin poison in her apartment. Bryce found it intriguing that an outsider knew what kind of poison had been used. They'd been careful to keep that detail away from the public eye. It was more than interesting to discover the tipster had also specifically referred to castor beans.

Aware that his men were waiting, Bryce gave the order to move in. Jett knocked loudly on the door that led to Chanel's apartment and then stood aside for Bryce. A moment later, the door was opened.

She was dressed in a pretty sundress that ended just above her knees. It was white and patterned with hot-pink polka dots. Her hair was pulled back into a bouncy ponytail and her lips were newly glossed. She looked fresh and calm and composed. She looked beautiful.

"Chanel Munro," he said, "I have a warrant to search your apartment. I have a copy here for you. If you step aside and let us in, we'll be out of your way as soon as possible."

Her eyes never strayed from his face. Her chin lifted and she stared him down, not even glancing at the warrant in his hand. Bryce couldn't help the surge of admiration that rushed through his veins and settled warmly in the vicinity of his heart.

A moment later, she stepped back and allowed him and his men to enter. Taking refuge on the couch, she quickly became engrossed in her phone. Bryce had to give her points for holding it together. She looked like she couldn't care less that she was the suspect in several murders and that her apartment was being tossed. It only strengthened his sure knowledge that she was innocent.

"I've found something!"

Jett's triumphant yelp came from the direction of the kitchen. Bryce frowned and hurried to find him. Jett held a small brown bottle in his gloved hand.

"Give it here," Bryce demanded. Jett handed it over. Bryce looked at the nondescript medicine bottle and turned it over in his hands. With his gloved hands making it more difficult than it needed to be, he carefully unscrewed the lid.

It was filled with a fine pale powder. Bryce's heart went into overdrive and he reeled back in shock. *What the fuck?*

Careful not to inhale it or come into contact with it in any way, he screwed the lid back on and deposited it into a plastic evidence bag.

"Where did you find it?" he demanded.

"On a shelf in the kitchen," Jett replied. "What is it?"

"I'm not sure. We'll need to get it tested, but first we'll ask Doctor Munro. She should be able to tell us."

"She's hardly going to tell us it's ricin powder," Jett said, shaking his head.

Anger surged through Bryce and it was all he could do not to smash something. His mind spun with shock and confusion and overriding fear. He was sure he wasn't wrong about Chanel, but what if his judgement had become skewed?

He'd been attracted to her from the moment he'd seen her and for all his vagueness about whether or not he was going to investigate her complaint, he'd always intended to do so. And he had. And he'd believed Doctor Baker. Until he hadn't. Then he'd believed Chanel.

His thoughts spun faster and faster out of control until he didn't know which way was up. He could see Jett frowning at him, but he couldn't seem to stop his mind racing at breakneck speed.

"It's okay, Bryce. I'll go and talk to her." Jett muttered the words and disappeared. Bryce sucked in a savage breath.

Scrubbing at his hair, he did his best to get his heart rate back under control. His anger slowly subsided and the noise receded in his head. He was the leader of the task force. This was his investigation. He needed to pull himself together and act like he was in charge. *Had he been duped by a very clever criminal?* He wouldn't be the first cop to be taken in by a beautiful girl.

The awful thought had entered his mind, but now sat heavily in his gut. *Had he fallen for the oldest trick in the book? Had his cock blinded him to the truth? Was she so confident of her ability to hoodwink him that she'd left the evidence out for all to see?*

He ground his teeth until his jaw hurt and cursed his

foolhardy dimwittedness. It was his fault. He'd fallen for her innocent act and the promise in her eyes. With steely determination, he got himself back under control. With a last look around the kitchen, he headed into the living room.

Chanel was still seated on the couch as if she didn't have a care in the world. He'd thought her demeanor was proof of her innocence. Now it only seemed to emphasize the level of her arrogance and deceit. Jett turned to him as he entered.

"Doctor Munro claims she's never seen the bottle before. She doesn't have a clue what's in it."

Bryce stared at Chanel with narrowed eyes and his anger stirred again. "Is that right, Doctor Munro? You've never seen this bottle before?"

Something in his eyes or maybe the coldness in his voice gave her pause. She looked up at him in surprise and her brows came down in confusion. Fear chased itself across her face and her eyes darkened with uncertainty. In other circumstances, he would have gone to her and assured her it was all right.

But he didn't move and it wasn't all right. As if sensing something was terribly wrong, Chanel stood and crossed her arms over her chest. She lifted her chin and once again, stared him down.

"What are you implying, Detective Sutcliffe? Should I know what's in that bottle?"

"It was found in your kitchen. I assume you know what it is."

Her eyes blazed into his, anger setting them on fire. "Like I told your partner, I've never seen it before in my life. I'm not the only person who lives here."

Jett looked from her to him, then back to the bottle in Bryce's hands. "What do you want to do, Bryce?"

Bryce stared at Chanel for another long moment and breathed through his hurt and disappointment.

"Arrest her."

Chanel gasped and her cheeks went pale. She stared at him in confusion. "What the hell? You can't do that!"

"I'm afraid we can, Doctor Munro," Jett nodded and pulled out a pair of cuffs.

Her gaze flew to Bryce and this time, it was tinged with panic. Her eyes narrowed in anger. *"Handcuffs?* You have to be kidding!"

"Bring her in, Jett," he said and turned away, unable to remain near her another minute.

# CHAPTER 17

Chanel paced the tight confines of the holding cell and tried to stem her panic. The pale blue bars that surrounded her were lined with thick Perspex and no doubt would hurt if she hit it. She clenched her fists and resisted the urge to find out.

She still couldn't believe she'd been arrested. She'd been curious when Bryce's partner had shown her the small brown medicine bottle, but not overly concerned. Although she hadn't seen it before, like she'd told Bryce and his partner, she wasn't the only one living there. It was quite likely her roommate had left it in the cupboard. Tanya was always cooking exotic Indian curries using genuine herbs and spices. Chanel didn't know the name of half the things the woman had stacked on the shelves.

She couldn't believe Bryce had arrested her without even acknowledging the possibility that the bottle belonged to someone else. The closed look on his face had cut her to the quick. It was like looking into the face of a stranger. Overnight, he seemed to have morphed into a cold and unfamiliar figure. A man she didn't recognize.

So much for his assurances that he believed in her innocence and that innocence always won out on the day. Somewhere during the hours of lovemaking and his return to her apartment with his men, his attitude had undergone a total about turn. She couldn't explain it and most certainly didn't understand it, but it was the truth. The hurt it caused deep inside her was a physical thing.

"Chanel Munro, you have a visitor," said the young constable on guard outside her cell.

The announcement caused Chanel's heart to leap with hope. *Could Bryce have come to his senses? Was he even now doing what was necessary to affect her release? Would she accept his apology that it had all been a terrible mistake, or would she give him the silent treatment and make him suffer?*

She was still debating the wisest course of action when her brother Tom appeared outside her cell. On his heels were two more brothers, Brandon and Clayton. All three of them looked furious.

"Tom! I'm so glad you're here!" She looked from Clayton to Brandon. "How did you both know—?"

"Tom called us as soon as he got off the phone to you," Brandon explained. "He thought the more manpower on your side, the better. I agree." Brandon shook his head in disbelief. "What have you gotten yourself into, little sister?"

Clayton stepped closer to the cell. "How are they treating you, honey? Have you eaten today?"

Tears welled up in Chanel's eyes at the care and concern in his voice. She shook her head and answered in a shaky voice.

"No. They came by with some sandwiches an hour ago, but I wasn't hungry. I just want to get out of here. Take me home, Clay. Please."

Tom moved closer, his expression grim. "We're working on it, Chanel. Don't worry, we've made it clear we're unhappy about how they've dealt with this. They don't even know what's in the fucking bottle! To have you arrested on the flimsiest of excuses is unforgivable. Someone's going to lose their balls over this. Mark my words."

Tom's anger was gratifying and worked to soothe Chanel's battered nerves. If Tom thought her arrest was unjustified, it was good enough for her. He was a veteran cop with more than two decades of experience. There wasn't anything about the law and policing her oldest brother didn't know.

"Thanks, Tom," she whispered. "And thanks to all of you for coming. This cell's doing my head in."

"They put her in a *cell*, for Christ's sake!" Brandon shouted, his expression darkening.

"Like a common criminal!" Tom added.

"Let's hope the buffoon responsible gets his ass into gear and gets her out of here," Clayton growled.

Right on cue, Bryce appeared outside the cell. He stared at Chanel, his face a blank mask. She held back a sob of distress. It was as if last night had never happened. *Where had the tender and loving man gone, the man who'd held her and kissed her all night long?* The morning had brought her a stranger and a cold and unforgiving one at that.

Well, two could play at that game. With a surge of determination and stubborn pride, she deliberately turned her back on him and focused on her brothers. She listened in satisfaction as Tom tore savage strips off the man who'd been her lover.

Unable to stand it, Chanel peeked at him from the corner of her eye. To his credit, Bryce remained unmoved, never once reacting to the anger in Tom's words. Instead, he merely lifted the keys in his hand and inserted one into the lock.

"You're free to go, Doctor Munro, but don't go leaving town," he said coldly. "We'll be in touch."

Hurt warred with anger deep inside her. Anger won out. She spun on her heel and opened her mouth to tell him exactly what she thought. Clayton grabbed her by the arm and hurried her along. He shot her a warning look that meant she was to keep her mouth shut. She left without speaking, but threw Bryce a look so cold and venomous, she was sure he'd get the drift. Inside, her heart broke into a thousand tiny pieces.

---

Bryce kicked at the loose stones lining the path that wended its way through the park across from the building that housed Doctor Baker's private rooms. He'd dropped his grandmother off outside the entryway nearly thirty minutes earlier and once again was waiting for her text to tell him she was done.

Of their own volition, his thoughts turned to Chanel and he winced at the way he'd treated her. Now that the initial shock of finding the medicine bottle had worn off, he could look at the matter rationally. He still didn't know anything about the person who'd called in the anonymous tip, but the truth of it was, the tipster had known far more than they should.

To know the specific type of poison was more than suspicious. It wasn't like people were poisoned with ricin every day and yet, the anonymous caller had known about it.

Right up until the moment Jett had discovered the bottle, Bryce was still very much of the opinion Chanel was innocent. Their night together had been magical and he liked to think he was a decent judge of character. Apart from her physical beauty, she was beautiful on the inside, too. Good and kind and caring... He couldn't imagine her being a killer.

And then there was her family. He'd met three of her brothers the day she was released. Large and impressive, their presence had dominated the police station. It was obvious they loved their younger sister and were quick to come to her defense. They were much decorated police officers—their characters, unimpeachable. It didn't seem possible that their sister could be guilty of murder. Call him naïve, but it plain didn't make any sense. Apart from the bottle that was found in her kitchen and the fact the patients were under her care, there wasn't a scrap of evidence that pointed to her guilt.

A wave of reproach washed over him and he compressed his lips in disgust. Her brothers were right: He should never have arrested her. He'd been acting through a haze of shock and hurt and disappointment. Still, it was no excuse.

The discovery of the medicine bottle had floored him, but the mysterious powder could be anything. It might come back to be nothing more than some herbal crap that could be purchased at any health store. The mere existence of a bottle in a woman's kitchen wasn't cause for arrest.

Not only an arrest, but she'd been handcuffed and put in the cells, all at his direction. *What had he been trying to prove?* That he was still the one in control after being blindsided by what he perceived was her betrayal? The blow to his pride was no excuse for his bad behavior. His heavy handedness was unforgivable.

And what about the roommate she'd mentioned? Tanya Singh? Chanel had reluctantly supplied him with her name and cell number. Though he'd left several messages, he had yet to track her down, but the fact was, she lived at the residence, too. It was just as likely the bottle belonged to her.

Hot shame raced through him and scorched his skin. No wonder Chanel had stared at him as if she wanted him to disappear off the face of the earth. After all they'd shared, he couldn't believe he'd fucked it up so monumentally. He'd be lucky if she ever spoke to him again.

His phone chirped to indicate a new text message and he glanced down at the screen. His grandmother had finished with Doctor Baker. He hurried back to his vehicle and met her a few minutes later outside the building. She waved to him from the pavement and he climbed out and helped her into the car.

"How did you do?" he asked and eased out into the traffic.

"Oh, not too bad, but Doctor Baker wants to admit me to the hospital. My ulcer isn't healing like it should. He wants to give me a course of IV antibiotics. I'm going to be admitted tomorrow."

Bryce frowned. Doctor Baker was still high on his suspect list, even though he didn't have any evidence linking the man to the crimes. It was more of a gut instinct. Unfortunately, he needed more than that to veto his grandmother's treatment. The fact was, she had faith in her doctor and for now, that would have to be enough.

"I'll make sure I'm free to take you in. What time do you have to be at the hospital?"

"Tomorrow morning, if that's all right. It would be nice if you could take me there."

"Of course, Grandma. I'll make sure it happens. Now, I'm going to have to drop you off at home and run. I have a heap of things to do at the office."

His grandmother looked at him. "You look tired, Bryce. I hope you're not overdoing it. A couple of days ago, you didn't come home all night."

He could see the questions in her eyes, but refused to acknowledge them. Instead, he forced a smile. "I'm fine, Grandma. Busy, that's all."

———

Chanel finished her umpteenth round of solitaire and shut the lid on her laptop with a sigh. It had been four days since she'd been summoned to the general manager's office and stood down from her job; three days since her arrest. She couldn't remember the last time she'd had so much spare time on her hands. Even when she was in high school, she'd studied hard. College was more of the same and after graduation, she'd been consumed with twelve-hour shifts, emergency call-outs and everything in between. She'd never been one for sitting around and the enforced idleness and the constant attention from her brothers were driving her crazy.

She loved that they cared enough to want to make sure she was treated right, but Tom and Clayton's over protectiveness and Brandon's determination to find the killer was doing her head in. The three of them had drilled her for hours over the details of the case.

When Tom admitted she'd told him a month earlier about

the indecent proposal from Doctor Baker, Clayton and Brandon were angry that he hadn't beaten the doctor into a pulp. She then spent an hour calming her brothers down and reassuring them she could look after herself. By the time they left, she was exhausted.

With another sigh, she tucked her feet underneath her and curled up on the couch. She reached for the TV remote and flicked through the channels. She stumbled onto a police drama and when the male lead filled the screen, her heart skipped a beat.

Tall and dark and brooding, he looked a lot like Bryce. She hadn't heard from him since her release from the jail cell and as angry as she was at him for her mistreatment, she still missed him. Their night together had been nothing short of wonderful. He'd loved her like no other. She yearned for his touch again and was saddened to think it might never happen.

Her phone chimed to indicate an incoming call. She leaned across and scooped it up from the coffee table. The Caller ID was blocked. She pressed the button to accept the call.

"Chanel Munro." There was a pause and then his familiar voice sounded rough and low over the phone.

"Chanel, it's Bryce."

She swung her legs over the side of the couch and planted them on the floor, suddenly tense and alert. Her heart pounded so loudly, she was afraid she wouldn't be able to hear him through the blood that rushed through her ears.

"You probably don't want to talk to me, but I wanted to call and apologize."

His tone was low and uncertain, as if he didn't know how she'd react. He had every right to feel nervous. She was just as angry with him now as she had been when it happened.

"You're damn right I don't want to talk to you. And why should I accept your apology? In fact, why should I listen to anything you say? You told me you believed in my innocence. Do you think if I were guilty, I'd have left the bottle there to be found? You told me the police were on their way. I had plenty of time to get rid of it. You convinced me that truth would win out on the day. Less than twelve hours later, you had me arrested on suspicion of murder."

"I'm not sure what else I can say. When Jett found that bottle, I...I lost my head. We'd just spent the night together— a night that was fantastic in every way. It'd been so long since I felt connected to another woman. I...I could fall in love with you, Chanel. You probably don't want to hear it, but it's the truth."

"You're right. I don't want to hear it. Along with anything else you have to say." She heard him drag in a ragged breath. He blew it out slowly before continuing.

"When it looked like you might have been involved in the murders all along, I was devastated. I reacted with anger and hurt and crushing disappointment. I didn't think it through. I should never have arrested you, certainly not cuffed you and put you in a cell. From the bottom of my heart, I'm sorry."

His voice hitched and she felt his remorse deep inside her heart. "You treated me so badly," she whispered, still hurting.

"I did and I'm sorry. My behavior was inexcusable. If I could have that time to live over again, I'd do everything differently. That's the worst part of it. I can't change a thing."

A part of her remained angry, but he sounded so sad and sincere, Chanel felt herself softening. Bryce wasn't the only one who'd been shocked at the sudden turn of events.

Because she knew she was innocent, she hadn't reacted to the existence of the medicine bottle, but she could understand how it might look to a police officer investigating the deaths of three women by a poison that could be kept in a little bottle like the one they'd found. On top of the anonymous tip off, she could see how it had al come to pass.

"I'm not the killer, Bryce. I'd never seen that bottle before. Someone's setting me up, just like you said before." She paused and then added in a calmer tone, "Do you know any more about the person who pointed you in my direction?"

"The caller refused to leave their details, but we know it was a male. The call came from a public phone booth out in the suburbs. That's all we have."

"But you must agree, it's suspicious. I had nothing to do with the murders, so the caller must be in on it. Whether he's acting alone or on behalf of someone else, I guess that's what you have to work out."

"How did the bottle get into your kitchen?"

"I don't know. I only moved in here a couple of months ago. Have you spoken to Tanya, yet? She hasn't been home since...the night you came over."

"No, I've left messages on her phone. I'm still waiting for her to contact me. I'll hunt her down at work if she doesn't call me back. So, it's been three days since you've seen her. Is that normal? Has she ever stayed away that long before?"

Chanel shrugged. "Sometimes, she goes to visit her father. Occasionally, she stays overnight. She's also been seeing someone lately. It's possible she stayed with him."

"Do you know his name?"

Chanel sucked in a breath and her heart thumped. She didn't know how Bryce would react to hearing Tanya was dating Doctor Baker, but she guessed he'd find the news odd, at the very least.

"She's been seeing Doctor Baker."

"*Excuse me?*"

"She's being seeing Doctor Baker."

"I heard what you said, I'm just...surprised. I take it you're certain of this?"

"He's collected her from our apartment on several occasions. She told me they're sleeping together."

"Oh, hell, I don't believe it."

Chanel frowned at the growing excitement in his voice. "What is it?"

"Tanya and Leo Baker. I think that's our connection. The bottle was found in your kitchen, a kitchen she has access to. Now you tell me she's sleeping with your boss, a man who already has a gripe against you. All along, I've felt you were being set up. I let my anger screw with my head for a while, but I know where I'm headed now. It's him. Leo Baker. It has to be. Or maybe they're in it together?"

Chanel shook her head, stunned at Bryce's summation. As much as she didn't want to believe it, the whole thing now made an awful kind of sense. Besides, there was no other way to explain how the bottle got into her kitchen.

"Oh, my goodness, you might be right," she breathed, her heart thumping.

"The only other possibility is that your roommate acted alone. It's possible your boss has nothing to do with it. We need proof, one way or the other. I need to speak to Tanya.

It's time she and I had a little chat."

# CHAPTER 18

Bryce scrolled through his contacts until he found the number for the general manager of the Sydney Harbour Hospital. Tanya Singh was still avoiding his calls. He'd tracked down her father who confirmed he'd seen his daughter that morning. He said he'd brought her coffee before she'd hurried out the door to work.

"Good afternoon. Deborah Healy's office. May I help you?"

Bryce identified himself and then told the receptionist he needed to speak with her boss.

"I'll put you right through, Detective Sutcliffe."

A moment later, the phone was answered by the general manager.

"Detective Sutcliffe, what can I do for you?"

"I'm trying to locate Doctor Tanya Singh. I was wondering if you could tell me whether she's rostered on today."

"I'll need to check with one of the doctors. Sit tight. I'll call you right back."

Less than two minutes later, his phone rang.

"Detective Sutcliffe, it's Deborah Healy. I've had someone check the roster and Doctor Singh is apparently at work today."

"Great. What time does she finish?"

"Around seven in the evening, unless there's an emergency. Then she'll be here longer."

"Thank you, Ms Healy. I appreciate your time."

"What's happening with Doctor Munro? I heard a whisper she'd been arrested. Is it true? I'm so pleased we acted when we did. When the media gets wind of this—"

"Doctor Munro was released within hours of her arrest. No charges were laid. I would appreciate it if you made no mention of anything to do with this investigation to the press."

"Oh, so... She's not the one responsible?"

"No."

"Then, who is?"

Steel determination surged through him. His eyes narrowed. "That's what I intend to find out."

---

Tanya peered over her shoulder and was relieved to see that the corridor that led into the ward was bare. Slipping into the staff toilet, she locked the door behind her and collapsed against the wall. Her heart pounded and her breath came fast. She felt like she'd run a marathon. The thought of running into Leo had her adrenaline pumping.

She'd heard about the police searching the apartment in North Sydney and how Chanel had been taken away in handcuffs. Apparently, the police had found the poison in her kitchen, in a bottle Tanya had put there just over a week before.

She couldn't believe it was the bottle Leo had given her. Even more shocking was the growing knowledge that he must have known what it contained. He'd told her it was some kind of herbal aphrodisiac. He wanted her to keep it on the shelf in the apartment so that next time he came by, they could indulge in it together.

At the time, the thought of having sex with him in her bed had her giddy with excitement. Until now, he'd taken her to hotel rooms. While the rooms were nice and the sheets were soft, there was something a little cheap about having sex with a married man in a hotel room. A couple of times, they'd even had sex on the back seat of his car. The first time it was exciting, but it wasn't like they were teenagers and it was hardly comfortable. To have him in her king-sized bed sounded like heaven.

Now, it seemed like the bottle hadn't contained an aphrodisiac at all. Why Leo would have her put a bottle of poison in Chanel's kitchen was beyond her. She had an awful feeling he was involved in the suspicious deaths of his patients and was trying to pass off the blame.

From almost the beginning, he appeared to have a gripe against Chanel. If she was to be believed, it was because she'd turned him down. Although Tanya hadn't wanted to believe it at the time, Chanel's assertion that he'd propositioned her and was rejected rang with the truth. After all, he'd done the same thing to Tanya.

*Only, she hadn't turned him down.* She'd been flattered by the attention and he knew how to work his charm. She'd also been relieved to have the issue of struggling for high grades disappear. If sleeping with him was all it took, she was more than happy to do it.

But murder was another thing entirely. And framing her roommate... There was no way she'd agreed to be part of that. Even as an accessory after the fact. She'd seen enough *CSI* and old reruns of *Law and Order* to know there was such a thing. By leaving the bottle of poison on the kitchen shelf, she'd put herself at risk. When the police found out she was sleeping with Leo, they'd think she'd been in on it from the start.

Fresh panic surged through her and she trembled from the strain. The phone in her white coat vibrated against her hip and she ignored it, like she'd been doing for the past four days. The screen showed a blocked Caller ID. It could be anyone, but she had a sneaking suspicion the call was from the police.

Chanel would have denied knowing anything about the bottle. It was natural the police would seek Tanya out. It was the only logical course of action to take. If Chanel didn't know about it, then her roommate might.

t was why Tanya had escaped to her father's place for a few days. She'd lied and told him she needed the peace and quiet to study for her exams. Her father was more than pleased to see her and quietly proud of her dedication. The lie had tasted sour on her tongue, but she didn't have a choice. She was afraid of going back to face Chanel. She was also afraid to talk to the police.

A knock on the bathroom door gave her a start and she gasped aloud in surprise. She put a hand up to her chest in an effort to steady her heart.

"Is anyone in there?" The impatient voice of another female sounded from outside.

"Um, I won't be a minute." Tanya gulped and hurriedly flushed the toilet. Turning to the sink, she quickly splashed cool water on her face.

She drew in a breath and eyed herself in the mirror. Her cheeks were flushed, her eyes were wide, but to the casual observer, she looked almost normal. She opened the door and brushed past the staff member who waited outside. With her head down, she made her way back to the ward.

———

Filled with the disquieting knowledge that Leo Baker might be involved in a murder spree, Bryce decided to stop by and visit his grandmother before he confronted Tanya Singh. He'd driven his grandmother to the hospital two days earlier and she'd been admitted with a view to commencing her course of IV antibiotics.

He stepped out of the elevator and made his way down the corridor. He was pleased to see an IV cannula still in her arm and a bag of fluid attached to the machine. He smiled at the sight of her in her pink cotton housecoat and matching nightdress. With her halo of soft, white hair and eyes that sparkled when she saw him, she looked a decade younger than her eighty-three years.

"Bryce, how lovely to see you! I wasn't expecting you until after you finished work."

He leaned over and kissed her on her cheek. "Hi, Grandma. I had to pay a visit to the hospital on a work-related matter, so I thought I might look in on you. How are you doing?"

"I'm fine. It will take a few days for the antibiotics to give the ulcer a kick-along, but I don't mind. Someone's cooking all my meals, my bed gets made and I get to catch up on my reading." She lifted the book she held in her hands. The cover showed the naked chest of a man in a passionate embrace with a woman who looked more than a little enamored of him. His grandmother winked. "Life doesn't get any better."

Bryce smiled fondly back at her and shook his head. "There's no doubt about you, Grandma. You're one of a kind."

"Hey, there's nothing wrong with being unique." She smiled. "How are you getting on? Did you eat something decent last night? What are you having for dinner?"

"I'm fine, Grandma. For the first two nights, I ate the lasagne you left in the fridge and tonight I'll start in on the meatloaf. You didn't have to cook and freeze meals for me, Grandma. I do know how to cook."

"I know. I taught you, remember? And taught you well. I just thought, with you coming home from work so late, so often, the last thing you'd want to do was cook. I was just looking out for you, Grandson."

Bryce looked at the old woman he loved so dearly and breathed through the sudden tightness in his chest. "You're always looking out for me, Grandma."

She shrugged. "I've been doing it for a long time. What can I say? It's become a habit."

"Well, I appreciate it." Bryce glanced at his watch. "I'm going to have to go, Grandma. There's someone I need to see." He leaned over and gave her wrinkled cheek a peck. "I'll see you later on. Probably tomorrow. I'll call you."

"Have a good night, Grandson and thanks for dropping by. It's always good to see you."

He waved to her on his way out and took the elevator up to Level Four. Upon his arrival in the ward, he looked around, hoping to spot Doctor Singh. According to her roster, she should have been there. He approached the nurses' station and smiled at the nurse who stood behind the counter.

"I'm looking for Doctor Singh. I understand she's here."

The nurse nodded. "Yes, I saw her coming out of Room Six only a few moments ago."

Bryce waved his hand in thanks and strode in the direction she indicated, but Doctor Singh was nowhere in sight. With a sigh of impatience, he pushed open the door to a treatment room and came up short.

He recognized her from the photo ID that was pinned to the lapel of her white coat. She looked at him and her eyes went wide with fear.

"Doctor Tanya Singh?" he asked, more as a matter of courtesy than anything else.

"Yes. I'm Tanya Singh. Is there something you need?"

"I'm Detective Sutcliffe with the City of Sydney Police. I'm part of the task force investigating the recent deaths of three patients. I'm sure you've heard about it."

"Yes, of course. I was interviewed by one of your colleagues about ten days ago. Is there something else you need?"

"Yes. I need you to come with me and answer a few more questions. Down at the station, if you don't mind."

Her eyes grew rounder and she stumbled and reached out for something to lean on. She shook her head, indicating she'd prefer not, before she spoke.

"No, no, no, Detective. We don't need to go down to the station. Let's just do it here. I'm at work. I can hardly just up and leave."

"I've approved it with the general manager. She has asked you to cooperate with me. Now, are you coming with me of your own accord, or do I need to pull out the handcuffs"

His words had their desired effect. She gasped and turned white and her eyes went wild with fright.

"Please, detective, please, no handcuffs," she begged. "I'll come with you, I promise. Just give me a minute to collect my things."

"I'll come with you," Bryce said, not trusting that she wouldn't disappear. "Where have you been and why aren't you answering your phone? I've been trying to get hold of you."

"I... I've been at work. I never answer my phone at work."

"What about earlier? Your roommate says she hasn't seen you for days. Where have you been?"

"I...I went to my father's. I do that sometimes. He... He lives on his own. He misses me."

"So he told me," Bryce replied, his voice dry.

What little color left in Tanya's cheeks disappeared. "You spoke to my father?" she gasped.

"As I said, I've been trying to get hold of you."

A short time later, he showed Tanya to his unmarked police car and opened the back door. She climbed in and reached for the seatbelt with an unsteady hand.

Good. He wanted her scared. She might actually tell the truth if he frightened her enough about what could happen to her if she lied.

He maneuvered his way through the afternoon traffic and pulled up outside the station. Helping her from the car, he led her into the building and up the stairs to the squad room that housed the detectives. He showed her into a vacant interview room. Not bothering with niceties, he got straight to the point.

"Why did you leave a medicine bottle in Chanel Munro's kitchen?"

Tanya wrung her hands together and stared at her lap. Her bottom lip wobbled, but she refused to speak. Bryce's temper ratcheted up a notch.

"Tanya, hindering a police investigation is a criminal offense and so is being an accessory after the fact. We're talking about a triple murder. You could be looking at some serious time. Now, are you going to cooperate, or should I just charge you now?"

If it were possible, the woman turned even paler. Bryce felt a surge of satisfaction. He was being a little heavy-handed, but it was necessary. He was sure the key to finding the killer lay in discovering the identity of the person behind the medicine bottle and Tanya, who'd been seeing Doctor Baker, knew a hell of a lot more than she was saying. Which right now, was zilch.

Bryce's anger stirred. Pushing away from the table, he strode to the door and opened it, intent on carrying out his threat. Tanya's head snapped up and her eyes went wide with fright.

"Okay, okay. I'll tell you what I know. Please, Detective, sit down."

Bryce turned and made his way back to the table. He picked up the remote control that operated the video camera mounted on the wall.

"I'm going to electronically record this interview. Are you agreeable to that?"

She gave a jerky nod. Tears glittered in her dark brown eyes and Bryce felt a twinge of guilt. It disappeared the moment she opened her mouth.

"I got the bottle from Doctor Leo Baker. He asked me to leave it on the shelf in Chanel's kitchen."

Bryce's gaze narrowed. "Did he specifically mention Chanel?"

"No, but he knew we shared an apartment."

"Did he tell you what was in it?"

She lowered her gaze and her cheeks flushed pink. "He told me it was some kind of herbal aphrodisiac."

Bryce decided to play dumb. It wasn't necessary to make Tanya aware her roommate had revealed her dirty little secret.

"An aphrodisiac? Did I hear you right?"

Tanya's cheeks turned crimson. She nodded and buried her face in her hands.

"Are you saying you and Doctor Baker are lovers?"

Her voice was muffled through her fingers. "Yes."

"I'm sorry, Doctor Singh, I need you to speak clearly. Are you and Doctor Leo Baker lovers?"

She lifted her head and stared at him, tears flowing down her cheeks. "Yes."

"For how long?"

"I don't know. A month, I guess."

"Who initiated it?"

"He did."

"How?"

She proceeded to relate a story that sounded strangely similar to the one Chanel had related.

"Did Doctor Baker coerce you in any way?"

She shook her head. "No, apart from offering me a free pass through his residency program. It was an offer I couldn't refuse."

"Did he give you a choice?"

"Yes, of course, but to tell you the truth, I was flattered he'd asked. He might have a few years on me, but he's still a very attractive man. Gaining good grades was an added bonus."

"Do you know anything about the deaths of three of his patients?"

"No, only what I've heard around the hospital."

Did you ever talk about it with Doctor Baker?"

"No."

"When did he give you the medicine bottle?"

She shrugged. "I don't know. A little over a week ago. It wasn't that long before you found it."

"Have you talked to him about it since?"

"No, I've been too scared to talk to him. What if it does contain the poison? I don't know what I'll do!"

Bryce's phone rang and he checked the Caller ID. It was Samantha Wolfe from the morgue. Hoping she had news of the lab results, he paused the recording and took the call.

"Doctor Wolfe, how can I help you?"

"Detective Sutcliffe, I have those results back from the lab. The powder in the medicine bottle contains a very high strength ricin."

Even though he guessed it would turn out that way, Bryce took no satisfaction from having his suspicions confirmed. Doctor Baker had given a bottle containing ricin to his infatuated student and made sure it was found in Chanel Munro's kitchen. Bryce was sure the good doctor was the anonymous tipster. Nothing else made sense.

After thanking Samantha for her time, he ended the call and immediately made another.

"Boss, I'm sorry to call you at home. I was told you're not well, but I'm in the middle of an interview with a witness in relation to the hospital murders. She's told me it was Doctor Leo Baker who gave her the medicine bottle we found in Chanel Munro's apartment. I need to get a voice analysis of the male person who called in with the anonymous tip. I'm betting it's him."

Bryce answered the questions posed by Holt and when his boss approved Bryce's request, he breathed a sigh of relief.

"Thanks, boss. I'll keep you informed. I hope you're feeling better soon." He ended the call and turned back to Tanya, who remained drawn and pale in her seat.

"The bottle you left in Chanel's apartment contained the poison ricin. It's the same poison that was used to kill three patients under Doctor Baker's care. If you had any knowledge about what he was doing or if you participated in any way, I will bury you so deep inside the bowels of a correctional facility, you'll never see the light of day."

Her expression turned frantic with fear. "No, please, Detective. You have to believe me. I knew nothing about the women who died, I swear. My only involvement with Doctor Baker began when I was stupid enough to start a relationship with him. I was sleeping with him. I...I thought I was in love with him. Now, I realize I've been used. I was nothing more than a pawn to assist him in his vendetta against Chanel."

Bryce nodded grimly. I'm afraid you're right, Doctor Singh, but lucky for you, there's no crime for being stupid or for making poor choices. I believe you when you say you had nothing to do with the deaths, but you don't get to walk away scot-free. I need you to help me."

Tanya nodded with an eagerness that would have been comical if the whole situation weren't so serious.

"Of course, Detective. I'll do whatever you want. Does this mean I'm not going to be charged? I won't have to tell my father?"

"What you tell your father is your business, Doctor Singh. I can't help you there. But no, you won't be charged provided you cooperate with our investigation. You're going to help me get the evidence I need against Doctor Baker."

"What must I do?"

"I'm going to get approval for you to wear a wire. Then you're going to meet with Doctor Baker and do your best to get him to talk about the medicine bottle. You're going to tell him about Chanel's arrest and that the police suspect the bottle contains the poison that was used on her patients. You share an apartment. It's not too much of a stretch for him to believe you'd be privy to information not necessarily in the public domain."

Tanya looked fearful. "What if he guesses there are people listening? What if I can't get him to talk?"

Bryce smiled without humor. "You're a smart woman. You'll think of something. Right now, I need to check on my grandmother."

# CHAPTER 19

Chanel watched the final segment on the six o'clock news and then switched off the television. She was relieved there'd been no mention of Bryce's investigation. Although it meant the killer was still on the loose, she was relieved her name hadn't come to the attention of the media. It was bad enough that her brothers had called her parents, her sister and her other two brothers and told them of recent events. For the past few hours, she'd done nothing but field concerned phone calls from members of her family.

Not that she could blame them. They were a close family. If it had happened to one of her siblings, she'd have reacted just the same. 'All for one and one for all' was the unofficial motto of the Munro family. They looked out for one another and were there for each other when the occasion demanded. She loved that they cared so much, but would be happy when they backed off a little and went back to their normal lives.

The phone rang again for the umpteenth time. She bit back a sigh and reached for it where she'd tossed it on the coffee table. It was probably her sister again. Josie was about to undergo another round of IVF treatment and was on edge about everything. Chanel's arrest was her sister's latest worry project.

Checking the Caller ID, she frowned. The number was blocked. She thought about ignoring it, but then answered the call.

"Hello?"

"Chanel, it's Bryce."

Her heart skipped a beat and then took off at a wild gallop. Just the sound of his voice was enough to send blood rushing through her veins. Despite everything, she wanted to see him again.

"Bryce, how are you?"

"I'm fine. I'm still at work. I wanted to bring you up to date on the investigation."

"I just watched the news on TV. There was no mention of it. I take it there haven't been any new developments."

"Well, actually, there are. I found Tanya. We had a chat. She admitted to planting the medicine bottle in your apartment, although the way she tells it, she was unaware of its contents. The lab confirmed it contained ricin."

Surprise surged through her, even though a part of her resisted the fact the bottle found in her home was linked to the deaths and had been placed there by her friend. Bryce's original assertion that someone was trying to set her up for murder seemed more and more on the mark.

"Where did she get it from? I don't believe Tanya's capable of murder."

"No one knows what they're capable of until they're put in the situation, believe me... But I agree, I don't think she's the mastermind behind this."

"Then who?"

There was a pause and then Bryce said, "She told me she got it from Doctor Baker. According to Tanya, he led her to believe it contained some kind of herbal aphrodisiac."

Chanel digested his words and then winced. She didn't want to imagine her roommate and Doctor Baker getting down and dirty. The very thought was repulsive.

"Have you arrested him?"

"We only have Tanya's word he gave her the poison. You can bet your last dollar he'll deny knowing anything about it. Right now, it's her word against his. We need more. I'm waiting for fingerprint analysis on the bottle. You never know, we might get lucky with one of his prints."

"Surely, he wouldn't be so stupid. He's a very clever man."

"Not clever enough. He chose an assistant who didn't know how to keep her mouth shut, especially when put under pressure."

"What did you threaten her with?"

"It doesn't matter. The fact is, we got results. You should be thankful you're well and truly off the hook."

His words stung. "I thought you said earlier you believed me?"

"I'm sorry, that came out wrong. I do believe you, but it doesn't hurt to have irrefutable evidence of someone else's involvement. We're also looking into the identity of the anonymous tipster."

She mulled over his apology and decided he was being sincere. He was a cop. He couldn't help thinking like one. It was all about evidence and proof. She'd lived with a family of police officers. She knew how it was.

His voice pitched lower. "What are you doing?"

"I'm on the couch. I was watching the news, remember? I was relieved when there wasn't any mention of your investigation."

"Yeah, we're keeping this under wraps until we have more proof. I'm confident we'll have something more definite soon."

"Good. The possibility that Doctor Baker might be the one indiscriminately killing his patients is beyond belief."

"I'm hearing you. He's my grandmother's physician. He admitted her a couple of days ago for treatment of her ulcer. She's a diabetic."

Chanel digested his words and did her best to contain her disquiet. "Doctor Baker's an outstanding physician. One of the best we have. It's why I'm finding it so hard to reconcile him with a cold-hearted killer. Not that we have any solid proof. At least, not yet. I'm... I'm sure she'll be fine."

Her reassurances were met with silence. Finally, he answered. "Yeah, of course she'll be fine. She has a lifetime of confidence in him and he's never treated her in an untoward way. Like you said, we don't even know if it's him. Tanya's hardly an impartial witness. Besides, I phoned my grandmother right before I called you. She said she was fine."

"Good."

There was another pause, this one a little more awkward. Bryce broke it by asking, "So, have you eaten yet?"

"No. Have you?"

"Nope. I was just finishing up a report. I have my grandmother's meatloaf defrosting on the kitchen counter, but I have a hankering for pizza."

Chanel's stomach growled, reminding her she hadn't eaten since lunchtime. She loved pizza.

As if he read her mind, he added, "We could share one, if you like."

"I'm...um... I'm not exactly dressed for going out. I'm in my pajamas. I had an early shower, washed my hair. You know, that kind of thing. I didn't have anything better to do."

"I could get takeaway and come over."

His words sent a wave of excitement rushing through her. She drew in a breath and eased it out and did her best to get some control over her frantic heart rate. It had taken off the moment he mentioned coming over. They both knew if he did, it would lead to far more than sharing pizza.

She drew in a deep breath and then jumped off the cliff. "Pizza's just about my favorite thing to eat. Do I get to help you choose the toppings?"

She heard him let out his breath on the other end of the phone in a soft sigh, as if he'd been holding it.

"Of course. Whatever you like."

"Thin and crispy super supreme, hold the olives and anchovies, double the cheese."

"That's it?" he said dryly.

"Yep, that's it."

"Just as well I like supreme. I'll be there in forty minutes."

---

While Bryce waited for the pizza, he sent a quick text to his grandmother. His need to stay in contact with her might appear like paranoia, but with all that had gone on with her treating physician, he wanted to be sure she was all right.

Much to his relief, she texted him back straight away and assured him once again that she was fine and resting comfortably. Doctor Baker had stopped by earlier and was pleased with her progress. He even thought she might be able to return home in the next day or so.

Bryce thought again of the questions surrounding his grandmother's doctor, but forced himself to let it go. What was he going to do? Charge into the ward and demand that she be discharged?

She was resting comfortably. She'd told him so. In a day or two, she'd be home and he could forget all about his unease. Besides, Baker was an excellent physician, one of the best, Chanel had said. If she had any concerns about him treating Bryce's grandmother, he was sure she'd have voiced them.

At the thought of Chanel, his gut twisted into a knot of excitement. There was no doubt in his mind he'd end the night in her bed and the knowledge had the blood pumping through his veins.

Ever since their first night together, he'd yearned to be with her again. She'd made him feel alive for the first time in too many years to remember. Now that he'd finally laid his wife to rest, he was in a better state of mind to contemplate the future.

He'd never dreamed he might find love again, but ever since he'd been with Chanel, the possibility seemed very real. She couldn't be more different from Angela, in every single way, yet he was still drawn to her. When he thought of the two of them together, he was filled with hope.

"Thin and crispy super supreme, no olives or anchovies, extra cheese," the man behind the counter shouted.

Bryce stepped forward. "That's me." Handing over a few bills, he collected the pizza and headed back to his car.

Less than ten minutes later, he parked outside Chanel's

apartment complex and jogged up the steps, the pizza box in his hand. With his free hand, he knocked on the door and waited for her to open it. He wondered if she'd changed out of her pajamas and hoped she hadn't. He was curious about her sleepwear. The image of a short, sexy black nightie skimming slim, tanned thighs crowded his mind.

And then she was there, on the other side of the open door, smiling and looking a little nervous. She wore a faded cotton T-shirt and long, striped pajama pants that should have looked anything but sexy, but on her... He winked at her.

"I come with pizza."

"*Mm,* it smells good. Come in and let's eat. I'm starving."

His gaze roved over her and he paused to take in the way her T-shirt moulded to her breasts. It was obvious she wasn't wearing a bra. Her choice of sleepwear suddenly rose in his estimation. It wasn't the only thing on the rise.

She turned away from him and headed in the direction of the kitchen and he swallowed a sigh of relief, but the view from behind was just as tantalizing and his relief was short-lived. The soft pajama pants outlined the sweet curve of her butt and it was all he could do not to reach for her. The hot pizza box in his hand reminded him there were other things to attend to and he resigned himself to having a hard-on for the duration of the meal.

Chanel chatted amiably while she went about gathering plates and napkins from the cupboard and he could only assume she was oblivious to his predicament. A small wooden table was wedged against one wall of the modest kitchen and a chair at either end provided enough room for two. She placed the crockery and napkins on the table and then urged him to sit.

Bryce set the pizza box down and opened the lid. The delicious aroma of freshly baked pizza made his mouth water and for the moment, he was happy to concentrate on satisfying a different kind of hunger.

They ate in silence amidst soft groans of appreciation. Chanel chewed on a long piece of stringy cheese, working away at it with her lips and her tongue until she finally captured it in her mouth. Her lips glistened and Bryce couldn't drag his gaze away. She blushed and with a self-conscious swipe of her tongue, removed most of the sheen. Need surged through him, hot and fast and heavy.

His cock hardened almost painfully. Without thinking, he pushed away from the table and stood. He closed the small distance between them and pulled Chanel up from her seat. She stared at him, her eyes a deep cobalt, tumultuous as the ocean on a dark and stormy night.

He bent his head and grazed her lips with his, tasting the spicy warmth of the pizza on her tongue. He kissed her again, more urgently this time and was gratified by her response. She moaned quietly and pressed against him. Her arms crept up around his neck.

"Wait," she gasped and hurriedly wiped her greasy hands on a napkin. "I don't want to stain your jacket. It looks like it cost a bomb."

"I don't give a damn about the jacket," he muttered, kissing her again. "All I want is you."

"I want you, too," she whispered and smiled up at him.

His breath caught at the invitation in her eyes and another thrill of desire coursed through him. With his hand against her back, he pressed her to him, needing to feel her close. She moved until there was nothing between them but their clothes.

He kissed her face, her lips, her eyes. He nuzzled in the sensitive spot behind her ears. She moaned deep in her throat and a surge of masculine pride rushed through him. His cock felt near to bursting and his breath came hard and fast.

She was equally affected. Her face was flushed and her eyes glittered like she was in the throes of a fever. He picked her up and carried her into the living room and put her down on the sofa.

"Wait, what about Tanya? What if she walks in?"

"She's staying with her father tonight."

Chanel frowned. "You're sure?"

"I'm sure."

At that, she relaxed against the cushions and reached for him. He gladly joined her on the couch. They sank into the soft leather and groaned their mutual need. Chanel tugged at his tie, got it loose and tossed it to the floor. She went to work on the buttons of his shirt and it went the way of his tie. A moment later, he felt her hands at his belt.

"Hang on a sec, why don't we get the condom now? That way we won't have to stop again."

She growled her discontent, but nodded and climbed off the couch and left the room. She returned shortly afterwards with a fistful. He raised an eyebrow in silent query and she smiled.

"Who knows? It might be a long night. A girl can remain hopeful, can't she?"

He grinned and swatted her on the ass. "Cheeky woman. Now, get over here and finish what you started."

She pushed him down on the couch until he was lying on his back, but instead of following him, she knelt beside him on the carpet. Her fingers worked the buckle of his belt and slid it out of the loops of his pants. The button popped open and down went his zipper. She reached inside his underwear and caressed him. He growled in satisfaction.

She took hold of the waist band of his suit pants. "Lift your hips."

He did as she ordered and she slid his pants and underwear down. He kicked at them, until they disappeared and sighed when she tightened her hold on his cock. Once again, she stroked him, her fingers soft and cool on his heated skin. When she bent her head and took him in her mouth, he couldn't hold back a gasp.

"Oh, that feels so good. Keeping doing that."

She ran her tongue up and down his shaft and swiped it across his slick head. She dipped it into the slit that was oh so sensitive and brought forth another groan of need. He tangled his fingers in her hair and held her head in place and prayed for it to never end. She continued to suck him hard until he was almost ready to explode.

"I'm going to come if you keep that up any longer..."

She lifted her head for a few seconds and stared at him, her eyes dark with desire. "So, come," she murmured and then returned to her unbearable torture.

Once again, she took all of him in her mouth, deeper than he'd ever been. She sucked and stroked and tightened her hand in a rhythm that increased in pace. Having her permission to find his release, he bucked hard against her mouth. His fingers tightened in her hair until it was probably hurting, though she didn't protest.

"Oh, God, oh, babe. I'm gonna come."

With her hand still pumping his shaft, she released him from her mouth. Hot fluid spurted out and landed on his stomach. He groaned and reached down to cover her hand with his and make the most of the final moments of his climax. With a deep sigh of satisfaction, he closed his eyes for a moment and relaxed against the cushions.

"Now, it's my turn."

He opened his eyes and smiled. "You bet."

---

The words fell out of Chanel's mouth and she couldn't believe she'd said them. *When had she become so bold?* She was hardly experienced in the bedroom. And yet, with Bryce, the passion seemed to come so naturally. She wanted to know every intimate part of him. She wanted to please him. She'd made him come with her hands and her mouth and the knowledge filled her with a glow of satisfaction. She'd only given oral sex a few times in her life and had basically relied on instinct. She couldn't help but feel pleased with the result.

Bryce sat up and reached out and cupped her cheek in his palm. His skin was slightly rough against the softness of hers. She leaned into his hand and he stroked a thumb across her lips.

"You're so damn beautiful. How did I get so lucky?"

She pressed a kiss against his palm in answer and he growled low in his throat.

"Lie down," he commanded softly.

Desire surged through her at the determination in his eyes and with it a rush of heightened excitement. She wiggled down on the other end of the couch. Bryce leaned forward and slipped his hands beneath her T-shirt. His fingers splayed across her stomach and then stroked up and around the sides. He reached her breasts, bare beneath her shirt, and skimmed over her nipples. They hardened under his touch.

"Do you like it when I touch you?" he asked, his voice husky.

"Yes," she whispered and fought back a blush.

"Good, because I'm going to do a whole lot more of it."

Her insides quivered at the promise in his eyes and heat tingled deep in her core. He bunched up her T-shirt and then lifted it over her head, baring her breasts to his gaze. A moment later, his lips found them and his tongue stroked across her hardened nipples. Over and over and over again, he caressed her, until she was mindless with need.

While he laved one, his other hand squeezed and shaped her other breast and playfully pinched her sensitive nipple. Then his mouth fused itself to her breast and sucked greedily. She twisted and writhed beneath him and was surprised to feel his cock pressing hard and needy against her thigh. She melted at the thought of him once again deep inside her.

While he switched his focus to her other breast, his free hand stole under the waistband of her pajamas. It moved lower and lower still until his fingers slid in and out of her folds. She was slick and burning for his attention and squirmed beneath his palm. When two of his fingers slid inside her, she gasped with relief.

"Do you want me?" he rasped and worked his fingers in and out.

"Yes."

"How much?"

"I'm going to explode from the inside out if you don't take me."

"Do you want me to fuck you?"

His crudity sent another wave of white-hot desire rushing through her. She surged against his fingers.

"Yes."

"Good. But it will have to wait. I have other things to attend to."

He withdrew his fingers and she groaned aloud from disappointment. "Bryce, please..."

He kissed her hard on the mouth to quieten her. "Be patient. It'll be worth it. You'll see."

With that, he stripped off her pajama bottoms and positioned himself between her legs. He bent her knees and spread her thighs wide and then licked her soft, slick folds. She gripped the sides of the couch, too surprised to utter a sound. The feel of him on her sensitive flesh—his mouth, his lips, his tongue. It was like nothing she'd ever felt before. His fingers returned to where they'd been and stroked her in a strong, sure rhythm. Once again, need built up inside her.

She squirmed and moved against his hand. His tongue was relentless. She clutched at his head, not sure if she wanted to hold him in place or tear him right away. Just when she didn't think she could bear the torment a moment longer, he pulled his fingers from inside her and eased one into her ass.

She gasped with shock at the alien feel of it. "Bryce!"

He lifted his head and looked at her. "Do you like it?"

"I...I don't know. I think so. No one's ever done that to me before."

His expression filled with satisfaction. "Good. I'm glad I'm the first. Relax. Trust me, you're going to enjoy it."

She wasn't too sure about his reassurances, but was soon distracted when he buried his face back between her legs. His tongue kept up the rhythm of his finger and she was soon once again, mindless with desire. Her body was tense. She was hot all over. He increased the pressure of his tongue and his finger moved in and out faster.

"Oh, Bryce! I'm going to come. Oh, God, please..."

"Go with it, babe. Let yourself come. You've earned it."

His words tipped her over the edge and she cried out in exquisite relief. Her muscles clenched around his finger.

A few moments later, he moved up and joined her on the couch. His cock protruded, thick and hard and nudged at her slick entrance. She didn't think she could bear any more, but when he sheathed himself and plunged straight into her on a single, long swift stroke, she sighed with satisfaction.

"Oh, God. You're so wet. You feel so good. I'm gonna come again," he murmured.

She clung to him and rode the waves of his pleasure. It was a long moment before their breathing returned to normal.

"That was amazing," she said softly.

"You were amazing." He smiled and reached over to tenderly brush a loose strand of hair off her face.

She blushed and looked away. "Thank you."

"How about we move to the bedroom? I'm just about spent."

She quirked an eyebrow and grinned. "Only just about? I'll have to try harder next time."

He stood and pulled her up with him and swatted her butt again. "Cheeky girl. I might need to teach you a lesson."

She pulled an innocent face. "Who me?"

He laughed and pulled her close to his side and together, they left the room.

# CHAPTER 20

Bryce's phone rang in the middle of a police briefing about the listening device which was to be worn by Tanya Singh. He glanced at the Caller ID and noticed it was Chanel. His heart tripped over. Ever since he'd left her bed earlier that morning, he hadn't been able to stop thinking about her. He couldn't wait to see her again.

But it wouldn't be happening today. Tanya Singh would be making contact with Doctor Baker that afternoon and all members of the task force were needed. He'd also spoken with his grandmother. She'd told him she was going to be discharged later in the day. He needed to be there to collect her. It was going to be a busy one all round. Letting Chanel's call go through to voicemail, he swallowed his disappointment and switched his phone to silent.

He looked around at his boss and the other members of the task force. Everything had been put in place. The tech guys were standing by. All they needed was for Tanya to arrive and get kitted up with the wire.

"Has anyone prepared a script for the witness?" Holt asked.

"I have," Bryce replied and slid a copy across the desk to his boss.

"Good. Make sure you go over it with her as much as you can. The more familiar she is with it, the more likely she'll stay on track."

"No problem. I asked her to be at the station by midday. She should be here any minute."

"Good. Is that all?" Holt looked at the officers gathered around the table of the major incident room and was met with a series of nods.

"I think so, boss," Bryce replied. "Let's hope we get what we need."

"You think Baker's the killer?"

"I'm not sure, but he knows something about it. He gave the bottle containing ricin to his lover to hide in Chanel Munro's apartment. Ricin was never mentioned in the press releases. It can't be a coincidence that he had it. I'm hoping he'll let something slip about who or where he got it from."

"Were there any prints on the bottle?"

Bryce shook his head. "I heard back from the lab this morning. The only prints on it were Singh's."

"So he wiped it clean before he gave it to her. Not exactly the actions of an innocent man," Holt said dryly.

Another surge of unease filled Bryce's gut. His grandmother was still a patient under Doctor Baker's care. If there was a real possibility the doctor was the killer... He pushed the thought aside. She was being discharged later that afternoon. Her ulcer had improved enough that she could come home. She'd been treated just fine by everyone at the hospital. He was being paranoid thinking anything different. It came with the job.

"What about the voice analysis? Do we have anything back on that, yet?"

Holt's question interrupted Bryce's troubled thoughts. "No, sir. The same old story. 'They have a backlog. They'll get to it as soon as they can. They'll call us when they have the results. It could be another day or two.' You know how it goes."

"All right, if there's nothing else, you can go and find something to eat and prepare for this afternoon. Bryce, I want you to stay with the techies while they hook up Doctor Singh. She'll be nervous and you can calm her down.

Besides, you need to go over the script with her, make sure she understands."

"No problem, boss."

"Keep me in the loop, Bryce. I want to know how it all goes down."

"Of course. Jett and I will be in the tech van outside the hospital. We'll hear everything that's said."

Holt nodded and strode out of the room, behind the other departing officers. Bryce glanced at his watch and sighed. It was ten after midday. Tanya was late.

---

Chanel called Bryce's phone a second time and listened while it dialed out. Once again, it went to voice mail. This time, feeling deflated, she left a message.

"Hi, Bryce. It's me…Chanel. I…I just wanted to tell you I've had a call from the general manager. They're reinstating me at the hospital. I'm allowed to return to work this afternoon. I…I just wanted to tell you. I'm so excited to be going back." She cleared her throat. "Anyway, I'd better get going. Maybe I'll see you later tonight?"

She ended the call and tossed her phone down on the bed, still rumpled from the night before. She thought of how they'd rolled around in the sheets twice more before they'd fallen asleep. She couldn't believe his stamina. And hers, too, for that matter.

She sat on the bed and her thigh muscles protested. They hadn't been worked out like that in a very long time. In fact, they'd never been worked out that much, not even when she attended the gym. Not that she was complaining. Sex with Bryce was out of this world. He was an attentive and imaginative lover and she was more than happy to succumb to his will and apply her own…

He'd told her about his parents and how they'd been killed when he was eight. He also spoke in more detail about the simple service conducted on behalf of his wife. She was at peace now and he felt he could finally move on with his life. He'd stared at her as he'd said it, his gaze intent.

She wanted to believe he meant he saw a future for the two of them, but it was all too new, his wife's death too soon for her to be voicing such hope. Still, Bryce didn't seem like the "love 'em and leave 'em" kind of guy. He'd remained faithful to his wife. That told her a lot about his character and she was confident they'd work something out.

She hoped so, anyway, because she was falling for him fast. It might have taken her twenty-seven years to find him, but now that she had, she wanted to hold on to him tight. Her family would love him, once they'd gotten over the fact that he'd had her arrested and thrown into jail. Tom and Clayton and Brandon might take a little more convincing that he was a great guy, but she was sure she could bring them around.

The thought of having a boyfriend left her giddy with excitement. For too many years, she'd done nothing but work and study and do whatever it took to get ahead. It hadn't been until she'd met Bryce that she realized sometimes her devotion to her career didn't count for as much as she hoped.

With nearly a quarter of the program already over, it wouldn't be long before she started the next part of her life. Even without Doctor Baker's direct recommendation, she hoped to be able to apply for her dream job.

She wanted to go into pediatrics. She'd always adored being around kids. Her brothers had enough between them to fill a bus, but there was always room for more. And her sister Josie was trying for a baby, too. Chanel could only hope this time the IVF would be successful. There wasn't a woman on the planet who deserved to be a mother more than Josie Munro, but Chanel knew full well, life didn't always work out the way you planned. Bryce was a prime example of that.

Josie and her husband, Chase, had set up a halfway house for troubled kids. Their farm in the country on the outskirts of town was often home to a dozen or more. Foster kids, mostly, who'd been in and out of care. Chanel couldn't believe the love and dedication her sister and husband showered on them. That couple was truly turning lives around.

As inspirational and fulfilling as Josie found it, she still yearned for a child of her own and Chanel understood her need. She felt the same yearning. It had come upon her slowly, sometime after meeting Bryce. She supposed until she found a man she could imagine having kids with, she hadn't allowed herself such thoughts.

Now, those thoughts almost consumed her and she wondered how he'd feel. He hadn't been able to have kids with his wife. According to Bryce, Angela's need for a child had become an obsession and it nearly ruined their marriage. *Would he want to contemplate the possibility all over again?* Did he care enough to want to even think about it? Was she brave enough to ask him and find out?

He liked her well enough and she believed he cared, but did he love her? Did she love him? Yes, she probably did. They hadn't known each other very long, but what was time when it came to true love? Her father had known the instant he met her mother that she'd one day become his wife. It was the same for all of her brothers and they were still in love with their wives. In fact, sometimes it was downright embarrassing to see the devotion in their eyes.

*Would Bryce look at her like that someday?* She could only hope. For now, she had work to do. Making the bed and tidying the apartment were at the top of her list. Then she'd get ready to return to her job at the hospital. She couldn't wait.

---

Chanel finished pulling on her white lab coat and closed the door to her locker before heading in the direction of the elevators. She got out on Level Three and strode around the corner to Doctor Baker's rooms. She knocked and opened the door, but the reception area was unattended.

"Hello? Is anyone here?" she called.

A few moments later, the door to Doctor Baker's office opened and he stepped into the room. When he saw her, his eyebrows flew up in surprise.

"I was told you were arrested on suspicion of murder. How could they let you come back?"

Chanel clenched her jaw, but replied with as much courtesy as she could. "I've been cleared of any wrongdoing. The general manager called me today and reinstated me. Do you have my list of patients?"

He stared at her a moment longer and his expression grew petulant. "I don't know what the world's coming to these days," he muttered and stormed off into his office. He returned a short time later brandishing a sheet of paper.

"Here you go and make sure you get around to all of them. I haven't managed to see the last four on the list today, so I'd like you to start with them."

Chanel nodded and took the list from him and then turned to leave.

"It's good to have you back, Doctor Munro," he threw at her on her way out the door.

She turned and stared at him in confusion. Only moments before, he'd seemed annoyed about her return. Now he was showing her encouragement and support—if she could call it that. She couldn't work it out and right then and there she didn't want to. It was enough that he hadn't threatened to have her removed from his program. She'd half expected he would.

"Thank you, Doctor Baker," she murmured and made her escape.

Most of the patients at the end of her list were in Ward Three, on the same level as Doctor Baker's rooms. She approached the nurses' station a little uncertainly, unsure of the reception she'd receive. No doubt news of her arrest had made its way around the hospital.

A young nurse greeted her with a friendly smile and only the slightest hint of curiosity. If she wondered about Chanel's role in the investigation, she didn't voice it. Chanel breathed a sigh of relief and proceeded to record bed numbers beside the names on her list.

The first patient was a woman by the name of Virginia Tilocca. Virginia had been receiving treatment for a chronic ulcer on her foot that was simply refusing to heal. She was a diabetic, which made the healing process worse and had been admitted to undergo a course of IV antibiotics. Along with the drug therapy, the wound was being cleaned and dressed twice daily.

According to the hospital notes, the ulcer was healing nicely. The patient was due to be discharged later that afternoon.

"If you could complete the discharge papers and organize her medication, that would be great," the nurse said after Chanel enquired about them.

"I'm sure I can do that," Chanel replied with a smile and headed off in search of the patient.

The woman was in a four-bed room. There was only one other patient in the room, asleep in the bed opposite. Chanel spied the nametag above the bed and smiled in greeting. A mass of white hair surrounded the woman's head, framed by a sweet, wrinkled face.

"Ms Tilocca?"

"Yes, honey. That's me."

"I'm Doctor Munro. I work with Doctor Baker. I believe you're going home later today. I'm here to complete your discharge papers. I notice Doctor Baker hasn't been in to see you yet. Do you mind if I take a look at your ulcer and just check that it's okay?"

"Of course, Doctor."

The petite woman in the bed pushed aside the covers and stuck out one pale, skinny leg.

"It's my left leg that's been giving me all the trouble, but it's looking so much better than it did. Doctor Baker's a miracle worker."

Chanel nodded, but remained silent. Drawing the curtains around the bed, she switched on the overhead light. After removing the dressings on the woman's left foot, Chanel got a good look at the wound. A large ulcer was visible on her foot. Although it still looked painful, the skin around it was a healthy pink and it was free of discharge.

"It looks good, Ms Tilocca. It looks like the antibiotics have done the trick."

"That's good news, Doctor. I'm keen to get home. My grandson tries to behave as if he doesn't miss me, but I know he does and I need to know he's eating right. He's a detective in the city and he works long hours, so I like to make sure he has a good meal at night. I baked lasagne and meatloaf to tide him over while I was in here, but he's just as likely to leave them in the freezer and order pizza."

Chanel frowned. She remembered Bryce saying something about his grandmother's meatloaf and that she was a patient under Doctor Baker's care. *Could Virginia Tilocca be Bryce's grandmother?*

Chanel re-covered the wound with the dressings and then drew up the bedcovers before coming to stand beside the patient at the top half of the bed.

"Ms Tilocca, I don't suppose your grandson's Detective Bryce Sutcliffe?"

Surprise lit up the old woman's face and she smiled widely. "Why, yes it is! Do you know him?"

Heat stole up Chanel's neck and spread across her cheeks. She lowered her gaze to the bed.

"Yes, I do."

"Are you one of the doctors he spoke to? He told me he's in the middle of an investigation involving the hospital."

"Yes, I met him through work. He's a lovely man. You're very lucky to have such a wonderful grandson."

The woman looked at her, curiosity bright in her eyes. "Are you single, Doctor Munro?"

Chanel blushed to the roots of her hair. "Ms Tilocca, why on earth would you ask me that?"

"No reason, but my grandson's just gone thirty and he needs a woman in his life. He's had to endure a lot of sadness in his short years. He needs someone to love."

"Oh, Ms Tilocca, I don't think we should be discussing this. Your grandson would be appalled you've even mentioned it."

"I've known him all his life. He was orphaned when he was eight. I raised him on my own from that point on and I couldn't love him more. But I'm old and tired and won't live forever. I need to know he has someone who cares; someone who'll look out for him and love him. He needs that."

"He might disagree with you."

"You're right, he might, but I know him better than he knows himself. He's been alone for far too long. It isn't good for the soul. I should know. I lost my husband to cancer right before the accident that claimed Bryce's parents. If it weren't for that little boy, I don't know what I would have done. But it's time for me to give back, to help him, like he helped me. I want to die knowing he's taken care of, knowing he has someone who loves him like I do."

The old woman's voice cracked with emotion and Chanel bit down hard to stop the prick of tears. Bryce's grandmother had painted a picture of him that tore at Chanel's heartstrings.

She wanted to be the one who loved him; who eased him through his pain; who cooked for him and laughed with him; who was there for him each and every day. But she couldn't tell his grandmother that. It would cause confusion and raise too many questions. And much as she longed to learn more about the Bryce his grandmother knew, she had more patients on her list.

"Ms Tilocca, it's been lovely meeting you and even more so because I know Bryce, but I'm going to have to keep moving. I have a lot to do this afternoon."

"Of course, Doctor. Do you know what time I can get out of here? It's just that Bryce is coming to collect me. He's very busy most of the time, so I wanted to give him a time. That way, he won't be sitting around waiting for me."

"I need to get a supply of antibiotics from the hospital pharmacy for you to take home with you. I'll also give you a prescription for an additional week. That should be enough. You'll need to make an appointment with Doctor Baker to see him in ten days' time. Hopefully everything will be healed by then."

"How long will it take to get medication from the pharmacy?"

"I'll drop the request in now. It might take them an hour or so to fill it. It depends on how busy they are."

"Fine, I can wait an hour or so. I'm not sure what Bryce is up to, anyway. He might not be able to get free until much later this afternoon. He usually doesn't finish work until six."

Chanel nodded and did her best to keep her thoughts away from the woman's grandson, but she was filled with disappointment. His grandmother was being discharged from hospital. He was taking her home. There would be no visits to Chanel's apartment that evening.

" must be off, Ms Tilocca, and I'm so pleased to see that your ulcer is better. You take care, now."

"You too, Doctor Munro and I'll be sure to put in a good word for you to my grandson." She gave Chanel a wink. "Sometimes men need a little push in the right direction, if you know what I mean."

Chanel returned the old lady's smile before bidding her another good-bye and heading out of the room. She shook her head and mused about the coincidence of running into Bryce's grandmother.

The woman was as sweet and lovely as salted caramel ice cream on a hot summer's day and she could see why Bryce thought so much of her. He was lucky to have such a staunch supporter and someone who loved him so unconditionally. Chanel was fortunate to have that kind of parental love in her own life, but there were many people who didn't. She sent up a silent prayer of gratitude for her family and moved on to the next patient on her list.

***

Bryce stared at Tanya where she sat on one of the seats inside the unmarked van that housed the police department's finest technicians and their equipment. The wire was in place and she was ready to go. They'd rehearsed her lines over and over until Bryce was confident she'd get it right. Now all they needed was for Leo Baker to play his part.

"When you spoke to him on the phone and set up the meeting, did he ask what it was in relation to?"

"No, but I told him it was important I see him."

"What did he say?"

"He didn't sound too happy about it, but he agreed just the same."

"Good. Now, remember, we're not exactly sure how he's involved in all of this, but anything you can get him to say about it will be good. He knows he gave you that bottle and he must be aware we found it in Chanel's apartment. I'm sure the hospital rumor mill would have reached him by now. It won't come as a surprise to him that you want to talk about it."

"What if he fobs me off?"

"Then you'll have to try harder. Remember the script. Do what you need to do."

She was pale and looked scared and Bryce had to stop himself from offering her comfort. It was important that she approach the doctor with a realistic level of fear. Any girlfriend finding out they were possibly an accessory to murder would be feeling jittery. Tanya's fear wouldn't come as a surprise.

"Now, don't worry about the wire. It's completely invisible beneath your clothes. Asking him about the bottle won't come across as strange. In fact, he's probably already guessed that's the reason you want to talk. Everything that's said will be heard by us in here. If things get out of control, we'll be there in less than a minute."

If it were possible, Tanya paled even more. "Wh-what do you mean if things get out of control? What do you think he might do?"

"I don't know, probably nothing. It's just a figure of speech. Either way, we have your back. Just try and behave as you normally would and get him to talk about that bottle."

Her head bobbed up and down as if on autopilot and Bryce cursed beneath his breath. He could only hope she'd hold it together long enough to get them what they needed. Refraining from voicing his concerns, he squeezed her arm in reassurance.

"You'll be fine. Now, it's almost time. Where are you meeting him?"

"In his office on Level Three."

"Have you met him there before?"

"Yes, we go there to get our daily patient lists at the start of every shift and once... Once we had sex on the examination table in his office."

Bryce refrained from commenting but made a note to himself to never trust his judgement again. Some "Husband of the Year."

"What about his wife? Doesn't she work there?"

"Yes, but sometimes she's out running errands. I'm sure he wouldn't have arranged to meet me there if she was in."

"Okay. It all sounds good. Are you ready?"

Tanya drew in a deep breath and let it out on a shaky sigh. "I guess so."

"Great. Let's do it."

# CHAPTER 21

Tanya drew in several quick, short breaths and tried to steady her nerves. She was more scared than she'd ever been in her life. How she came to be in the middle of a triple murder investigation, she didn't have a clue. She wished she'd never set eyes on Leo Baker. If only she'd resisted the urge to sleep with him. She cringed at the thought of what her father would say if he knew about her recent behavior.

She'd spent the past six nights at home. Her father had been curious about her reasons, but hadn't pried. She was thankful he hadn't asked her any questions. She honestly didn't know how she would have replied.

He assumed she'd had an argument with her roommate and she'd allowed him to think it was true. The deceit sat heavily in her stomach. Guilt weighed her down at the disservice she was doing Chanel, but hurting her friend's feelings was the least of her problems. Besides, her roommate would never be any the wiser.

Tanya didn't know what to think when the detective announced the bottle she'd taken from Leo contained the same kind of poison that was used to kill Leo's patients. The knowledge that she'd handled it and had maybe played into the hands of a killer made her ill. The detective said the police didn't know the extent of Leo's involvement, but they didn't know how much he had it in for her friend. There was no other reason for him to ask her to store it in Chanel's kitchen.

And now she was about to meet with the man who could be a cold-blooded murderer. Wearing a wire. Trying to entrap him. It was like something out of a movie—and a scary one at that. She didn't have a clue if she could pull it off.

If she wanted any chance of making it work, she needed to act as normal as possible, but how was she expected to do that? She was scared out of her wits. She couldn't imagine Leo hadn't known what the bottle contained. When she told him the police had tested the contents, he'd know straight away why she was scared. She'd use that to mask the fact she was quaking inside at the thought he'd discover she wore a wire. If he knew she'd turned police witness, there was no telling what he might do.

The detective assured her they weren't far away, but anything could happen before they got there. She was meeting Leo on the third floor of the hospital. The police surveillance van was parked in an alley behind the main building. Even at a flat-out run, they wouldn't get to her in less than five minutes. She didn't care what the detective said.

She drew in another breath and tried to slow her racing heart. She wiped her sweaty palms down the sides of her white lab coat and was reminded of the wire taped to her skin. Determination surged through her; she squared her shoulders and held her head high. With an effort, she quelled the nausea swirling in her belly, and entered the foyer of the hospital. She went straight to the bank of elevators.

Too soon, she stepped out on Level Three and rounded the corner. She stopped outside the door with Doctor Baker's nameplate. The first time she'd come there was the first day of the program. She'd been full of hope and excitement, tinged with more than a little awe: This is what she'd dreamed about; this was going to be the start of the best time of her life. Now that day seemed like a lifetime ago. She couldn't believe how naïve she'd been.

She gave a brief knock on the door and entered, as per

usual. She was greeted with silence and breathed a small sigh of relief. Susan Baker was out. She heard a sound behind her and turned.

"My dear Tanya, how nice to see you again."

---

Chanel looked at the next two names on her list and headed down the corridor toward Ward Two. Both gentlemen had been in hospital for the past three days under the care of Doctor Baker. She smiled a little cautiously at the staff who milled around the nurses' station, hoping they'd be just as kind as the nurse she'd spoken to earlier.

"Good afternoon, ladies. I'm seeking information on a couple of patients under the care of Doctor Baker."

Two of the nurses looked at each other. One of them leaned closer to the other and whispered something in her ear. The other nurse turned to look at Chanel, her eyes narrowed.

"I understand that you were told to stand down from Doctor Baker's staff, Doctor Munro. We're not at liberty to discuss his patients with you."

Heat scorched Chanel's cheeks, both from anger and embarrassment. It came as no surprise that her recent fall from grace had made the rounds of the hospital. She straightened her shoulders and stared the nurse in the eye.

"I'm sorry to inform you, but your information is out of date. I was reinstated this afternoon. Feel free to contact the general manager if you don't believe me. Now, would you tell me where Alex King and Jack Lineman are? Doctor Baker has asked me to check on them."

Once again, the two nurses looked at each other. The one who'd spoken frowned.

"Both of those men went home yesterday on Doctor Baker's orders. Are you sure you have them on your list?"

Chanel glanced down at the paper in her hand and checked the entries again. "Yes, I'm sure."

"Well, I'm sorry," the nurse replied, sounding anything but. "Perhaps it hasn't been updated. Maybe you should speak to Doctor Baker about it?" The look the nurse threw her was even more pointed than her words. Chanel held her stare and refused to feel intimidated. Instead, she replied in as steady a voice as she could manage, "I'll do that."

Chanel headed out of the ward and back toward the elevators, her cheeks blazing. She couldn't imagine why Doctor Baker had given her an old list, but she was determined to find out.

Stepping out of the elevator on Level Three, she turned the corner and walked the short distance to his office. It was possible he'd left, but it was as good a place as any to start looking. As she drew nearer, she heard him speaking. A moment later, a woman replied.

Chanel stilled. It was Tanya. *Surely, after all that had happened, she wasn't still under his spell?* It seemed impossible and yet, there was no mistaking it was Tanya who stood on the other side of the door.

Chanel was wracked with indecision. *Should she wait and see if her roommate was there for work-related reasons? Maybe it was best to intervene, no matter what the reason?* Tanya had proved she was more than a little susceptible to the doctor's dubious charms. Then again, it wasn't Chanel's place to decide who her roommate dated.

Perhaps it might be better for Chanel to wait and see whether she could determine the cause of the visit? It would be horribly embarrassing for Chanel, and Tanya would be more than annoyed, if the meeting was legitimate. After all, Chanel was there for work-related reasons. It was highly possible Tanya was, too.

The only thing to do was to eavesdrop a moment or two and be certain either way. With her mind made up, Chanel cracked open the door.

———————————

Leo came toward Tanya with outstretched arms. She deftly sidestepped his embrace and turned her head away from his lips. His kiss landed awkwardly on her cheek.

"What's this? Have you tired of me already?" He chuckled and waited for her to join him in his joke.

Chanel was relieved to note Tanya remained unmoved. Apart from the paleness in her cheeks, she looked calm and composed. *Perhaps it was a work meeting after all?*

"Leo, I'm not here on a social call. I need to know about that bottle."

Chanel's heart stood still. She had no idea Tanya had decided to confront their boss. She waited with bated breath for his reaction.

He frowned in confusion. "Bottle? What bottle?"

Tanya's hands fisted and it looked like it was all she could do to stop herself from slapping him.

"The medicine bottle you told me held the herbal aphrodisiac. I left it in Chanel's apartment, just like you told me to."

"Oh, that bottle. Now I remember. Yes, I thought we might have a lot of fun with it."

She shook her head. "What are you talking about? The police raided the apartment. They took the bottle and had it tested. It contained ricin. They told me it was the same poison used on those women."

"*Poison?* Are you sure?"

"Of course I'm sure. Why would they lie to me?"

"My dear Tanya, you're so innocent. It's one of the things I love about you. The police lie all the time. They'll say and do whatever it takes to make their case. Surely, you know that?"

Tanya stared at him and Chanel was proud of her friend when she held her ground. Her eyes narrowed on the man in front of her.

"You *knew* what was in that bottle. Don't tell me you didn't. I won't believe it."

"I don't care what you believe. Why would I give you a bottle that contained ricin? Do you know it can be fatal even if you inhale it? Imagine how those elderly women felt when they swallowed it in their food."

*How did he know the victims had swallowed it?* The thought had no sooner formed in Chanel's mind when Tanya frowned and said, "How do you know they swallowed it?"

Doctor Baker shrugged, unconcerned. "It's just an educated guess. Swallowed, inhaled or injected—it works as a lethal poison either way."

Tanya stared at him, her face filling with uncertainty. "How do you know so much about it? You're freaking me out. I'd never heard of ricin before the police told me about it."

He smiled in an almost paternal way and reached out to cup her cheek. Chanel's skin crawled.

"My dear Tanya," he replied in a tone of condescension. "You're still so young. You've barely begun to live. You've been sheltered and pampered all of your life by a father too doting for his own good. Try living like some of the rest of us— poor, hungry, motherless. I was ten when my mother died of cancer and I went to live with my dad."

He scoffed at the last word. "Huh! He was my father in name only. I believe he contributed the genetic material necessary to give me life, but he wasn't a father in any way you could imagine. Right from the very start, he didn't want me. When my mother died, he was forced to take me in, but he never let me forget he'd done it under sufferance."

He moved away and began to pace, tension evident in every line of his body. From her vantage point, Chanel watched him through the crack in the door, transfixed.

"I was treated like little more than a servant, forced to sleep outside. Winter or summer, hot or cold, my father didn't care. I either sweated to death in the hayshed or froze lying huddled amongst the cows. I slept beside them, stealing their warmth. It was the only thing that kept me alive."

"How did you escape? You went to college, med school?" Tanya whispered, her expression filled with horror and disbelief.

His bark of laughter contained no humor. "Despite the lack of care and concern at home, I was a bright boy. My teachers recognized my ability. I was tutored, free of charge. One teacher in particular went out of his way to help me. He was the reason I got into college. I was accepted into medical school on a full scholarship."

His eyes turned distant and his voice lowered. Chanel strained to hear him.

"It was the best thing that ever happened to me. I finally found somewhere I belonged. Nobody cared about my background. They were too busy borrowing my lecture notes. I managed to leave my past behind me. I vowed never to be walked on again. My father died quietly in his sleep after a short illness. He was found dead in his bed by my stepmother. He was sixty-four."

He turned to face Tanya. Chanel started in surprise at the feral smile on his face.

"The official cause of death was heart attack. He was overweight and a heavy smoker. There was no surprise that he'd met with a premature death. No one thought to test for anything else, least of all, poison. After all, he owned very little. There was no motive for murder. Nobody remembered the son he had who'd left two decades before."

Chanel's heart pumped fast. She was as stunned as her roommate looked, frightened at what he might reveal next. His voice was almost conversational now, as if he were talking about someone else. She held her breath and waited for him to continue.

"It had been twenty years since I'd lived there, in the filth and squalor of the shed, but I hadn't forgotten. I hadn't forgotten a moment of the humiliation and the pain he made me suffer. I was ten years old when I arrived there, grieving the loss of my mom. He treated me worse than an animal and I never forgot it. The day I left, I swore revenge and I got it in the end. I'd studied hard all through college. It wasn't a coincidence I did my thesis on the effects of different poisons on the human body."

His eyes took on a wild light. He smiled and came toward

Tonya and reached out for her hand. Chanel watched her roommate take a step backward, but then bravely hold her ground. Doctor Baker put his arms around her and rested his chin on the top of her head. Chanel noticed Tanya's quick indrawn breath and the tension in her body and realized the girl was trying hard not to shudder.

"I experimented on several patients before I perfected my technique," the doctor continued in a tone so calm and conversational that nausea swirled in Chanel's stomach.

"At first, I'd force them to inhale it, but it wasn't as easy as it sounds. I had differing results. Some died a long and horrible death, others didn't die at all. I learned from each experience until I got it right. Now, I know exactly how much to administer, down to the final grain. I filter and extract the ricin from castor beans and turn it into a powder. From there, it's a simple thing to add it to someone's food. My father found out just how easy."

The meaning behind Doctor Baker's words struck Chanel with a force that left her gasping. Her heart thumped so hard, she was sure they would hear it.

His bark of laughter quickly escalated into more, turning harsher and louder, as if he'd lost control. Tanya was in the room with a man who was clearly unhinged. Chanel had to do something. She had to help her friend.

With a surge of determination, she opened the door and pushed her way into the room. Doctor Baker and Tanya looked up at her in alarm. Her sudden entry had startled them both. It was Doctor Baker who recovered first.

"Doctor Munro, what a nice surprise. To what do we owe this pleasure?"

Chanel looked from him to Tanya and thought hard about what she should do. He looked different from the Doctor Baker she knew. His eyes were unfocused and distant, his expression was of a man who'd lost his mind. She wanted to feel sorry for him, but she couldn't. From what she'd overheard, he'd had a terrible childhood. He was sick and needed help. But he'd also become a cold-blooded killer and it hadn't ended with revenge.

*Who knew what he was capable of?* She needed to get Tanya out of there, away from him. In an effort to distract him, she began talking to him about his past. Perhaps he if thought she was on his side, he'd let them go without a fight.

"Doctor Baker," she said gently, "I'm sorry to hear about your childhood. It must have been tough growing up like that."

He turned to face her, his eyes wide, as if surprised by her words. "You overheard me speaking, Doctor Munro? Never mind... And you're right; it was tough. You simply have no idea. Like I was saying to Tanya, you young people have it easy. You have no idea how some people are forced to live. We hide our atrocities like we hide our shame, so that no one is any the wiser. Who wants to hear about another abused kid? The world's full of them. Nobody wants to know and nobody cares. If it hadn't been for my teachers, I'd probably have ended up in jail. Or dead. Not many street kids live a long life. It's just the way it is."

"I can't imagine your pain, Doctor Baker or the fear and the anger and hurt. But you could have used all that for good and yet you chose evil."

His face turned red. "I do good work. I do God's work. Besides, I didn't choose evil; evil chose me. It was in me from the start. My father never tired of screaming at me that I was bad from the inside out. After awhile, you begin to believe it, even when others don't see. That's how it was for me."

"What about your patients? Amelia Arncliffe, Robyn Evan and Eileen Green? Why did they have to die? Were their premature deaths a by-product of your evil? You cut their lives short and it wasn't fair. They didn't deserve to die before their time."

She asked the questions quietly, careful to keep her voice free from accusation. He stared at her for a long time, as if he didn't know who she was. Finally, he spoke and his voice was full of defeat.

"Fair? Where does fair come into any of this? A long time ago, I had a conversation with God. I was halfway through med school. He told me I was there for a higher purpose. I was there to help bring His people home. As a doctor, I had an elevated position of trust in the community. In the hospital, I was treated like a god. I *was* God. At least, I was His foot soldier. I followed His will. I did as He asked.

'At first, I only took the lives of those who needed to find relief. The terminally ill, the ones who couldn't be healed. The accident victims who begged to be allowed to die in peace. I did them a favor and God was pleased."

Chanel stared at him in horror. "What about the recent deaths? The women on my list? They weren't seeking a release from pain. They were on their way to getting better. They'd come to you for help. They trusted you to make them well."

He shrugged. "That was their mistake. They should have known better. I can't save everyone." He offered her a smile. "Only God can do that. It was through God's wisdom I came up with the plan to frame you for their deaths. Given that the police have released you, I suspect my plan hasn't been entirely successful. Never mind. All will be well. I have God on my side."

He encompassed both girls in his gaze. "Now, as much as I've enjoyed our little chat, I have things to do, places to go, people to see." He stared at Chanel, his expression bordering on crazy. "Patients to kill," he added with a maniacal laugh.

He turned away, dismissing both of them as if they were of no consequence. Finding his white coat hanging on a hook behind his office door, he shrugged it on and headed toward the door. Chanel stood watching him, aghast, unsure. *Surely, he'd been joking?*

He came to a sudden halt and then strode back to where she and Tanya stood. Before she knew what was happening, his fist came out and connected with the side of Tanya's head. With a little cry, the girl fell down hard.

Chanel gasped in horror. She looked around for a weapon, but there was nothing. When he came at her, she fought and kicked and sunk her teeth into his arm, but she was no match for him. With his fist clenched and his manic eyes flashing, he brought back his arm and hit her full force on her jaw. She cried out in shock and pain. Stars danced behind her eyes. A moment later, her legs gave out and she crumpled to the floor.

---

Bryce strained to listen through the headphones, but heard nothing but silence. He was still reeling from the knowledge that Chanel was also in the room. He'd recognized her voice the moment she spoke and his gut had filled with dread. Now, the room had gone ominously quiet.

"Something's happened," he said, panic spreading quickly through his veins. "I heard two cries and something that sounded like a thump and now there's nothing. Those girls are in trouble. We have to get in there."

Jett heard him through his headphones and nodded. "I agree, and we have enough to take him down, anyway."

Bryce threw down his headphones and checked the safety on his service revolver. "Let's go."

The short distance to the hospital yawned like the width of the widest valley. He took off at a run, not waiting for Jett who followed closely behind him. The noise he'd heard over the headphones just seconds before everything went quiet reverberated in his head. *If that bastard has hurt them...* He wouldn't even let himself complete the thought.

He tore through the front doors of the hospital and pushed a group of people out of his way. "I'm sorry. Please, excuse me... Police, let us pass."

He mumbled the words without hearing them, focused only on getting to the third floor. He found the fire exit and took the stairs two at a time, cursing every second it took to reach his destination.

He never imagined Chanel would walk in on Tanya and the doctor. He should have made sure the room was more secure. He should have placed men outside to guard the door. His only defense was that until that moment, he hadn't a clue how unstable Baker was. Bryce was just as shocked as everyone else when he heard the man confess.

Still, he should never have sent Tanya in there alone. He shouldn't have taken the risk. If he'd known how sick Baker was, he'd never have done it.

The fact that they had enough evidence to lock the prick up for the rest of his life didn't matter if it came at the cost of the girls' lives. The thought of Chanel, bruised and broken, had him gasping from an agony of pain. Despite the turmoil of the last few years, he'd learned to love again and he had her to thank for that. He couldn't lose her now. Not when he'd just found her.

He burst through the heavy fire door and raced down the corridor. An engraved nameplate identified Doctor Leo Baker's rooms. Without pause, Bryce barged in and came up short in the reception area. Both Chanel and Tanya lay still and silent on the floor.

With a cry, Bryce ran to Chanel and turned her over, his heart lodged deep in his throat. His fingers went to her neck and felt for a pulse. *It was there*. He was sure of it. Faint and erratic, but there all the same.

Jett ran in a moment later and took in the scene. "Jesus, are they alive?"

"Chanel is, but she's hurt. I haven't had a chance to check on Tanya."

Jett raced over to where Tanya lay and searched for signs of life. "She's still breathing!" he shouted and Bryce swallowed a sigh of relief.

"I think the bastard knocked them unconscious. Chanel has a mother of a bruise on her jaw and I can feel a lump on the back of her head."

"It looks like Tanya took a direct hit to her cheekbone. She'll have a hell of a black eye tomorrow."

"Call for a doctor. They both need to be taken to the ER."

Jett tugged out his cell phone and disappeared the way he'd come and Bryce leaned over Chanel. He gently slapped her on the cheek.

"Come on, Chanel, wake up for me. Open your eyes, honey."

She groaned and her eyelids fluttered and he smiled in relief. "That's it, sweetheart. Open your eyes. I need to see you're okay."

This time, her eyes came open and she blinked against the light. "Ouch, it hurts. What happened?"

Before he could offer her an explanation, comprehension flooded her face. "Doctor Baker! It's him! He hit me!"

Bryce pressed a quick kiss against her forehead. "It's okay, we caught everything on tape. He won't be hurting anyone else again."

"You have him? You were listening?"

"No, not yet. And yes. Tanya was wearing a wire."

"Oh, my God! She's such a brave woman. He hit her hard. Is she all right?"

"Yes, she's going to be fine. She'll sport a shiner about as good as yours, but I'm sure she'll be okay."

Chanel's expression turned somber. "He killed his father."

"Yes, and a lot of other people, from what I heard."

"I was listening through the door. He had such a sad childhood. Nobody should be allowed to treat a child like that. It...did something to him. It warped his way of thinking."

"I love that you're finding excuses for him, but don't. Many people have it tough and don't become serial killers. I'm not as kind and compassionate as you and I'm definitely not ready to hear any more excuses. He hit you. I could have lost you. God, I can't bear to think about it."

She smiled groggily up at him. "So, does this mean you care for me, even a little?"

Emotion rushed through him and choked him up. "More than a little. Are you okay with that?"

Her smile widened. "More than okay." She looked around and her smile faded. "Where did he go?"

"We're not sure, but we have a van full of officers who'll find him. He won't get too far away."

She frowned. "He said something about having to go somewhere and kill another patient. He laughed when he said it and I thought maybe he was joking, but what if he wasn't? What if he's crazy enough to kill someone else?"

Bryce froze. He wanted to deny that it could happen, but it made a perfect kind of sense. Was that the reason Baker had hit the women? Was it because he needed them out of the way? He might have confessed, but in his warped mind, he hadn't done anything wrong. Perhaps rendering them unconscious was just a convenient way of getting rid of them while he went about his work.

"Grandma," he gasped, remembering she was waiting for him to collect her. "She's still here. I need to go and find her."

Chanel paled. "Ward Three. I spoke to her earlier. She told me about you."

Bryce started in surprise and wanted to stay and hear more, but the feeling of dread that now consumed him wouldn't be denied. It urged him to go to his grandmother and make sure she was safe. He leaned down and pressed a quick kiss on Chanel's lips.

"Stay here. Help's on its way. Don't leave the hospital without me."

She nodded and Bryce was relieved by her calm acceptance of his order.

"Go and find her," she whispered. "I'm not going anywhere."

***

Doctor Baker strode down the corridor of Ward Three with something akin to a skip in his step. He always felt that way right before he set into motion a chain of events that would eventually lead a patient to their Maker. The thought the police were onto him gave him pause, but he didn't break his stride. God would look out for him. He always had.

It was God who'd given him the words that had put that detective off the scent. Ha! Taking his wife out on the harbor! As if that would ever happen. It had been years since they'd done anything together. What a joke!

He took the return of Doctor Munro to the hospital as a sign from up above. It made his choice of victim very simple. He assumed she'd already attended upon the one who was to receive his healing touch. She was at the bottom of the doctor's list. He found the room he was seeking and greeted the patient in the bed.

"Virginia, how lovely to see you. I thought I might have missed you. Aren't you supposed to be going home today?"

"Yes, Doctor Baker, I am and your nice young Doctor Munro came to sort out the paperwork. I'm just waiting for my grandson to come and collect me."

"I see your meal has arrived. You might as well eat while you're waiting."

"Thank you, Doctor. I wasn't sure what time Bryce would arrive, so I went ahead and ordered dinner."

Leo came closer and lifted one of the lids. "*Mm*, it smells good. Better than the hospital food they used to serve when I was a kid." He laughed and the woman laughed with him. He loved it when they died with a smile on their face. Not that she'd be smiling in a few hours, when the poison took effect.

Surreptitiously, he pulled a vial from out of the pocket of his white coat and carefully prised open the lid.

"Would you like me to pour you a glass of water, Virginia?" |

"Thank you, Doctor. That would be very nice of you."

"What about a little salt and pepper? Do you need a hand with that? Those little paper thingies can be tricky to get opened."

"Yes, a little salt would be lovely."

The doctor shot her a smile so bright he was sure she'd feel it all the way down to her toes. All was going as planned.

---

Bryce charged into Ward Three and skidded around the corner. Nurses looked up from their posts, curiosity clear on their faces.

"Doctor Baker— Have you seen him?"

"Yes, he went by here a few minutes ago. He headed that way."

The nurse who'd spoken pointed in the direction of Bryce's grandmother's room. He spun around and raced down the hall. He reached his grandmother's room and bolted through the doorway. The doctor stood beside his grandmother's bed, shaking something in his hand. Bryce pulled his service revolver out of his holster and shouted.

"*Stop!* Police! Step away from the bed and put your hands up where I can see them. Grandma! Don't touch anything. Move, quickly! I need you to get out of there!"

"Bryce, what's going on? Whatever are you doing?"

His grandmother sounded bemused rather than scared and he implored her once again. "Grandma, I have reason to believe Doctor Baker's trying to poison you. Please, get out of the bed and move away."

Bryce eyed the tray of food and his heart nearly stopped. "Have you eaten anything?"

"No, it only just arrived. Doctor Baker was helping me open the salt. You know how much trouble I have with those tiny little packets."

With his gun still trained on the doctor, Bryce closed the distance between them. He flung the covers across the bed and helped his grandmother out of it. She shook her head and fussed at him, still convinced he had it wrong. Bryce preferred to be more safe than sorry and his gut was telling him he'd gotten there just in time.

With his grandmother safe on the far side of the room, he pulled a pair of handcuffs off his belt. He'd just finished securing the doctor when Jett arrived, Chanel in tow.

"What the hell are you doing here? I told you to get her to the ER!"

Chanel stepped forward. Apart from the bruise shadowing her jaw, she looked almost like her old self.

"I insisted he bring me here. I needed to see your grandmother for myself. Is she okay?"

"Yes, she's fine." He shot a narrow-eyed glare at Doctor Baker. "I got here just in time."

Jett looked at the doctor in disbelief, but directed his comment to Bryce. "I don't believe it. You mean, he was trying to poison your grandmother?"

Fresh anger surged through Bryce and he nodded. "Yes, it's my guess that's exactly what he was trying to do."

More staff arrived, confusion and concern in their eyes. Within moments, the room was full of people, including more members of the task force.

"Bag up everything on that tray," Bryce ordered when the forensics team arrived. "And search the prisoner's pockets. He must have it stowed somewhere."

A few moments later, one of the officers gave a triumphant shout. "I've found something in his coat. It looks highly suspicious to me."

Bryce stared at the small clear vial filled with white powder and could only guess what it contained, but he was willing to bet everything he had that it wasn't sugar crystals. The knowledge that he'd gotten there just in time began to set in and then it hit him hard. His legs weakened.

Chanel frowned, as if she knew exactly how he felt. She moved closer until she stood beside him and held onto his elbow. Her support was just what he needed and he breathed a sigh of relief. She was fine. His grandmother was safe. It was over.

# CHAPTER 22

Susan finished arranging the vase of roses she'd picked earlier that day from her garden and stood back to survey the result. The crimson buds were on the verge of opening and promised a perfect display. Already, the sunroom was filled with the heavy scent of their perfume. She couldn't wait for them to bloom.

The phone on the wall of the kitchen rang, disrupting her thoughts. She walked out of the sunroom and made her way across the polished floorboards of the living room and at last picked up the phone.

"Hello?"

"Mrs Baker?"

"Yes, this is Susan Baker. Who am I speaking to?"

"It's Detective Bryce Sutcliffe from the City of Sydney Police Station. I'm calling to let you know we've arrested your husband on suspicion of murder. He's being held here at the station. He asked me to contact you."

Susan frowned in confusion and tried to hear the detective over the roar in her ears. "Arrested? Leo? Murder? There must be some mistake."

"No, Mrs Baker. I'm afraid there's no mistake. He was arrested at the hospital a couple of hours ago. He was caught red-handed with the poison in his hand. We have reasons to suspect it's not the first time he's killed a patient. In fact, at the moment, we're looking at him for three murders. There could be a lot more."

Susan caught snatches of the detective's response, but her mind refused to comprehend. Leo wasn't a murderer. A lying, deceitful philanderer, perhaps, but a murderer? Surely, not.

And yet the detective was speaking like there was no contest to be had. Leo had been caught in the act.

But Leo loved his patients. She'd come to believe it was the only thing he loved. *Trying to kill them with poison?* It didn't make sense.

"What kind of poison?" she demanded, interrupting the detective.

"Ricin. It comes from the castor bean. Somehow, it's been extracted. It's not the normal kind of thing we see."

Her mind went back to the night she'd found Leo in the basement and she thought again about what she'd witnessed. It hadn't made sense at the time, but all of a sudden, it did. Like a piece of a complex puzzle falling into place, she knew with unexpected certainty she was right. He was using the house as a laboratory to concoct his murderous intent.

"I... I'd like to see him. Is that possible?"

"Yes, I'll make sure the guards know you'll be stopping by."

"Thank you, Detect've. I'd appreciate that."

Susan hung up the phone with a hand that was far from steady. Her thoughts were in turmoil, filled with anger and disbelief. *How could he? How could he do this to her? Was the man completely unhinged?*

Arrested and charged with murder? It would be splashed all over the news. Everyone would hear of it. She'd never live down the scandal. Her life would never be the same again. *What was he thinking? Did it always have to be about him?*

The thought of him murdering his patients shocked her beyond all comprehension. He'd always spoken so lovingly about them. For years, she'd been a little envious over the attention they were given, but she'd learned to accept it was just the way he was. For all his other failings, there was no denying he was a kind and brilliant doctor who truly cared about the people in his care. It was an admirable way to be.

Yet, if the police were to be believed, he'd been intent upon their murder. She didn't have a clue what had happened to change him and now it was all too late. The damage had been done. The charges had been laid. The only thing she could hope for was to end things before the trial.

The publicity during a trial would be beyond unbearable as the prosecutor picked over every aspect of their lives. She shuddered in horror at the thought of it and pressed her hand against her mouth.

A sob escaped and then another, but she refused to allow him to best her. For too long, she'd let him do what he wanted, sleep with whatever slut he found... But no longer. Enough was enough. Her patience had come to an end.

This time, he'd pay for what he'd done.

---

Leo turned at the sound of the keys rattling in the steel door that held him prisoner from the world. He didn't have a clue what time it was, but he guessed night had fallen. The prison cell was made of solid concrete without a window to be seen. It was only because there had been a change of shift that he had any idea of the passage of time.

He looked around and spied an officer outside the door to his cell. The door swung open and Leo's heart lifted. God had saved him in time.

"You have a visitor." The surly guard grabbed him roughly and turned him to face the wall. "Hands behind your back."

Leo winced at the feel of the handcuffs biting into his skin. "Handcuffs, officer? Is that really necessary?" he asked in his most cajoling voice.

The only response was a shove in the side and then he was led down a cold and silent hall. A moment later, a door was opened and he was pushed inside.

"Fifteen minutes. I'll be right outside. Don't try anything stupid."

The thinly veiled threat from the officer should have filled Leo with foreboding, but he smiled and even gave the man a wink. God was on Leo's side. There was nothing he would fear.

Susan sat on a plastic chair with her elbows resting on a small table. Clad in Dior from top to bottom, including a matching handbag, she presented a striking image. Another chair stood opposite, completing the furniture in the room.

"Darling, how nice of you to come." He greeted her with a genuine grin, pleased to see her. While he'd been pacing his cell right after the arrest, it had come to him to call her. God would work through Susan. She was the key to setting him free.

Her expression remained dark and forbidding and he wondered briefly if he'd made the right call. *Perhaps he should have phoned his lawyer, like the officer who charged him had suggested?*

"What are you doing here, Leo? The police officer said something about you being charged with murder. Is it true?"

He stared at her and knew it was time—time to reveal to her who he was—who he *really* was.

"I wouldn't call it murder. I'm just doing as I'm told."

She shook her head and her brow creased in a frown. Anger glinted in her eyes.

"Don't talk in riddles," she snapped. "Just tell me the truth."

He stared at her, remaining calm. "I speak the truth. It is you who doesn't understand it. I was chosen very early on to carry out God's work. God chooses who I heal and...who I don't."

"So, you admit it. You poisoned those women. I looked it up on the Internet. It's already all over the news."

He smiled, pleased to discover his gift was finally being recognized. "I am a disciple of God. I live to do His will."

"So, you're God's chosen one, murdering people in His name. Is that what you're trying to say?"

He frowned at the sarcasm in her tone. "I'm not sure I'd

use the word *murder*. I help them on their way. For many, their time on earth was over. There was no hope of them ever getting well. God doesn't like to watch them suffer, and neither do I. He tells me when it's time for them to meet their Maker."

"I see," she said in a tone much more to his liking. "Is that what you intend to tell the court when it comes time to explain your actions?"

"I don't need to explain God's work. I'm merely a vessel for the Almighty. God decides who lives and dies, not me."

He thought of Amelia Arncliffe and Robyn Evan and even to some extent Eileen Green and did his best to ignore the guilt that flooded through his veins. He'd taken their lives at his own behest. God hadn't factored in on those. Still, he was sure God would approve. He wouldn't abandon him now. God had sent him Susan, hadn't He? It was a sign He was still on side.

"I need you to do something for me," he said and his wife frowned at him again.

"What is it?"

"There's a small brown bottle in the safe in my office. I need you to find it and destroy it. Don't say anything to the police. They wouldn't understand. Will you do this for me? Please?"

He shot her his most charming grin and hoped it would have its desired effect. It had always worked in the past. To his relief, she smiled back.

"You mean this bottle?"

She held up the medicine bottle he'd filled with the ricin powder only a week before. He quickly got over his surprise and nodded.

"Yes, that's the one. What made you look for it?"

"As I said, I've been researching on the Internet. I found some very interesting facts. Did you know ricin can be injected?"

A sudden wariness crept up inside him. There was something about his wife's calm expression that he didn't like. Still, he offered her a nod. "Yes."

"I's usually more lethal that way. You can be assured the recipient receives the full dose. Injected straight into a vein, it quickly works itself around the body. Soon, every tissue is filled with it. It almost certainly leads to death."

She leaned forward as she spoke, until their faces were just inches apart. Her eyes glowed with excitement and something else. He stared at her, transfixed, like a field mouse poised before a snake.

The tiniest prick of pain in the side of his neck was all he felt. He reached up to touch the skin and a spot of bright red blood stained his fingers. He frowned in confusion and focused back on his wife. The syringe was barely visible, clutched inside her hand. A second later it disappeared into the vastness of her handbag.

Panic fluttered inside him and built into a flood of dread. *She couldn't have...? Surely, she didn't...?*

He shook his head back and forth, his movements becoming more frantic. No, he was mistaken. She wouldn't dare. Besides, God would protect him. God would keep him safe. With that, he relaxed and the tension eased out of him. He had nothing to worry about.

When his wife stood and pushed back her chair, he even managed a tiny smile. She smiled back and he relaxed some more. He even offered her a wave as she collected her bag and turned and headed for the door.

All was good. All was fine. God would see him through.

———

Susan Baker slid her handbag over her shoulder and smiled at the young officer stationed outside the door. He flushed, just like he had when she'd greeted him upon her arrival. Her practiced charm worked then as it did now and he grew flustered once again.

"I'll see you out, Mrs Baker. Do you have everything?"

"Yes, I only came in with my handbag. Thank you once again for letting me bring it in. It cost five thousand dollars and is very dear to my heart. My children bought it for my birthday last year."

"Well, I'm sorry I had to check through it, but it's standard procedure."

She shot him another brilliant smile. "I understand. I do. And I appreciate that you didn't paw through it. A woman's handbag is an extension of herself. It's a very private thing. You don't know how nice it is to find a man who understands."

She pressed her hand to her heart, making certain her cleavage was elevated to full advantage. She was rewarded when his gaze lowered to her chest.

"I was happy to help, Mrs Baker. You deserve better than that man in there." He indicated with his head the room where she'd left her husband.

She nodded. "You're right. You're absolutely right. I thank you once again for doing what you could to make this whole experience a little less awful."

"My pleasure. It's the least I could do for a beautiful woman such as you."

She smiled and dropped her gaze and pretended to blush at his words. "Thank you, officer. You're very kind to an old woman."

The officer opened his mouth as if to protest, but Susan pressed a finger against his lips.

"Hush, let's just leave it there. It's been nice meeting you, officer and I thank you once again."

He stammered out a few words on his way out into the main part of the station, but she paid them no heed. She'd accomplished her mission. It was done. It was time for Leo Baker to meet his Maker.

———

Bryce pressed a satisfied kiss on the tip of Chanel's nose and sighed. "You're going to kill me if you keep going like that. I'm not sure I can keep up."

She chuckled and snuggled against him, as naked and replete as he. His hand found the curve of her hip and idly caressed her. They'd only just finished making love and yet he still craved her touch. It was like she was a drug and he was an addict. He couldn't get enough.

"How did things go with your interview yesterday? Did Doctor Baker give himself up?"

He shook his head. "Believe it or not, despite the fact we played him the recording, he continued to deny everything. Lucky for us, his wife wasn't so good at keeping her mouth shut."

"Really? What did she say?"

"We spoke to her this morning. Apparently she visited her husband in the cells last night. She told us about a house in Mount Druitt. We executed a search warrant on the place a few hours ago. It was empty, save for what we found in the basement."

He went on to tell her about the equipment they'd found, including a supply of castor beans full of seeds. Coupled with the evidence from the tape, a guilty verdict was almost guaranteed.

"You did good," she said and pressed a kiss against his chest.

"*You* did good," he declared firmly. "If you and Tanya hadn't gotten him to talk, we would never have known. We're going to be busy for many months going over old records from the morgue. It's possible he hasn't stopped killing since he was in medical school."

She nodded her agreement and sighed. "I'm afraid that might be true."

"I was going to talk to him again this afternoon, but he's taken ill. He's been sent to the prison infirmary. Not that it matters. I can catch up with him when he's brought back to the cells. It's not like he's going anywhere. With the evidence we have against him, there's no way in hell he'll make bail."

"I'm glad to hear it."

With a sudden movement, Bryce rolled Chanel over and

kissed her softly on the mouth. "Let's not talk about it any longer. I can think of far better things to do."

He pressed himself against her, leaving her in no doubt as to his intentions. She moved to accommodate him. Her legs fell open and he eased his cock inside. They sighed in mutual satisfaction.

"I love being inside you," he whispered against her lips.

"I love having you inside me."

He moved slowly, enjoying the exquisite feel of her warmth surrounding him. Eventually, passion overtook them and by the time they reached their peak, they were panting. Chanel cried out as she toppled over the edge and a moment later, Bryce followed her over.

When they'd caught their breath, he kissed her sweetly on her lips. "I love you, Chanel Munro."

Her eyes widened in surprise and she sat up on one elbow, half dislodging him. "You love me? You mean it? You really love me?"

He grinned. "Yes, I really mean it. I love you."

She turned and threw herself against him, her arms tight around his neck. "I love you, too. You can't imagine how much."

He kissed her again and then again. "I think I can."

She sighed and relaxed back against him. "I don't think I've ever been this happy."

"I know I haven't. Don't get me wrong; Angela and I loved each other, but we were still kids when we met and fell in love. We didn't have a clue how we'd grow and change as adults. We weren't quite the same people in our twenties as we'd been in our teens." He shrugged and continued quietly. "Maybe if we hadn't had the strain of having a baby, we would have made it without the added pain, but we'll never know. I guess it wasn't meant to be."

She was silent for a moment. When she spoke, her voice was low and uncertain. "How do you feel about babies now?"

He was a little taken aback at her question, but the fact that she'd voiced it told him how important it was to her. He answered as honestly as he could.

"I love babies. I always have. The fact that it didn't happen for Angela and I saddened me at the time, but I guess I resigned myself long ago that fatherhood wouldn't happen for me. I haven't given it any thought since. Why do you ask?"

"I've always wanted a big family. I have five brothers and a sister and between them they have about a hundred kids. Family gatherings are loud and noisy and crowded and I love every minute of it. I'd love to have a heap of kids, if you're willing."

He eased her away from him until he could look into her eyes. The hope in them stole his breath. "I can't think of anyone else I'd rather have a heap of kids with. I love you, Chanel, with every breath that I take and I'll love our children just as much." He grinned. "Can we get started on one now?"

# EPILOGUE

*Nine months later*

**B**ryce turned the car into the driveway of Chanel's parents' place and switched off the ignition. She let out a sigh of relief and turned to him and smiled.

"I can't believe it. We made it. Our first long road trip with the girls and we're here."

Bryce glanced at the three babies who slept peacefully in their capsules, blissfully unaware of the stress they'd put their parents through over the twelve-hour haul from Sydney. The trip had taken almost double the time it usually did because they'd had to stop and feed the infants three times and then Zoe had developed a gas pain and had refused to settle down. Charlotte had gone out in sympathy and had exercised her lungs with such ferocity, Chanel was sure she'd suffered permanent hearing loss. Only Ginny, the smallest of the triplets, slept through the whole ruckus, much to her parents' amazement and relief.

"I can't believe it, either. Remind me next time to book plane tickets. The distance between Sydney and Grafton is mammoth, way too far for a road trip with three new babies. I thought with them being barely a week old, they'd sleep most of the way. Boy, was I wrong."

Chanel reached over and ran a hand tenderly through his hair. "Thanks for driving us. It wasn't easy. I'm not sure how you managed to concentrate over all that crying, but you did and you got us here, safe and sound. I love you."

He turned his head and pressed a kiss against her palm. "I love you, too, but remind me again whose crazy idea it was to do this?"

Chanel rolled her eyes at him. "It's Christmas. Okay, I didn't exactly plan on driving up with week-old babies, but that's the way things turned out. They arrived a month early." She smiled and offered him a helpless shrug. "What was I supposed to do?"

He shook his head, but grinned back at her. "You're a cheeky girl, Chanel Sutcliffe. I don't know what I'm going to do with you."

She widened her eyes and stared at him, her expression a picture of innocence. "I'm sure you'll think of a suitable punishment."

Bryce growled low in his throat and his eyes darkened with desire. He pulled her closer and kissed her hungrily on the mouth. His hand reached down to cup her breast, full and tender. Her nipple jutted out against his fingers and he brushed it back and forth. Chanel gasped into his mouth and angled her body toward him. He took advantage of her silent invitation and pressed against her as much as possible in the confined space of the car.

"We'd better get inside. Mom and Dad will have noticed our arrival. Any second we'll be surrounded by about one hundred Munros vying to get a look at the girls."

Bryce groaned against her mouth, but reluctantly pulled away. "I'm going to find you later and steal you away so that you can attend to this." He grabbed her hand and rubbed it against his cock. It was hard and thick and pulsing.

"I'm sorry I got you in such a state. How are you going to manage to ignore it while we play nice with my family?"

"Hey, they're my family too, remember? They claimed me from the time you introduced me at the engagement party. Are you done with sharing them already?" he teased.

"Of course not. Everyone loves you, Bryce and they'll be besotted with the girls. I can't wait to meet Josie's little boy. Mom says he looks just like Chase."

"I can't believe their baby and ours were born just minutes apart. How freaky is that?"

"Freaky or not, I couldn't be happier for them. They've wanted a baby for so long."

"What did they call him? Has anyone heard?"

"Clancy Duncan Barrington, I believe."

"Your family's going to have a tough time with our three. They look so much alike, even I get mixed up."

Chanel giggled. "Me, too. Especially when they're dressed the same." She glanced over her shoulder at the triplets. "I couldn't resist those little Santa suits. They were so tiny and cute. I just had to have one for each of them."

"They're beautiful, just like their mom. Grandma thinks so, too."

"How is she? When did you see her?"

"I dropped by her cottage yesterday afternoon on my way home from work. She was thrilled we'd named Ginny after her."

"How's that cough she's been suffering from? Is she over it now?"

"Yes, I think so. She seemed in high spirits when I spoke to her, talking about the bus trip she's taking over Christmas with some of the other senior villagers. Moving her into that retirement place was the best thing we've ever done. She has people her own age to talk to, a social life that's busier than ours and medical care at her fingertips. She's thrilled with her cottage and is already talking about expanding the garden." Bryce shook his head and smiled. "She might be nearly eighty-four, but you wouldn't know it. She's amazing."

Chanel's chest tightened with emotion and she had to blink back tears. She blamed it on the hormones that were still pumping through her body. Nowadays, the slightest thing turned her into a blithering idiot.

"You're amazing, too," she whispered in a husky voice. "I love every moment of our life together."

Happiness beamed from his face. "I love you, Chanel Sutcliffe, more than I dreamed possible. I'll love you forever and ever and ever."

"Amen."

# NOTE TO READERS

I do hope you have enjoyed reading Bryce and Chanel's story. If you've enjoyed this story, please feel free to leave a review for The Maker. Every review is very much appreciated.

If you would like to receive news on upcoming stories, release dates, book launches and other snippets, go to my website at www.christaylorauthor.com.au and subscribe to my newsletter. I love to receive feedback from my readers. Please feel free to contact me at chris@christaylorauthor.com.au

**The Perfect Husband** is the first book in my next series. The Sydney Harbour Hospital Series follows the lives and loves of the men and women who work in the Sydney Harbour Hospital, many of whom you've already met in the Munro Family Series.

Here's a sneak peek:

Isobel Donnelly has a perfect life. Married to a renowned orthopedic surgeon who's employed at the illustrious Sydney Harbour Hospital, she also has a successful and satisfying career as a pediatric nurse. Life couldn't get any better.

But then her babies arrive and the husband she adores turns into a cold and angry stranger. Her perfect world is shattered the first night he hits her.

Now, she's trapped in a violent marriage with nowhere to

turn. Her husband has threatened to kill her and the kids if she ever dares to leave. In public, they're the perfect couple, but inside, she's slowly but surely dying.

Mason Alexander has relocated to the city to take up his dream job as a pediatric doctor at the prestigious Sydney Harbour Hospital. Recovering from a failed marriage, he's determined to put the change of scene to good use. The distractions and demands of his new job are just what he needs to get his life back on track.

Then he runs into Isobel Donnelly and his world is once again turned upside down. He's loved her since they were children. She's the reason his marriage failed. But Isobel's still married to his nemesis: the incomparable Nigel Donnelly. From all accounts, the two of them are still blissfully in love.

Vowing to steer clear of the woman who's haunted his dreams for far too many years, Mason does his best to avoid her, but Isobel continues to seek him out and he can't help but notice her assurances about her happy marriage appear a little forced.

When she arrives at work with a blackened eye, he's immediately suspicious: There's no way she fell over toys left in the way.

The thought that Nigel might be abusing her is abhorrent, but the signs are there for all to see. Will Mason be able to convince her to leave her husband...or will they both die trying?


**The Perfect Husband** will be released on 1 November, 2015 and is AVAILABLE NOW for pre-order from your favorite digital retailer.

# About the Author

Chris Taylor grew up on a farm in north-west New South Wales, Australia. She always had a thirst for stories and recalls writing her first book at the ripe old age of eight. Always a lover of romance and happily-ever-afters, a career in criminal law sparked her interest in intrigue and suspense. For Chris to be able to combine romance with suspense in her books is a dream come true.

Chris is married to Linden and is the mother of five children. If not behind her computer, you can find her doing the school run, taxiing children to swimming lessons, football, ballet and cricket. In her spare time, Chris loves to read her favorite authors who include Richard North Patterson, Sandra Brown, Kathleen E Woodiwiss and Jude Devereaux.

You can find out more about Chris and sign up for her newsletter at her website:

http://www.christaylorauthor.com.au

Follow Chris on Twitter at:
http://www.twitter.com/christaylorbook

Join Chris on Facebook at:
http://www.facebook.com/christaylorwriter